EXISTENCES

A COLLECTION OF SHORT STORIES

Shuvashree Chowdhury

CINNAMONTEAL
DESIGN & PUBLISHING

First published in India in 2018 by CinnamonTeal Publishing

ISBN 978–93–86301–98–7

BISAC Code: FIC029000/FICTION/Short Stories

Typesetting and Cover design: CinnamonTeal Design and Publishing

CinnamonTeal Publishing
an imprint of CinnamonTeal Design and Publishing
Plot No 16, Housing Board Colony
Gogol, Margao
Goa 403601 India
www.cinnamonteal.in

Praise for Shuvashree Chowdhury's debut novel,
Across Borders

'A moving and evocative novel that vividly captures our past.'
— TIMERI N MURARI, novelist & playwright, recipient of the
R K Narayan Award

'An urgent tale told with utter vividness. An important addition to
the literatures from India's North-East and Bangladesh.'
— SUDEEP SEN, author of *Fractals: New & Selected Poems |
Translations: 1980-2015*; *The HarperCollins Book of English Poetry
& EroText*

'The book is unputdownable. How many people can write as
powerfully as Shuvashree Chowdhury?'
— PRANAY GUPTE, journalist & author

'Across Borders holds you with its vivid descriptions and its
delineation of characters. Moving across the important decades of
our early independence, it tells stark and often poignant stories.'
— RUCHIR JOSHI, writer & columnist, *The Telegraph* (Kolkata)

'An engrossing storyteller .... The delineation of characters is
superb, so true and real that they come to life. I was able to identify
myself with many situations. I finished reading the novel in two
straight sittings.'
— P V KRISHNAMOORTHY, (first) Director General,
Doordarshan

'The author has surpassed herself in fleshing out the primary
characters. But her strength lies in linguistic flair, especially in
descriptive prose. There are myriad evocative turns of phrase
throughout the novel, each a delicate brushstroke that adds
luminosity to a master canvas. It is in these compelling details
that Across Borders stands out as a commendable body of work, its
vivid details evocatively blending history with fiction.'
— *The Telegraph*

For My Parents

Contents

Prelude: A Game of Snakes and Ladders

"I slept and I dreamed that life is all joy. I woke and I saw that life is all service. I served and I saw that service is joy." – Kahlil Gibran

"You, young lady," said the general manager from the head office, assessing me curiously through his rimless glasses. I instinctively looked both ways among the five women and six men, wondering whom he was referring to. He caught my eye with his steady gaze, then added firmly, "Yes, you. I'm talking to you lady. Why didn't you join the cabin crew?"

It was this apparently innocuous comment, on the first day of my airline job, at twenty-three years of age that propelled me into making it a career. I had gaped at the salt-and-pepper haired gentleman quizzically, taken aback by his question. But by his warm expression, I realised he meant it favourably, since I had the physical attributes of good height, slimness and facial charm, all vital for the role in question.

"Sir, I wish to be in your position before long," I replied resolutely, to impress him, the idea occurring to me just then. "This ground job will enable me to do that. I feel I have the intelligence to lead teams, not merely follow instructions as required by the cabin crew."

The general manager, looking stumped, merely nodded in response. Then, he turned his attention to the rest of our group of new inductees and started his welcome speech. This was in the first-floor office of the airline at Calcutta airport. Till this exchange, any thought I had invested in this job had been aimed at being occupied till given away in marriage by my well-meaning father. My parents had been single-mindedly scouting for a suitable groom since I was twenty-one. I had quit the MBA programme I was pursuing at the behest of my mother, a professor, to take up this job, much to her consternation. Academic studies bored me since I was a child. A graduation in commerce, followed by a degree in public relations, was as much as I could bear.

The airline job was, in fact, the second in line, after I quit my first at a travel agency, within a year, due to my father's incessant disapproval. He had maintained a stoic silence for a fortnight since my joining, thereafter goading my mother to compel me to quit, in lieu of the amount of my salary. He was anxious about the snide opinions his friends and our neighbours would have, about him allowing his daughter to parade herself in frivolous jobs. His wife's career as a professor was honourable in his view, also that of his friends and the world at large, thus she had been allowed and encouraged to pursue it lifelong. A businessman, reasonably well off at that, father considered he was competent in finding his daughter an economically stable groom, who would ensure her never having to work. That I had the attributes of a good homemaker, skills in cooking, sewing, along with an even temperament and good looks, boosted his confidence in the matter.

However, father had no qualms in my pursuing academic qualifications, or learning foreign languages – I was enrolled in a German class at Max Mueller Bhavan, till as long as I wished, before marrying me off. I had a boyfriend at college, who was also from a business family, whom my parents knew nothing about. But he, too, was expected to marry a girl of his parents' choice, the veracity of which he had accepted, as in joining the family business he would not have economic independence to go against them. So, I relented to meet one prospective groom after another, though, I was given the choice to turn them down till I was convinced I could consider spending the rest of my life with the man. My friends, to whom I narrated the details of these meetings, referred to them as the, 'Sunday matinee show' in jest. It was little wonder then, with my conditioning – raised as I was to be married off after a basic education till graduation, that I had not taken a career seriously, up till the general manager's observation on the day of my joining. Though well intentioned, as cabin crew and pilots are the cream of an airline's employees, and highly paid as compared to ground staff, the remark was hard hitting on me.

Was I seemingly fit only for glamorous roles, I had thought indignantly, unintelligent for responsible ones? Then why was I, in a group of women, judged for my looks, which apparently overshadowed the other skills I might possess? Raised in an all-girls convent boarding school since the age of five, I had never considered myself as good-looking, let alone consider it an asset. My spontaneous response to the general manager had been triggered, I presume, by my mother's ideology that I had been raised with. Mother never ceased to emphasise to me, that a person's good looks are merely transitory, and that it is one's abilities, effort towards and beyond it, and the resultant work and service to people and the society, that one is justly appreciated and remembered by. It was then that I realised I had subconsciously been well indoctrinated. In my view, 'good looks' was a gift I was bestowed with, even thankful for, but since it was due to no effort of mine, it did not make me proud.

My appointment in the airline, at Calcutta, in the November of 1995, had been confirmed after several rounds of interviews, out of a large crowd of us applicants. I had been called for the interview by a quirk of fate: from having submitted my resume to the airline, rather informally during my travel agency days, on one of my regular visits to their office as an international-travel sales executive. By the time I received the letter for the interview I had left the travel agency well over a year, and abandoned all interest in pursuing a travel or aviation industry career. However, the interview letter lured me back quite by chance to my destiny into becoming a working woman. The series of interviews were held, both, one-on-one and in groups, by a panel of top-level employees from the head office in Mumbai. The interviews, group discussions, and psychometric tests through games, were aimed at evaluating our attitudes, confidence, resilience, communication skills, and above all, our team spirit. Three of the women whom I met in the final round and who joined the airline along with me are close friends till today.

On completing the initial formalities, the eleven of us — six women and five men, who were recruited in time for the commencement of the Calcutta-Bangalore sector, were put on a two-week training schedule. It was only on passing the three examinations, scoring over ninety per cent marks in each, as was mandatory, were we put on the job. On the one hand, it was exhilarating to be at the airport, with its fast paced activities and constant buzz amidst so many different types of people. On the other hand, it was physically challenging, with few moments to sit, large areas to briskly walk over, and getting used to the rigorous timings. I was initiated to the job in the afternoon work shift from 2pm to 11pm. After a month, I was put on the morning shift, from 5.30am to 2.30pm. The night shift, which was never assigned to women in Calcutta, contrary to Mumbai and other cities, was from 10.30pm to 7.30am.

The most difficult part, though, was the constant prodding and pestering by seniors, to grab us out of our innocence, naivety, remould us into tough, resilient men and women, to survive in the airline industry. Every now and then, one or the other of us inductees would be in tears, being rebuked by a passenger, but more often bullied by a senior for some perceived incompetence. At such times, we, the new inductees, morally and emotionally supported each other, often huddled together in the restrooms at the departure or arrival halls. But it was I who was ragged the most by seniors, usually males, including duty officers, supervisors, the airport and the regional manager. Assuming from my appearance I was not serious, that I did not need the job, they made it their job to make my life difficult. They perhaps aimed to make me flee from a perceived charade at working, making a career, thereby creating space for someone better deserving and certainly more in need of the job in their view.

In spite of constant intimidation by seniors, being yelled at in retaliation for my repartees only in exasperated defence, I never shed a tear. There were also a few sympathetic senior staff and batchmates who did try in vain to shield me from the constant volley of reprimands. All of it, however, made me tougher, strengthened my resolve to stick on, and to rise above the perpetrators of my humiliation. In fact, it was from here in working at the airport, that I began to closely view people, for an insight on them, and to understand the workings of the human psyche. I began to look out for the motivations of human behaviour, trying not to judge, rather empathise with jealousy, insecurities, and what made people tick. In less than six months, the next batch of recruits joined. I didn't want them to go through the same agony that I had gone through. So I involuntarily became their guardian. The pretty and smart ones, also the ones with aptitude and potential for growth, were

   Shuvashree Chowdhury

invariably ragged the most. I would then try to console and shield the uninitiated sensitive women from the harsh reality of the world they had inadvertently stepped into – just as I had only recently.

I never discussed the tough time I was having at work with my parents. They would be very distressed, but more so into compelling me to quit. It is only now – twelve years after my father's passing away, in writing this prologue to set the tone for these short stories written over the last decade that I appreciate his being so protective then. In his years in self-employment, dealing mainly with corporates, he perhaps knew that good looks were actually a hindrance for a woman. It is a different matter if a woman wishes to use her looks to her advantage, at the cost of her conscience and morality. Then, too, other women try to tear apart those they consider having an advantage due to their looks, to appease their own insecurities. How I wish father were alive, so I could admit to him that he was right. I appreciate that he was only trying to safeguard his daughter, from the perceived harshness of the chauvinistic working world.

However, having said that, in looking back, I also realise I would not have done anything differently myself. The tough times I endured, made me soon excel at my job. Also, the HR and regional managers noticed my inherent tendency to look out for juniors, shielding and inspiring them, rather than adding to their harassment. High profile corporate passengers also began to appreciate and leave feedback on my sensitivity and sharpness in identifying their needs, solving their problems at the check in counters or the departure and arrival halls. All this led to the enhancement of my job profile at the end of a year. I was chosen to set up and manage the newly built, swanky, twenty-four hour reservations and ticketing office adjacent to the airport, also the Special Handling Cell that was responsible for all VIP and commercially important passenger movement, that operated out of that office. Then, after two years, in applying to a Post Vacancy Advice, that was a notification to employees for internal job vacancies, and interviewed at the head office along with a large number of applicants, I was elevated to the position of a service quality co-ordinator for the airline's network.

By now, though my 'Sunday matinee shows' continued, my

parents, in understanding my need to have an identity of my own, stopped pressurising me to marry. During this time, I also had my share of boyfriends and heartbreaks, which my parents knew nothing about. In the year 2001, transferred to Mumbai with an enhanced role, not wanting to leave my hometown and my family, my father very ill then, I quit the airline. I joined a premium luxury hotel chain, as reservations in-charge of their new property opening up in Calcutta. After six months, the hotel by now inaugurated and functioning smoothly, I felt compelled to leave even without due notice, due to severe harassment by the front office manager, a man of about thirty years. I was wiser from this experience, but my spirit was not yet deflated to give up working.

I now joined a reputed pan-Indian jewellery brand as manager of their flagship store. In this stint, I had close interactions with people that truly nurtured my personality and my understanding of human existences. It also gave me good exposure to sales, marketing, public relations functions, and gave me a lot of creative satisfaction. By now my father was proud of me and was confident of my working. He looked forward to my random and frequent television interviews representing the brand, especially before and around the festival times of Diwali, Dhanteras and Christmas. He also made it a point to remind his friends to tune in, when my interviews were to be telecast, the last being a few days before his sudden death in early January of 2005. I left this assignment a year later in May when I got married and moved to Chennai. This was followed by another two retail assignments in Chennai, managing large format stores, which gave me a much larger, yet close view of people. With each assignment, I was getting adept at empathising with people, nourishing my well of humanness. Then, in July 2007, I joined a multinational executive search firm as a senior consultant in the consumer, retail and services vertical. It was this experience, with the training on psychometric tests, personality groupings, the close attention to human behaviour and its motivations, that gave me more clarity, and insights, into my observations of human existences. Now I had the opportunity to meet and assess top rung executives of premium companies, enhancing my maturity more than I could have on my own from working another decade.

Thus, moulded in adversity at every step, my life has been

            Shuvashree Chowdhury

much like a game of Snakes and Ladders. Just when I thought I had climbed a tall ladder and was getting closer to the finish, I inadvertently stepped on the head of a sneaky snake like circumstance, not in my control. Then, I had to restart the climb over again, on another ladder. However, though I switched a number of ladders, both professional and personal, stepping on debilitating circumstances that tended to bring me down, crush me emotionally, I never quit the game, or the spirit of playing, each relationship garnering my personality. It is out of this deep well of experiences of almost two decades that I have drawn these short stories, feeling equipped to review with profundity the tapestry of existences I have encountered. In fact, they help me see with clarity all those simple things that give true meaning to our lives.

A Slash Of Blue

A slash of Blue—
A sweep of Gray—
Some scarlet patches on the way,
Compose an Evening Sky—
A little purple—slipped between—
Some Ruby Trousers hurried on—
A Wave of Gold—
A Bank of Day—
This just makes out the Morning Sky.

by Emily Dickinson.

Existences: The canvas of a woman's life at birth is like the pristine blue sky. She can paint it with all the rainbow coloured perspectives, she finds in the box of crayons, we're all given and accumulate, as we walk through the hill or valley track of life, whether in cloud, rain or sun.

Conversely, she can sulk, envy and deride those who risk using all the brilliant hues, trusting life will supply them superior crayons, even if they have not been privileged to be born with a trusted brand through family and circumstances.

1. A Job Done Well

It was 8am, on a January morning, at Calcutta airport. As customer service staff, I was assigned to look after the arrivals that day. I walked down the tarmac, passing the arrival lounge, to a remote bay. Our flight from Delhi was due to land any minute now. The sun was up, nice and bright, but in spite of its warmth, the chilly breeze sent shivers down my spine. Due to the cold, I had my hands tucked into the pockets of my uniform's navy-blue blazer, worn over a printed silk-blouse, a knee length straight skirt and pump shoes. Overall, I was well groomed as per guidelines; my long hair pulled back tightly into a chignon, the eyeliner, lipstick and blusher in place. I balanced a walky-talky precariously with the inside of one elbow. The other forearm held a clipboard pressed against me, the passenger special-handling list for the incoming flight on it. The list included two unaccompanied minors and a wheelchair passenger.

I walked briskly, the heels of my shoes clip-clopping on the metal road, hoping to make it before the aircraft touched down. Why do they assign the farthest bay in this cold weather, I mentally cursed, rather than an aerobridge?

"All stations come in," a heavy male voice bellowed on the walky-talky at my elbow. "Flight no 801 is taxing-in on bay no. 14."

Pulling my hands out of my pockets, clutching the walky-talky and clipboard in them, I broke into a run. I was late. But, hopefully, I would be in time before the chocks were put to the wheels of the aircraft. In fact, as per standard operating procedure, I should have been the one to alert all stations, of the aircraft taxing in. I made it just in time to record the actual arrival time, that at which the chocks are put to the wheels of the aircraft.

"All stations come in," I announced, into the walky-talky, pressing hard the 'talk' button at the side. "Flight no 801 … chocks on at 0810 hours."

"Roger, copied" came a succession of replies from across the airport.

I watched the stepladder lugged towards both doors of the aircraft. By the time the front door opened, I was positioned in the front. I had stridden up the front stepladder, even as it was being aligned by two loaders.

At the opened door was a tall, broad shouldered, sharp-featured, very good-looking purser.

"That was fast, you're already up here," he said, as he gave me a friendly wink, grinning as he handed me the incoming passenger manifest.

It was only a few weeks since I had joined the airline, and was still shy, especially with the crew who was an affable, flirtatious lot.

"Please keep the unaccompanied minors and the wheel chair passengers on board," I briskly replied, ignoring his friendliness. "I will come back for them in a while."

I walked down the stepladder, to wait at the base, for the business class passengers to deplane. After the last of them got into the coach, I got on, latching the entrance behind me. The first one getting off at the arrival hall, after unlatching, I waited till all the passengers had walked inside. Then I hurried to check the signage, reading the correct flight on the baggage conveyor belt. As the baggage started to move up on the belt, I returned to the aircraft, on a coach going that way, to fetch the two unaccompanied minors. The wheelchair passenger, a lady, was by then already transported to the arrival hall in a coach, by a loader.

By the time I returned with the two minors and handed them over to their guardians after standard procedures, all the baggage had been picked up, off the belt. With all the passengers on their way outside, I was about to leave for the departure hall, to assist with the boarding for the turn-around flight to Delhi, when I noticed a young man, in an olive green t-shirt, blue jeans held with a tan belt, tan shoes, striding towards me. He was short, stocky, with a boyish face about which fell his long wavy brown hair. A rucksack was slung on his one shoulder, a brown jacket on the other.

As the man came close, I noticed the distress on his plump face, brown eyes.

 Shuvashree Chowdhury

"My baggage has not come as yet," he announced, worriedly looking at me.

"Are you sure, Sir?" I asked earnestly, "I mean, were you here all the time? All baggage has come on the belt already."

"Yes, I've been looking out since the first baggage came on the belt," he replied.

"Then, please wait, Sir," I said, "I will check behind and let you know."

I walked towards the start of the conveyor belt, the loading point. Suddenly, I noticed something show up, and then move up on the belt towards me. It was like a large black boulder floating up on the sea, moving steadily towards the shore. The conveyor belt of steel plates, reflecting the strong lights around, was like the shimmering sea. As the thing came up close, I recognised it for what it was – a soft-bodied suitcase that had burst open, misshapen.

Before I could approach it, its contents started to spill about its course. At first, shocked at the condition of the baggage, I panicked. It didn't strike me to stop the belt right away. A few weeks at the job, I had no clue how to deal with this situation. I had theoretically learnt to deal with lost, damaged baggage. Through role-plays, I had trained on irate passenger handling, but this situation was a tad too complicated. What with the owner of the destructed bag in full view of its contents spilling out in public view.

"There's my suitcase," the young man announced cheerily, sounding relieved. Then his voice rising sharply in alarm, he shrieked, looking in my direction.

"Oh my God! It's open. Everything's spilling out of it."

As I stood transfixed, a sea of people, passengers on other arriving flights, spilled into the arrival hall. In a while, the lounge was crowded and noisy from the passengers, but over that the intermittent announcements. I turned to look at the young man, the owner of the suitcase. Suddenly, the innocent, boyish face turned into an arrogant, grown up one.

"What the hell do you guys think of yourselves," he bellowed, looking at me with hostility. "Is this an airline you are operating or a local bus? Now stop this goddamned conveyor-belt, will you, instead of staring at it."

Stunned at his anger and ferocity, stinging with embarrassment at being its sole recipient in public view, I stood rooted to the ground. My silence was spurring his anger. He glared at me, almost like he was about to strike me. My mind seemed to blank. Through the film of tears that had spurted to my eyes uninitiated, I noticed the arrival lounge was packed, it being prime time for all operating airlines. I turned towards the belt, to find to my horror, bottles of imported toiletries – perfumes, soaps, creams, and cosmetics, spilling from the suitcase.

I rushed to the power switch to the side of the belt and switched it off. The bag came to an abrupt halt, a little ahead from where we stood. With the kind of stuff spilling out of his suitcase, I assumed the man to be a retailer, returning with merchandise possibly from Bangkok or Dubai. But walking up to the suitcase, looking at the varied baggage tags closely, I learnt he was actually coming from London, transiting through Dubai and Delhi. I took a deep breath, trying to focus on the testing situation at hand. It struck me to ask for help.

"Sir, come in," I called for the airport manager, holding the walky-talky to my mouth. As he responded with a crisp, "Go ahead," I replied, "Sir, I need help in the arrival hall urgently, there's a badly damaged baggage case. The passenger is very irate."

"Hold on for a while, try and pacify the passenger till then," the airport manager responded, after what seemed like a long pause. "I'm at the departure gate and will be with you once boarding for this flight is complete. I'll try and send someone to help you before that if I can."

Aware that no help was forthcoming soon, I braced myself for the man's tirade, turning to face him squarely. A number of people had surrounded us by now, in the crowded arrival hall. I found we were enclosed by people in a semi-circle, against the conveyor belt. While the baggage's owner was busy accumulating empathy from the passengers around, I started picking up his spilled stuff, placing them atop his suitcase, a little distance from the conveyor belt on the floor. By now the baggage of another flight was doing the rounds on that belt. Two loaders returning from the car park, carting vacant wheelchairs, seeing me surrounded by a crowd, came over to join me in gathering the fallen articles. The people around us, after a while, criticising our airline's

          Shuvashree Chowdhury

services vociferously amongst themselves, started targeting their complaints at me.

"You are no better than Indian Airlines," one man said. "In fact, you are worse," another added tartly. "Your claim to better them is a sham," a third said.

This incident is of a time much before low-cost carriers came into business in the Indian aviation industry. The expectation of service quality was not yet reduced to mere on-time and safe transportation. There was no concep of apex-fares yet, only full-value pricing around the year on domestic sectors, as compared to low-season fares available on international travel. Airline travel was as yet the privilege of either the corporate traveller or the moneyed one.

"Sir, I understand how you must feel," I said, in a very low, steady voice through the volley of accusations, to the owner of the damaged baggage, looking him in the eye. "In your place, I would have been equally upset, if not more."

He looked at me, first curiously, in registering what I had said, and then his expression abruptly turned to that of embarrassment.

"I am really, sorry. I didn't mean to shout at you," he said, in a soft voice, apologetically. "I know this is not your fault. It's just that I am so frustrated."

He marched outside of the ring of people surrounding us. With his change in attitude, realising the show was over, his well wishers dispersed, merging into the crowd without a trace. It's so common for people to fan the fire, watch the fun, for a few cheap thrills. When someone is complaining, shouting, everyone around joins in, at times without knowing the real cause, a typical mob-mentality. I escorted the man away from the conveyor belts, asking the two loaders to follow us, with the torn baggage and its strewn contents on a trolley.

"I'm Arup Basu," the man said, turning towards me as we walked, exiting the arrival enclosure, past the security guards. "I'm a student at a European university, and I'm returning home after two years." Then, after a few steps, in a cynical tone, he added, "See the grand welcome I get here in my hometown. In fact, my parents are expecting me only late this evening. I thought I was lucky to get a seat on this flight, in order to surprise them. Now look at the mess I'm in."

"I apologise for the inconvenience, Sir," I replied earnestly. "I understand how you must feel. But please don't worry. From here, things will be taken care of."

He nodded; his youthful look having returned, now that his anger had subsided. We sat down on a row of seats, not far from the elevator that led to the airport manager's office on the first floor. The loaders left his baggage on a trolley in front of us. As we sat, I noticed we were facing the Oberoi snacks counter.

"Would you like some coffee while we wait, Mr Basu?" I asked politely. "Meanwhile, I'll have someone shift your stuff to our office upstairs."

"Yes, that would be nice. In fact, we could both use some," he replied, looking in the direction of the coffee shop, "but let me buy the coffee."

"Thank you! But you're still our guest," I replied, smiling.

"Thanks," he replied.

I got up, and walked to the snack-counter. In those days, the staff got coupons we could exchange for snacks and beverages from any airport counter, which I carried in my pocket. In this situation, I could get the bill signed by a duty manager, instead of spending my coupons, but decided to use them nevertheless.

I returned with two large disposable cups of coffee, handing Arup one.

Why don't you call up your parents after coffee," I suggested, sitting beside him. "They will be pleasantly surprised you're at the airport, in Calcutta, already."

"That's a good idea, I'll do that," he replied, his eyes lighting up.

"So, is all this shopping from Europe?" I asked, indicating the strewn stuff, now balanced over his baggage in a plastic bag. "It must have cost quite a lot?"

"No, I came via Dubai, so that I could shop for my family. Everything's cheaper there," he replied. "I landed in Delhi late last night, so I took the earliest flight this morning, instead of waiting for the evening one I was booked on, in ModiLuft. In addition to the Doctoral degree I'm pursuing, I work part time, so I had

     Shuvashree Chowdhury

some money saved to shop for everyone back home. I'm the only member of my large joint-family who has ever gone abroad. They are so proud of me."

"I'm so, so, sorry about your baggage," I repeated sincerely. "It must have been so distressing, to see all the stuff purchased with your hard earned money strewn around like that. I can truly empathise with your being so livid. But please don't worry about your things I've had them all collected safely. We will lend you a suitcase to carry your baggage home and either mend or exchange yours."

Arup didn't reply. He merely nodded, looking downwards thoughtfully.

After we finished coffee, I stopped a passing loader, and asked him to carry Arup's belongings on the trolley, upstairs, and keep it safely in the airport manager's cabin. I then escorted him to our ticketing office, right behind us, to make the telephone call to his parents. This was before the advent of the mobile phone, so rather than a call from the public pay booth I got him to call from our office. After his call, relieved his parents would be arriving shortly, Arup returned with me to our prior seats near the elevator that were still vacant.

"I am ashamed of my earlier conduct," Arup said abruptly. Then, looking at me sheepishly, he added, "It was truly unjustified, whatever the provocation. I mean, screaming at you, at a lady, like that in public. And you're still being so kind."

"That's alright," I replied softly, in a placating tone, "I can understand it wasn't intended. I'm pretty new at this job, so I was initially puzzled."

"I'm still sorry," he insisted. "And I must say you are one brave girl."

"Thank you!" I smiled shyly; glad he was at ease now. "But I have to admit I was shocked, upset, by your shouting, the volley of public accusations that followed. But all in all, it's been a lesson well learnt for me today. That you can always expect an exigency working at the airport that you're never prepared for. Over that, to get an upset man away from a crowd as soon as possible...."

"Yeah, sure, I agree," he laughed. "I'll take a lesson in positivity from you."

"Now come on," I smiled. "It was a shocking, more so, an illuminating morning. I'm glad for this experience early on in my career."

"Your service recovery has been splendid, considering you claim you are new," Arup said. "You ensured every moment of truth in my interaction with you, since my learning of my damaged baggage, was positive."

"I don't understand all that jargon yet," I replied. "I just followed my instincts."

"They say the word RATER comprises the first alphabets of the attributes required for excellence in service quality," Arup continued. "R – is for Reliability; A – for Assurance; T – for Tangibles; E – for Empathy; and, finally R – for Responsiveness. Your handling of this situation was excellent customer service. You were prompt in responding to my need, you empathised with me, assured me to loan and then repair or change my baggage – a tangible thing. I'm thereby convinced of your personal reliability and that of your airline, since you are its brand ambassador. Thus, in spite of just having one of the worst experiences of my life ... I will continue to patronise your airline. You seized the opportunity, converted a bad experience to a pleasing and perhaps a memorable one."

"Your knowledge is very impressive, I must say," I exclaimed. Then joking, I added, "Did they teach you all this at the course you're taking in Europe."

"Yeah, I once learnt all this in theory," Arup replied smiling, "But you've demonstrated it so well to me this morning, even though you are so new at your job."

"I'm usually sensitive to people's needs, I also pick up cues easily," I replied. "So it was really simple. I don't think sophisticated training is required for customer service, if you have an attitude to help. Even if you don't know procedures, you can resolve problems, by asking your seniors how."

"Aha! An attitude to help," he replied. "You're right. That's most important. It's why recruiting the right people is crucial in the service industry or training will not suffice in delivering quality customer service. Attitudes are difficult to imbibe. Yet, a lot of young people are attracted to this industry, merely for the

    Shuvashree Chowdhury

perceived glamour, not what it entails in way of humility and servitude."

"You either have the right attitude, or you don't, difficult to imbibe it in a short time," I replied. "Hopefully, I've made the right career choice. Today's experience also gave me early on, a glimpse of the adversities packaged in the glamour."

Suddenly interrupting our conversation was my name called aloud on the walky-talky in my hand. It was the airport manager.

"I will be with you in a few minutes," he said. "I hope you're fine."

"Yes, Sir," I replied into the walky-talky, "I'm waiting near the lift."

The airport manager walked up to us shortly. He was handsome, of average height, sturdy built, in his mid-forties. With a pleasant face, and a warm smile, he had a charming disposition. His grey-white hair, rimless glasses, and tasteful clothes, lent him an air of elegance.

"Sir, this is Mr Arup Basu," I said, looking from one to the other men, "and this is Mr Soumen Roy, our airport manager."

"Good to meet you, Sir," Arup replied, proffering his hand to shake.

"I hope she has taken good care of you," Mr Roy said to Arup, shaking his hand. Then turning to me he added, "I'm sorry, I got held up at the boarding hall. Moreover, I knew you could manage here."

"Sure, she has undoubtedly taken good care," Arup replied.

We walked towards the lift together. Inside, on our way up, Arup said, "Sir, I would like to reiterate that she has indeed done an excellent job, handling this situation by herself in the crowded arrival hall."

"Thank you!" I said, smiling.

"I'm really sorry for the inconvenience," the airport manager added.

Once we were inside his office, the airport manager sent a loader to the adjacent Oberoi restaurant to get breakfast for Arup. A suitcase, little bigger than Arup's own, was handed to him, in which he could carry his stuff home now. His damaged one didn't seem to be in a condition to be fixed, so it was communicated that he would be given a new one shortly. Arup, accepting the loaner suitcase, set about shifting the contents of the damaged one, including the fallen items, into it. As Arup had his breakfast of a cheese-chicken sandwich and coffee, I filled out the damaged-baggage form. He had barely signed on it, after eating, when a middle-aged, very Bengali looking couple stepped into the outer office. The man was lean and tall, with greying hair and a moustache, wearing steel framed glasses. The woman, stocky, a plump face with a liberal dash of vermilion on the parting of her head of greying hair braided to her waist, wore thick gold, coral, and conch-shell bangles, symbols of a Bengali married woman.

One look at the worried expressions on the couple's faces, and I recognised them as Arup's parents. On seeing their son, Mr Basu, his eyes lighting up with joy, retained his composure. Mrs Basu spontaneously went up to Arup, hugged him warmly, a relieved, joyful look on her face. Then pulling away abruptly, she looked up questioningly into his eyes.

"What happened? Arup, is everything all right?" she asked anxiously. "Your father and I were so worried on getting your call to come over immediately. You look rather thin. You haven't been eating, I know, poor boy. But how can you eat well in a faraway place when you're so used to my cooking?"

Arup and his father looked embarrassed, as I smiled understanding her sentiments. Arup interrupted his mother's mollycoddling, to recount to his parents the incident of his damaged baggage, and how I had taken care of it.

"Thank you so much!" his parents said earnestly, almost in unison.

Mrs Basu then proceeded to open, and take a look at the packed loaner suitcase, ensuring her son's belongings were neatly arranged. Mr and Mrs Basu accepted a cup of tea, each, they were offered, sitting down to drink it.

When they were ready to leave, Arup, turning to me, smiling, said, "Now I'll only travel by your airline. They recruit compassionate people."

His mother clutched my hand, tenderly saying, "Thank you so much!"

     Shuvashree Chowdhury

His father patted my shoulder, as he said, "Good job. Thank you!"

"You're welcome," I replied, smiling at all of them simultaneously.

As I saw Arup and his family out of the door, I had a warm, contented feeling that morning. It stayed with me all day. This experience was to set the tone for my long haul in the service industry. There is immense satisfaction in a job done well, but much more after facilitating people, from their gratified smiles.

2. *Stand Up to Bullying*

I was twenty-five years old, when I was dispensed without any ceremony, not even prior intimation, the responsibility of inducting, training on the job, and leading a team of fifteen young men and a woman. This was barely in my second year of joining the airline, and all in the team were just a couple of years younger than I was. It was to be the new twenty-four hours reservations and ticketing office, also the VIP and CIP handling cell for Calcutta. The front wall and gate, all of glass, from floor to ceiling, the office was on the ground floor of an isolated corridor, adjacent to the Calcutta airport, in a building that we referred to as the Link Building. Here, passengers, in addition to calling on the fifteen telephone lines routed through an Alcatel call distributor, also walked in around the clock. But seldom did anyone from the airline walk into this office to overview the activities.

I reported to the sales manager who was located at the city office in Park Street, who, in turn, reported to the general manager. The day before the new team was to report to me at the airport, I was called to the city office to meet them briefly. It was on meeting me that two of the young men actually recruited for the airport side activities, pleaded with the general and sales managers to join my team. After some questioning on their intentions, they were swapped with two others. A witness to this sudden keenness in the change of department, their pleading to joining me, I promptly realised, it was their assumption I was going to be an easy boss. Their workplace would then be a continuation of their college days – all of the men joining us from among the fresh pass-outs of St Xavier's College – a premier institute in Calcutta.

The day after I met them when the group reported at noon, the lone woman was reserved and withdrawn, but the men seemed as cheery as though the party had just begun. After they introduced themselves one at a time at my behest, and I did the same – along with a brief dialogue on what was expected of them here, they

     Shuvashree Chowdhury

settled down around me at the computers. In a while, in initiating conversation, one man wanted to prepare their work allocation roster for me, and another, the shift/timing roster – like one tries to help one's teacher in school or college. But I politely declined such help, as I was not intending the enactment of a college scenario here. This was a business module, for which I was solely going to be held responsible.

In the initial days, I allowed the team their lunch break two at a time. All of them would return in half an hour as allotted, but one man took almost an hour every day. After noticing this trend, I summoned the man who had just strolled in late again – to my desk, in view of all the rest. He was of less than average height – shorter than all the other men in the team, also somewhat pudgy, unlike the rest who were athletic – having played cricket or football for their college. Their sports acumen was an added criterion for their recruitment, so they could now represent the airline in corporate matches. As the man I summoned, walked over looking at me nonchalantly, the hint of a smile lighting up his moustached face, I looked back sternly. I noticed his large eyes set on his full face now shone with mirth.

"Why are you so late, Sourav?" I asked sharply, his amusement reflecting his defiance and disrespect, propelling my anger steadily.

To my utter infuriation, he now grinned wide. In a sweeping glance, I looked around me, to notice everyone else's eyes on us, though they looked indirectly, some even breaking into sly smiles now.

"Don't you hear me, Sourav, why are you late every day?" I lashed out at him. "You know that lunch break is only for half an hour!"

He grinned again, to my utter fury. I knew this was it. If I didn't act now – the team was going to be out of my control for good. Perhaps they had even put him up to this prank to bully me, I thought, as he was not as smart as the rest, and were now morally in this defiance with him. The single lady, who was of my age, more mature and reserved than the others, looked down shamefacedly.

"Get out!" I lashed vehemently now, "Wipe the grin off your face and then return if you must."

Sourav kept grinning defiantly, and rather foolishly, looking into my eyes that were slits of fire. The others openly smirked now, looking directly at the spectacle as one would a monkey show.

Sourav cheekily retorted, still smiling: "We were taught at the customer-service induction to smile all the time when on duty."

I looked at him sharply, and over and above my anger, with the realisation that I had to get the team to respect me, I menacingly replied: "That might be the case. But you will not smile henceforth, if you want to continue working in this office. If you see me anywhere, inside the airport or even outside, you will wipe your smile off your face instantly. Am I clear?" Then with a pause, with more verbal punch, I added, "You will never smile at me ever, do you get it!"

His smile finally froze, to my relief, and I noticed so did the rest of the teams. They were never to smirk at me again, and we were able to settle into a respectful working relationship. This incident had established my credence with them, contrary to their initial perception since seeing me on joining – as one of meekness. But our days ahead were, of course, peppered with random trivial tricks that I tended to allow the young team the liberty. This was so as not to kill their enthusiasm and vitality that needed to be harnessed and put to good use. There were, however, times when I pulled the carpet from under their feet, if they crossed the line, to upkeep workplace discipline.

It must have been over three months in this office, when one of the team – a man named Stuart, came to work one day with his head shaven, also sporting a well-groomed French beard. This was much to everyone's amusement but not mine, rather I was incensed. I knew this was his defiant streak surfacing again, from my recent coolness with the team. Stuart, of average height with an athletic physique, a good football player, was one of the intelligent and capable, but mischievous ones of the team. His new look now was in absolute rebellion to the laid down grooming guidelines for staff, of which they were made well aware, at their induction.

Only Sikh men were allowed deviations. So I firmly told Stuart I would not allow him to work here, with his new look, as this was

    Shuvashree Chowdhury

a passenger interactive office after all. He, in turn, kept giving me one excuse after the other, to justify to maintain his shaven head, and the unshaven face. I finally insisted he get a medical certificate for the acute dandruff and sensitive skin issues he complained of and meet the HR and general managers at the regional office with it.

It was a couple more months since the previous incident, when one morning, I received an urgent call, from the deputy general manager, Mrs Soni. A strikingly attractive lady in her mid-fifties, she called me up at home.

"Why are you not taking good care of those boys in your office?" she said crisply, without any prelude, just as I came on the line and said 'hello'.

"Ma'am, I don't get what you're implying," I blurted.

"The glass door at the Link Building office has collapsed. One of the boys is badly hurt. Luckily I had called there to check on something, and he told me of this incident in a rather harassed tone."

"Surprisingly, I haven't a clue, Ma'am," I replied, shocked. "Alright, I'm rushing to the airport right away; I will call you once I see things for myself."

As I stepped into the Link Building corridor, walking through the airport, as is the way we usually came in or out, I noticed the imposing glass door was indeed lying in two large parts against the wall across our office. I rushed inside concernedly, to find Sourav – the man who I had severely instructed not to smile on seeing me, sitting on the sofa facing the door. He was alone, as he was in the night shift along with one other staff who might have stepped out. To my surprise, he seemed rather calm and collected.

"Are your badly hurt, Sourav? What happened to this door?" I blurted.

He looked at me sombrely and replied: "One passenger pushed the door with all his might, as he didn't realise it was locked from inside – below, and it just cracked up. We rushed immediately to prevent it from crashing, and then set it outside. Luckily, I had been headed to the door to open it."

"Where did you get hurt and how ... show me!" I repeated concernedly, assuming it might be a muscle, a bone perhaps, or a ligament injury Mrs Soni had mentioned, as there was no visible sign of any open wound on him.

"It's alright now," he replied grimly.

"But Mrs Soni called me at home. She said you're badly hurt."

"She had called to check on a PNR so I just said I was hurt. I didn't say badly," Sourav promptly replied, but consciously averting my gaze, thereby raising my doubt on his intentions – in relating the tale he told Mrs Soni."

"Alright, show me what happened," I insisted. "Where are you hurt?"

He flourished his little finger and indicated to me a cut just below his nail. It was a fine red line of clotted blood, like it might have been a bruise by a penknife or a nail cutter even. On seeing it, I felt a surge of anger at the recall of Mrs Soni's stinging reprimand at my lack of concern and sense of duty towards my team. Also in promptly assuming Sourav might have told Mrs Soni the exaggeratedly dramatic tale to get even with me. It was highly likely he was finding an outlet for his squashed male ego, from my blow to it – on his coming late from lunch in the initial days. But I decided not to react further, or I stood the chance of his calling up Mrs Soni again and giving her another dramatic version of my negligence of my duties towards my staff.

"I think you should get a Tetanus injection," I said, thinking this would be in ensuring no possible harm came upon him, also not to give him any further chance to complain. "The doctor should be there in the medical unit."

"No, no injection! I'm very scared of injections!" he interjected sharply. "I've never ever taken an injection in my life!"

I looked at him quizzically, wondering what it was with him now. But, on closer look, I inferred he was indeed scared of injections. So I made up my mind right then, it was an injection that could best be used to prick his oversized male ego. The Tetanus medication would ensure the pain on his buttocks – where I would call the medical unit to ensure they injected so he could work easily with both hands on the computer – lasted at least a couple of days. Then, in spite of all his resistance, I sent him for the injection, along with a senior officer from the airport manager's administrative office whom he could not defy as he was

 Shuvashree Chowdhury

me. His post injection pain must have intensified, after I told him on his return from the medical unit, that the real need for the injection was not for his medical safety – but as my disciplinary aide.

After a year in the office, due to a lady cleaner absenting herself often, and when she was absent for over a week without intimation, I replaced her with another young girl. It was past two weeks of uninformed absenteeism when the first one returned to beg and plead that I take her back, even dramatically bending to touch my feet, as I moved away in exasperation. But I refused to be manipulated into relenting. I had given my word to the new girl – just over eighteen years, to keep her on, more so, as her mother suffered from cancer and she needed the money. After the first one, pleaded for two days, dropping into the office at whim, she didn't turn up for two days after that. I thought I was rid of her for good.

When suddenly late one morning, four tall, bulky, ruffian-looking men marched into our office, pushing the glass door by now reinstalled, shuddering the glass walls alongside.

They marched to my desk and resting their hands on it menacingly, one of them picking up the phone handset, shoving it into my hand, said: "*Mai Bapp ke phone lagao* (Call your bosses)."

I looked at them in horrified shock, as two of the young men from my team got up and stood beside me, even as the gangster men repeated in Bengali: "Call your owners! How can you sack the cleaner? Don't you know she is a member of our union?"

I explained to the goons the circumstances, but they were adamant and replied: "We will not allow the new girl to work, and in fact, we won't allow anyone to clean this office. We will break the new girl's legs if we find her outside. As for you … you're sitting in a glass office, so just think how easy it is for us to stone it down."

I just kept staring at them in horror, in deadly fear, but feigning a calm composure, as another added from behind, "We will not hesitate to use acid or a blade."

I was totally shaken, the pit of my stomach churning in fear, but this hooliganism made me very angry, and adamant, as I telephoned our GM.

"Take the old cleaner back …" he admonished, horrified,

listening to my hurried and crisp narrative - so as not to show fear to my crude audience. "Are you mad, don't you know what they are capable of doing?"

But I had made up my mind that a unionised employee, one who could resort to such threats through goons could not be taken back, as she would really be a troublemaker in the long run.

"Sir, I will not take her back," I said firmly. "And how can you even consider doing so … Now after learning that she is part of the airport union, which is so aggressive?"

Luckily I could stand my ground with the support of the HR and airport managers, who I telephoned promptly, even as these huge men marched out with a flourish, threatening to return shortly.

In an hour, I suddenly saw a group of over one hundred and fifty men and women of the Trinamool Congress union, come in procession and sit, filling the entire covered corridor outside our glass office. They stared at us, especially me, menacingly, even as a couple of men would come inside every now and then and threaten me in turns. I was scared … very scared, indeed. I had vivid imaginations of how it would feel to have a blade slit my cheek, acid thrown on my face, and how I would live with the scar … or what if they slit my skirt or trousers with a blade as they threatened. Was standing up to these bullies worth it? But I had taken responsibility of the new young girl's job now, and then the older previous girl would be a menace if we took her back. But worse still, would my team ever respect me again if I cowed down? I had just begun my career with the airline, where I had, at the time, planned to spend a very long time. I was also worried about my parents finding out of this situation and forcing me to quit the job. Also, the general manger kept pressurising me to take the girl back in worrying about my safety.

"You all are my responsibility, don't you understand?" he screamed at me several times over the phone, along with various other threats. But I firmly replied each time, "Sir, trust me on this. I'm in this for good or bad."

For the next three days, my team and I walked in and out of our office, in passing a group of about hundred to two-hundred people, including a number of women by now, staring at us in

          Shuvashree Chowdhury

the most menacingly disrespectful manner. I was getting sick of this intrusion into our lives and the office being unclean for days. But I didn't want my team to get a scope to complain that I had asked them to sweep and swab the floor, so I planned on doing it myself.

"Guys, let's clean the office ourselves. They cannot stop us, can they?" I suggested. "In fact, you all just help me carry the bucket, broom and swab, etc. inside. I'll sweep and swab the floor, let's see what they do to me! You all clean the computers and the phones with Colin spray, in the meantime."

"No, how can we watch you cleaning … we will do it," they said in unison. "You just supervise us."

So all of us cleaned together, we swept and swabbed the floor, with much flourish, really enjoying ourselves. We laughed and joked, showing off to the union watching us in utter shock. We thoroughly cleaned the computer screens and telephones. In a few hours, we saw the unionised group disperse. Then, the next day, as we were now used to their presence, we awaited their coming and sitting down to gawk at us. But they didn't ever return. I now got a new male cleaner, from one of the existing staff. I didn't want to risk the young girl's safety by taking her on.

In the course of the next two years, the trained and proficient men from this office, either one or two at a time, were transferred to the airport services department or the city office. They were replaced with the same number or more of fresh recruits – the ones who fared worst in the preliminary tests and interviews. The single lady remained with me and went on to become my pillar of support. Thus, now, in addition to running this office – with responsibility for its profitability, I was entrusted the job of coaching these men, freshly stepping out into the world after their college degrees. So I may bring them up to the standard of proficiency required, failing which they would be asked to leave the organisation. But these new men also invariably came with the baggage of male chauvinism and resistance that I needed to draw on track in their initial days.

All of these experiences, followed by numerous others such as these, I have been unluckily lucky to encounter in the organisations I worked for afterwards. They left me with the confidence that aggressors never leave you alone until you look them straight in the eye and deal with them. But over that, those watching you cowing down to bullies cannot respect you if you do. So then, how can you have any impact on them thereafter, if you happen to be a corporate leader or even a social icon?

3. A Dilemma

I drove to the airport very early that morning. The check in counters started around 5.30am, and I wanted to be there by then. It wasn't that I was taking a flight, but was getting to work as a service-quality coordinator for the airline I had joined six years back. My duties now comprised auditing the ground and in flight operations of the airline's network, for excellence in service quality. The nature of my job entailed my travelling extensively to all the stations we operated at, taking random flights through the length and breadth of the country. This morning, however, I had planned on auditing the cycle of services at Calcutta. I often made surprise visits early mornings and late evenings, picking on random flights, in a bid to check the implementation of standard operating procedures. There was no knowing when and where I might land up, or how long I would stay.

At the airport, walking in through the entrance, I hung my photo-identity-card that was on a chain, around my neck. I proceeded to the baggage screening, onwards to the check-in counters, followed by the departure-hall through the security checkpoint. At every point, I spent time quietly monitoring that the process was functioning smoothly, and that the staff was in their places, well groomed and helpful. By eight o'clock, I had a cup of coffee and a cheese sandwich from the snacks counter in the security enclosure along with two of the duty managers who were friends. It was almost time for the Delhi flight to land at 8.10am when I decided to move to the arrival hall through a boarding gate. On my way, I checked on the baggage offloading point outside the arrival hall to ensure the loaders were in place. I would go to the aircraft only before the boarding of this turnaround flight commenced, deciding on monitoring the arrival lounge services first.

At the entrance to the arrival lounge was a male staff, well groomed. Inside, another lady was at the conveyor-belt, waiting for the passengers and then the baggage to arrive. There would be a staff or two on the tarmac, to escort passengers in coaches to the arrival lounge. With the increase in flights over the years, there was more staff allocated to arrivals, as compared to a single one, when I was a customer-service assistant. After all the passengers of the Delhi flight came into the arrival hall, transported by three coaches, I walked over to check that their baggage was being loaded onto the conveyor belt smoothly. Then I hopped into the last coach returning to the aircraft. On the way, I exchanged pleasantries with the friendly driver named Amit, working since before I joined. Getting off the coach at the front stepladder, I climbed up, cursorily viewing the catering upload at the rear, the water tank and toilet cleaner in operation.

On seeing me, the cabin crew, at excessive proximity with each other, verbally, physically, put on a prompt show of formality. The ladies, slim and pretty, stashed away their open compact-cases, lipsticks and blushers into their handbags, the handsome men their smirks. They started goading the cabin-cleaners, also themselves folding open blankets, newspapers, arranging magazines, in reducing the turnaround time of the aircraft. On the walky-talky jutting out of the cabin cleaning supervisor's pocket, I overheard one of the duty managers alerting – "All stations come in … QC on board the Delhi aircraft."

I smiled to myself, recognising his voice, his anxiety of anything untoward happening in his shift that I may report to tar his image. The cabin-cleaning supervisor, a middle aged man with a friendly, pleasant face, promptly reduced the volume of his walky-talky, looking sidelong to decipher whether I might have overheard the alert.

I took a brisk walk down the aisle, to ensure the cabin was clean as per standard – the seat headrests changed, the carpet vacuumed, tray tables and pockets cleaned. The catering staff had finished loading the meal trolleys into the galleys behind. I mentally ticked off the audit checklists, to fill them out physically on my return to my office. After a peek inside each washroom, to ensure they were cleaned and sanitised, satisfied that the cabin was now clear for boarding, I climbed down the front stepladder. On my way out, through the open cockpit door, I caught a glimpse of the back of

     Shuvashree Chowdhury

the uniformed shirts, berets and epaulettes of the Captain and the Co-pilot.

I went across to the starboard side of the aircraft, so see if the loaders were impeccably groomed, loading the baggage into the holds systematically. As my gaze involuntarily moved upward to the cockpit windows, I noticed the two pilots peering at me curiously. I didn't recognise either of them, so looked away. Then, as the first coach of passengers arrived to board, I walked back to the departure hall, in time to catch the last and final boarding announcement for the same flight. In a while, assuming the aircraft had taxied-out by now, I was about to step out of the security-hold when a duty-officer named Levin – of average height, stocky built, with slanting eyes and the bridge of his nose low, suddenly walked up to me.

"The Delhi flight's commander, Capt. Chopra, wants to meet you in the cockpit," he said.

"Me? But why – and isn't it too late now?" I replied baffled. "The aircraft should have been airborne by now isn't it?"

"Apparently it isn't," Levin replied in an exasperated tone. "Captain wants to meet you right now. In fact, everyone's been trying to locate you on the walky since he asked the crew not to close doors till you come. If you don't rush, he will delay the flight, writing off the delay on Commercial. And you know how every minute of delay impacts our performance adversely."

I nodded, rushing into a coach at the departure gate, that was kept waiting to take me to the aircraft. On the tarmac, I noticed a number of curious staff eyes on me. As I rushed up the front stepladder, I noticed the rear ladder had been removed, and the door closed. I crossed a ground services supervisor named Deepak – tall, lean, with a thickset moustache, on his way down. He seemed to consciously avert my gaze, raising my curiosity.

At the entrance to the aircraft, the chief purser – a tall, athletic man, when I asked him why I had been summoned, feigned ignorance. I walked to the cockpit, stood behind the pilots laughing amongst themselves.

"Yes, Captain," I announced edgily. "Did you want to see me?"

The men turned around simultaneously, appraising me curiously.

The Captain, muscular, sharp-featured, and good-looking, with mocking eyes, in a sardonic tone, said: "As a matter of fact, I did, quite a while ago."

The Co-pilot, seemingly younger and somewhat shy now, averted my gaze, as I enquired firmly, their disdainful tone and look having put me on the defensive.

"May I know why?"

"I wanted to know why you are not in uniform?" the Captain replied, looking me up and down with a derisive look. "And how come you came here through the arrival hall rather than through the security hold?"

"In my job, I'm not required to wear a uniform, Captain," I replied crisply, impatient he had called me, held up the flight even, to ask such an inconsequential question, that in any case was not pertaining to him. "However, what is the relevance of that now, to the flight's departure?"

"What do you mean by you are not required to wear a uniform?" he persisted in an intimidating tone, "Exactly why are you not in uniform? Don't you know, you have to come through security-check to the aircraft, also you should not be carrying your handbag with you as you are?"

"I don't have a uniform, as I'm a service-quality coordinator," I replied indignantly. "I have a valid all-airport photo identity card which entails my entry into any part of this airport terminal. Moreover, though it isn't necessary, I passed through security to the arrival hall, before I came here."

"Ah! Now I get it!" he replied, trying to squash a grin.

I turned away in silence, seething from the harassment, and walked out of the aircraft, down the ladder, sullenly. On the tarmac, the ground staff and loaders waited anxiously for the aircraft doors to close and the flight to chocks-off. Their averted gazes, by now figuring out the bogus reason for the delay of the flight, heightened my humiliation. Women staff being called to the cockpit, delaying the flight, had connotations that were far from complimentary. The supervisor Deepak, who I had crossed on the stepladder on my way up to the cockpit, discomfited at my apparent humiliation but helpless to do anything looked at me sympathetically. He and I had joined about the same time six years back and were friends.

     Shuvashree Chowdhury

His primary concern now was to get the cause for the delay signed by the Captain. He briskly walked up to the cockpit.

I walked all the way back to the departure hall, rather than take a coach. My eyes smarted from the angry tears, the intensity of my indignity percolating in my psyche with time. The temerity of these pilots, I thought, to treat me like a new staff or one of their cabin crew, when I was totally outside the purview of their clout, by virtue of my work profile. Though these pilots had little way of knowing I was not a new staff who they could rag, since I didn't look much older than when I joined. The irony was that I had not faced a similar situation in my early days in the airline and to face this harassment now was indeed ludicrous. More so now since everyone was wary of us in the quality team. I was the only one based out of Calcutta, with two of my teammates in Delhi and another four, excluding our expatriate boss – the head of service quality and his secretary, in Mumbai.

On reaching the departure hall, I walked reverse through the security hold, proceeding to our office on the first floor. On my way upstairs, I met the airport manager – the same man since I had first joined, handsome, with greying hair, of average height, sturdy built, and a pleasant face.

"These Captains, I tell you …" he said to me sympathetically, "Think they can get away with anything, cow us down, because they control the 'delay', which has such a bearing on us."

"Yes, but I'm not going to let this go so easily," I replied resolutely, not surprised at his awareness of the incident that someone would have reported to him.

"Please be careful," he said. "Captains are a favoured lot in the company."

I nodded, as we resumed on our way, he downward and I up the stairs. As I walked into the outer office that enclosed the airport manager's cabin, I noticed the few staff present looking up at me from their desks curiously.

I took my seat at my desk ignoring the questioning looks, and turned on the computer. Then I placed my handbag inside the desk-drawer, waiting for it to start, for all the icons to load on its screen. With an overpowering sense of indignity, furious, unsure of what I could do to make the Captain pay, I clicked on my Outlook email icon on the computer screen, hitting the new message option. On the subject line, I typed: "Incident Report – Delay of Flight no … to Delhi, due to the harassment of staff by Capt. Chopra." This, I followed with a detailed description of the incident since my learning of his summon at the departure hall. Once I was done typing, my anger diffused, I sent off the email to the head of operations – all the Captains reported to him, as well as to my boss, the head of service-quality, both at the head office in Mumbai. I copied it to the general manager, eastern India, at the city-office in Calcutta. I viewed the word 'sent' with a sense of serenity.

I was going through my email inbox when the telephone – an extension line on my desk, rang. I answered it on the second ring, as usual announcing the airline, my name, location – "Airport manager's office," followed by "Good Morning. How may I help you?"

It was mandatory for telephone calls to be answered within three rings, with the standard text, and as an auditor, I never flouted the rules myself.

"Hello, have you thought of the consequences of your email before shooting it off using a word like – harassment?" the thickset voice demanded.

The voice was unmistakably the general manager's whom I had copied in the email I had just sent out. He was a shrewd man, in his mid-forties, who having worked in a number of domestic as well as international airlines for years, knew of its nuances very well. I was surprised at his reaction, his words, though not at the briskness with which he reverted, since he was a stickler for promptness in email, and overall communication.

"Why, what about it, Sir?" I replied indignantly. "Don't tell me you're supporting Capt. Chopra on this, over me. I've worked with you for so long."

"Don't be silly," he bellowed. "It's only because I know you well, I want you to be aware of the consequences. Act prudently. You know well the Captain will get hauled up to the head office. After days of interrogation, which can get unpleasant for all concerned, including you, he might lose his job. They might compel him to resign, or terminate his services if he refuses to resign. Now, if that

    Shuvashree Chowdhury

is what you want, and truly believe it is justified, then go ahead with your complaint. 'Harassment' is a strong word to use and I just want you to think over calmly, its repercussions. Though I'm not justifying the Captain's behaviour, be prepared to take this to the end. Once these interrogations start, you might feel compelled to press your point to save your dignity that might be further under attack then."

"I know what 'harassment' connotes, Sir, and what Capt. Chopra did, well amounts to that. He had no business to call me, and delay the flight. I don't fall under the purview of his authority," I said firmly. "But it's true I don't think it deserves him to lose his job. All I want is for him to learn a lesson to treat women respectfully, but terminating his service would be extreme."

"Now c'mon, don't be naive," the general manager retorted at the end of the phone line. "Once a woman makes a complaint of harassment, it is taken seriously. You will be compelled to prove it, or made to feel foolish for bringing it up. In fact, a fax message has already been sent to the Delhi flight-dispatch office, summoning Capt. Chopra to the head office after he lands the Delhi flight." Then, after a pause, he emphatically added: "Now don't you remember what happened to your good friend ... I forget his name, the one you told me of?"

"Yes, yes I do remember. What do I do now?" I said, sounding desperate in my confusion, he had got through to me finally. "Why does everything have to be so complicated? I only want him to be reprimanded, not severely penalised."

"I suggest, before the Captain lands in Delhi, you resend your email explaining your accusation of 'harassment.' Perhaps even replace it with 'bullying' or 'ragging'. Then they might let him off, seeking an apology."

The phone went dead in my hand, as the general manager hung up. I went over the incident in my head in detail, from the time I saw the two pilots peering at me through the cockpit window. The indignation the recall aroused, tempted me to think Capt. Chopra deserved to lose his job after all. It would set an example to those erroneous like him, who thought they could get away with this chauvinist attitude and behaviour, with their clout. Moreover, I mentally reasoned, my standing up for my dignity would set an example. It would boost the morale of other women employees, who feel inhibited and compromise their self-esteem for fear of losing their jobs or foregoing career advancements. But again, there is also the flip side to this. As the general manager had just reminded me, did Capt. Chopra really deserve to lose his job over this?

I was now truly in a dilemma over the impact my accusation of 'harassment' might have on the Captain's life. Would the severity of the penalty accorded to him, if it was by way of his losing his job, be justifiable for his paltry misbehaviour? I had little time to act now, weighing the odds with maturity – either in going along with my accusation of 'harassment', in retracting totally, or reducing its severity. Logging out of my computer, I decided to take a brisk walk over a cup of coffee downstairs, to resolve my dilemma clearheadedly. After all, it was my judgment to make, not be swayed by others opinions either which way.

* * *

As I walked downstairs, an image, fresh even after years, came to mind. It had been 10.30pm of a chilly November, in the year 1995, a week after I had joined the airline. Outside the airport terminal, in front of the ticketing counter, I awaited my official car-drop along with three colleagues. We had hailed for the car in the parking lot on the public address system. I stood at a little distance from the others, leaning on the ticketing counter windowsill, having stepped out of my shoes. My feet were sore from walking the colossal terminal and tarmac in the high heels. I had not received my uniform yet, so was wearing a black and white, printed, full-sleeved, *salwar kameez*. I pulled out one hairpin after another from my hair held in a French-roll. As not used to wearing my hair so tight, my head hurt. With each distracted pull of a pin, some hair fell loose.

After the last hairpin was in my hand, I shook my head with eyes closed, to let the hair settle down to the back of my waist. As I opened my eyes with difficulty after the long tiresome day, I noticed a man standing in front of me. It was the metal-wing above his navy-blue blazer's chest pocket that first caught my attention, as I curiously appraised him. I identified the broad chest, wearing

          Shuvashree Chowdhury

the full wing as belonging to a pilot. Flight stewards wore the half-wing, I knew. The pilot stood so close, I could smell his cologne. My gaze involuntarily went upward, meeting his large eyes that were prominent on his chiselled face. A few inches taller than me at 5'7", he didn't look more than thirty years. When the lopsided grin on his generous mouth reached his brown eyes, the laugh-lines emerging, realising I had been staring at him dazedly, I looked downward.

"Ma'am, I'm driving into town," he said, taking off his cap, revealing a short crop of thick hair. "Would you like a lift, if your vehicle's not here yet?"

"No, thank you! Captain," I replied, promptly standing erect now from the leaning position. "I'm staff and am awaiting the official car drop home."

"Aha! That explains the hurry in letting your hair down … a long tiring day!" he grinned. "I've never seen you around here before."

"Captain, I joined only a week back," I replied, giving him my name.

"I'm Capt. Aneet Dixit," he introduced himself, proffering his hand to shake, which I shook nervously, as he added, "I'm from Mumbai. I just brought the Bangalore flight in and am taking the evening flight back to Mumbai tomorrow."

I silently nodded, as my colleague Nandini in uniform, a spirited woman who burst into peals of laughter at the slightest, walked up to us.

"Hi, you ladies need a ride home?" the Captain asked, turning to her.

"No, thank you! Captain," she replied, "Our car will be here any minute now."

"So, as I was just telling your friend," he said to Nandini, "I'm here until tomorrow evening. Why don't we all go out? Give me your numbers."

Nandini quietly obliged, pulling out paper and pen from her handbag.

"Very nice to meet you," he said to me with a slight bow.

Then waiving to Nandini and the others, he got into his car that was waiting to take him to the hotel. The next morning, Capt.

Dixit called me at home, much to my surprise. I politely told him I could not join him for lunch at their hotel's restaurant, as I was on duty at 2pm. That evening at work, I was assigned to the departure hall, which by 7.30pm was crowded with passengers of all six domestic airlines operating in those days.

I had been repeatedly making announcements from the glass public-address booth, reading from my staff-manual, not very sure of them yet. One such time, as I stepped out hurriedly after making the announcement, I almost collided with someone holding the glass door open for me. As I distractedly tried dodging my way past him, I realised he was purposefully blocking the doorway in an attempt to get my attention.

"The most stimulating announcement I've heard in a departure hall," he said chuckling, as I looked up squarely in the direction of the voice.

"Capt. Dixit, good to see you again!" I smiled, embarrassed, then added: "I've announced the boarding for your flight, as your co-commander gave us the clearance."

Then taking a step forward, in a bid to get to the boarding gate I said, "Anyway, you have a safe and pleasant flight."

"Wait a minute," he said, and then from his black pilot's overnighter, retrieving two paper boxes of chocolates, he proffered them to me, adding: "Here's something for you and your friends."

I looked at the boxes curiously in his outstretched hands. Then recognising the packaging as those served on board the business-class, I accepted, smiling broadly at what I thought was a genuine gesture of friendship.

"I'd love to try some authentic Bengali food," he added suddenly. "Consider this a bribe to take me and my crew out on my next trip. Perhaps you'll also show us around your city. I've not been here much."

"Sure Captain, I'll take y'all to a nice Bengali place in town," I replied. "Also show you around town. I hope it's alright if my friends come, too."

A week later, Aneet was back in Calcutta, commanding a Mumbai flight. It was the evening of the 31st of December. I was at work, when he called at the backup office, on reaching their hotel, the Oberoi in Chowringhee.

            Shuvashree Chowdhury

"There's a crew party at the Airport Hotel," he said. "Why don't you join us? I'll have a car pick you up after the shift, from the airport. The driver could take you home to get dressed, and then bring you back to the hotel."

"I'm really sorry Captain, I won't be able to make it," I promptly replied. "I've got to go to a rooftop party organised by some friends here."

"Why don't you just go ahead to the crew party," Jessica interjected, in an undertone. "It will be fun, more interesting than Rina's."

She had received Aneet's call first, then handed the handset to me, thus knew who was at the other end of the line. Also, she had met him the first night while waiting for the car drop along with me. Now, putting the call on hold, I conferred with Jessica – a pretty, petite woman, with slant eyes and wavy hair, whose father was Anglo-Indian and mother was Chinese.

Jessica's persuasive enthusiasm rubbing off on me, she assured to excuse me from Rina's party. I tried to persuade her to join me, but she insisted Rina would be upset if both of us didn't show up since she was expecting us. I accepted Aneet's invitation to the New Year party, along with his proposal to send a car to pick me up. The car took me home to Salt Lake first. I was able to convince my parent's that my presence at the official party was mandatory, the waiting car justifying my claim. Just as Jessica asserted, I dressed trendily – in a halter-neck pink tube top, my hair left loose, with fitting blue jeans. The party at the hotel close to the airport, run by ITDC (India Tourism Development Corporation), was indeed as Jessica promised. It was enjoyable, with friendly, cheerful people, good food, drinks and music. Aneet introduced me to many of the other pilots, cabin crew, who took to me warmly as if I were one of them, as we danced. After the party, at about 2am, on their way to their hotel in the city, Aneet, along with another pilot, dropped me home.

After that night, whenever Aneet had layover flights at Calcutta, I went out with him and his crew for lunch, dinner, movies, or to the discotheque. I liked their company, and they mine, which added to the convenience of a local person to guide their jaunts. It was close to two years now that Aneet and I had developed a friendship above these outings, grown from our conversations in person or over the phone from Mumbai, if he was not rostered for a Calcutta flight for long. It was when Aneet had not come to Calcutta for more than three months or called me, that I thought something was amiss. I called his house several times but was always told he was not home. I gave up trying to contact him, waiting for him to call instead. Then one late evening, I came across a Co-pilot named Harish at the arrival hall, a friend of Aneet's I had met a few times. He was a tall, brawny man, with droopy shoulders, who walked with a swagger.

"I have not seen Capt. Dixit in a while," I said to him abruptly. "Do you have any idea, why he's not been coming to Calcutta?"

"Aneet's not flying now," he replied, averting my gaze. "He's been grounded indefinitely."

"Why, is he unwell or something?" I asked worriedly then almost to myself I added, "Perhaps that explains his not taking my calls."

"Actually he got himself into some big trouble," Harish replied hesitantly, sounding glum. "He's facing an enquiry committee, wherein every few days there is a long meeting at the head office. Poor guy, he is under pressure."

"An enquiry," I resounded in horror, "But for what, what's he done."

"I'll leave that for him to tell you. I will just tell him that I met you and ask him to call you." He replied, and then added: "See you around sometime."

Before I had the chance to press him to tell me more, not sure when Aneet would call, he walked ahead, to catch up with the rest of the crew.

I waited patiently for the next few days, but there was no call from Aneet. I wondered if Harish had informed him he had met me. It was after a fortnight when I had given up on hearing from Aneet, he called me at home one morning.

"Hi, it's me, Aneet," he said, in a strained voice, after I said, "Hello!"

I remained silent for a few brief moments, in registering my surprise at hearing his voice. I was happy he had called, but very worried by his tone.

 Shuvashree Chowdhury

"How are you, Aneet?" I asked very softly.

"You must have heard by now?" he enquired, sounding crushed.

"I heard from Harish," I lied, in the hope he would fill me in on the details assuming I had some idea already of his predicament.

"They asked me to resign," he stated flatly. "I just don't know what to do. If I resign, it's like accepting my guilt. And if I don't, they terminate my service anyway, thus ensuring I don't get a pilot's job again."

"Then don't resign," I said calmly, though shocked and still not having a clue of the nature of his alleged guilt. "You need to fight and prove yourself innocent." Then unable to hold my curiosity any longer, I blurted softly, "But what are you up against?"

"Ah! Now that's a long story," he sighed, and then after a pause, wherein he realised my ignorance of the issue, he inquired, "So, you don't know anything about it, do you?"

"Well, honestly no, I don't know anything," I admitted.

"I assumed Harish might have told you," he replied. Then, in a banal tone, he briskly announced: "There's a sexual-harassment charge against me."

"My God," I exclaimed, shocked to the roots. "How did this happen?"

So far I had assumed he had flouted some DGCA (Director General of Civil Aviation) rules or procedures on the aircraft, but little had I imagined this.

"I've been framed," he sighed. "It's my lot. What else can I say?"

"Now c'mon," I said zealously. "You cannot accept a wrong-doing as your fate. You've got to fight for your innocence. But what really happened?"

"I was the commander of a Mumbai-Chennai-Mumbai flight," Aneet started dejectedly at the recall, "when one of the Chennai-based lady stewards, reported late to the aircraft in Mumbai, delaying the flight by ten minutes. After reporting for duty at the flight dispatch office, she was waiting to meet someone at the departure hall. Also, she was not groomed as per standards when she came on board. I was obviously upset for the delay after all the passengers were on board. We assign delays to other departments, so it is not fair to cause it ourselves. I spoke sharply to the erring lady.

"I will file a complaint with your base in-charge in Chennai on landing," I said in my annoyance. "And see to it that you're grounded."

"Okay, so how's this connected?" I interrupted, impatient to get to the core. "Obviously, whatever you said would be in the presence of other crew."

"Well, that's true, but then so what?" he sighed exasperatedly. "When a woman decides to be devious, God help you. By the time I landed the aircraft in Chennai, I had forgotten about this incident. But the woman obviously nursed my words into a grave need for vengeance, even as she smiled and served the passengers. She feared losing her flight allowance of a fortnight, which is substantial, if true to my word she was grounded. We had a change of cabin-crew at Chennai, so this woman deplaned, and I brought the aircraft back to Mumbai with a different set of crew. In Mumbai, before leaving the airport, I went to the dispatch office, as usual, to complete signing out formalities. A complaint letter awaited me there."

"A complaint letter?" I exclaimed incredulously, "Whatever for?"

"To my gravest shock," Aneet continued, "This fax complaint the woman sent from the dispatch office in Chennai stated that I had harassed her on board the Mumbai-Chennai flight. She elaborated how she felt humiliated and would, therefore, request the company to take action on me, in order to reinstate her dignity."

"What nonsense," I retorted. "A reprimand is construed as harassment."

"Yes, that's the irony," Aneet stated, continuing his narration. "I was summoned by the head of operations and informed I would have to face an enquiry committee. During the interrogation, under pressure to prove her point that I was of capable of sexual-harassment, she said things like – I have lady friends among the ground-staff in every city in addition to the cabin-crew whom I hang out with, who come over to the hotel, my room. But what was most ridiculous was her claim that I had called her to the cockpit and showed her obscene literature before another flight."

"Where would you get obscene literature on board?" I blurted.

"You can well imagine the absurdity of her claims," Aneet replied dismissively. "She claims I showed her obscene pictures

     Shuvashree Chowdhury

from the magazines on board, asked her to come to my hotel room several times, and since she didn't come, I reprimanded her in front of everyone."

"What about the rest of the crew on board," I asked. "Weren't they interrogated as well? What about your co-pilot, didn't he say anything?"

"There was little they said that saved me, as I had indeed reprimanded her in their presence. Also, it is not untrue that I have a number of lady friends in various locations, though she had no witness to my showing her the obscene literature. The persistent pressure on this woman by the interrogators, to prove she was lying, made her resort to one story after another. Then caught in the whirlpool of stories, she could not re-track."

"Who is this crazy woman?" I asked angrily. "Was she a long timer?"

"No, in fact she is very new," he replied. "You've met her, though I'd rather not tell you her name. Born and brought up in Chennai, recently she eloped with her boyfriend, marrying him much against the wishes of her conservative parents. They were forcing her to marry of their choice."

"An angel of virtue, I must say," I mocked, "How hypocritical and ironic."

"Women go all out to save their husband, children and family, if they feel threatened. Her husband is a student, so she is the only earning member in their family of two. I suppose she feared my complaint, the one I threatened to make, might rob her of her job or at least get her in the bad books of the management. It was safer to turn the tables on me, in order to safeguard her job and position in the airline, now her haven."

"But that's very devious," I stated, and then earnestly enquired. "What are you going to do now? How are you going to manage if you do resign?"

I knew he needed the job. Then there was the risk of not finding another soon if word about this incident got around. Aneet had the financial responsibility of a four-year-old daughter who had barely started school, of retired parents and a wife who did not work. This added to the home-loan, also the one for his pilot's training in the US his parents had taken.

"I really don't know," he sighed heavily, and then after a brief pause, cheering up suddenly, he added: "But I'm glad I told you all this myself, rather than you heard from elsewhere. I value your friendship a lot. It really does not matter so much what the world thinks, so long as the ones I care about – my parents, wife, child and close friends are with me."

* * *

My coffee long over, tired now from the aimless pacing, I slowly climbed the stairs back to the office on the first floor. I was no longer in a dilemma. With the distinct recall of my association with Capt. Dixit, my mind was clear and made up. As I sat at my desk, I knew exactly what I had to do now. In my opinion, though Capt. Chopra was guilty, his offence did not justify what happened to Aneet. I knew how expensive, both in terms of time and money, it was to get a commercial pilot's license. Moreover, losing one's job was a blow to one's self-esteem, which often lasted a lifetime. Then, there was the risk of not finding another soon, due to the word getting around. I would perhaps be saving Capt. Chopra a lifetime of remorse, for a mistake he committed impulsively. It is crucial to remember, that any behaviour at work that is defined as inappropriate or offends a person of another sex, may be considered sexual harassment, and invites disciplinary action.

I made up my mind to revoke my complaint, judiciously thinking of its consequences on a man's life. However, I was glad I had made the complaint in the first place, thus registering my protest. Perhaps Capt. Chopra and others like him, on learning of it, would restrict their inappropriate behaviour in future. Hopefully, it would also send out a signal to women, that they need to stop playing the victim at work, fight for their dignity in a judicious manner when circumstances truly demand it. At my desk, switching on my computer, I retrieved the last 'sent' message from my Outlook sent-folder. I resent the message to the same addresses with a fresh note. I stated that though Capt. Chopra's behaviour was unacceptable, my previous report being true, all I expected was an apology from him and no more. As I saw the 'sent' message on my computer, I felt at peace, as nothing, in my opinion, is as agonising as being in a dilemma.

Shuvashree Chowdhury

4. My Earliest Leadership Training

I might have been in the fourth or fifth standard at the time. We were home from boarding school for the winter vacations. Mother, as she often did, took us sisters to work with her, to the residential teachers training college in Alipore, Calcutta. We girls would sit in the staff room for a while where mother had a desk cubicle for herself, entertaining ourselves with magazines and stuff lying around, and a teacher or two who would be at their own desk-cubicle. Then, before our boredom had crossed endurance, we would be rescued by some student or a group four staff (as they were referred to) who would take us out for a stroll around the campus. If we were lucky to bump into Kaloo-da, the in-charge of the large supplies room, he would generously give us a basketball, volleyball, and badminton racquets with shuttles to play in the sprawling, lush fields. There was an indoor basketball as well as a badminton court in the large gymnasium, which would be locked.

At times, we would peep into the principal's office where a number of administrative staff would be busy typing on manual typewriter sets, or peering into thick files behind huge piles of more in front. They would fondly talk to us, and even offer us biscuits out of their desk drawers. But they warned us, if mother, who occupied the inner principal's cabin, had external visitors or was talking to students who were free to come and meet her anytime, or if summoned by her. Mother would, if we had made it as far inside for her to get a glimpse of us, signal to us to go outside and play. She was always formal with us at her office, and on the campus, even though students, other teachers, and staff, were very warm and friendly. Some would even keep aside toffees and chocolates for our visits, pull our cheeks and walk us with hands around our shoulders, even do up our ponytails. They would be thoroughly entertained by our curiosity and awe at what was mundane work to them.

On one such visit, there was a ladies' hockey match in progress where we were seated in the pavilion at a distance from mother – who was seated along with a few teachers and students. A group of boys, riding bicycles, came into view and soon were circling the large field. They looked at the ladies at play amusedly, peering enthusiastically at the lean athletic legs under rather short divided skirts. As they circled in slow motion, the six or seven boys made comments and grinned as if they were in a public park. They commented and laughed loudly behind the ladies who were waiting as substitutes, also wearing shorts, in readiness to get onto the field. The lecturer-coach looked at the boys menacingly, but turned back to concentrate on the game. It was at the exact moment of commencement of the break in the match, that mother waved to the ladies panting by now, twenty-two in all, who were walking towards the pavilion in any case. A few promptly broke into a jog to find out why they were being summoned.

As I watched curiously, in awe, mother said to them in the crisply commanding tone that I recognised well from my visits to her workplace: "Go get those boys here, along with their bicycles."

The ladies did not even wait a moment, as about seven or eight of them jogged over to the boys – still merrily watching them, lustily now. The ladies forcefully gripped a bicycle each and then compelled the rider to get off, by sheer strength of voice and personality – after all, they were future teachers in the making. Then each bicycle was walked around the field by a lady, its rider following meekly – pleading apologies, to where mother stood with a 'dare me if you can', menacing look in her eyes.

"Put these bicycles away in the games store room," she commanded, and then looking at the boys she calmly added: "Collect your bicycles from the police station, where they will be handed over by tomorrow. They have been confiscated for trespassing private property."

"Ma'am, sorry, we are very sorry … really very sorry," one or two boys pleaded, while the others stood quietly with heads hanging low.

"Ladies, go on take the cycles away now!" Mother commanded, turning to those still clutching the handles of one each, without a

    Shuvashree Chowdhury

word more to the boys who by now had lost all steam and looked shaken.

As their cycles were taken away, the boys left the ground shamefacedly in view of a crowd now, even as my sister and I looked on in awe. One of the students, a dear friend by then, had been seated beside us. She patted us on the head and smiled comfortingly.

"Your mother is very strict, but the kindest teacher and principal I've known yet," she said to us. "Ma'am will not hand over the cycles to the police. She only wanted to teach us girls to be tough, and these neighbourhood boys a lesson, as they keep disturbing our evening games. Ma'am organises funds for the poor students who cannot buy books and gear, she also helps so many of the staff with their children's education."

It is with this lifelong learning – this being just a glimpse, I had grown up with, that I had stepped into my work life. There is nothing more ingrained than learning through one's experiences, that too since childhood. These were to form the instinctive basis of my performance, and my style of leadership and management in my varied work assignments.

5. A Dual Life

They were at a musical concert when his cell phone rang. Saumen had kept it on the silent mode, so merely felt the vibrations in his chest pocket. He disconnected after a few rings, engrossed in the medley of the *santoor* and the *tabla*. Then feeling a single tremor of an incoming text message, he mentally noted to check it along with the missed call after the concert. He and Parul looked forward to these concerts, plays, exhibitions, and any social event that could break the monotony of their long and free days, now that they had retired from service. These occasions additionally provided scope, as well as topics, for the flagging conversations between them lately. After retirement from their challenging, action packed aviation industry careers it was difficult to settle down into a mundane existence where one day was the same as the next.

Saumen, senior to Parul, had retired two years before her, at sixty years. During their thirty-five years of service, as many in marriage, the couple had at times worked in the same office in Calcutta, at others in Mumbai or other stations of the airline that I worked in. I had barely joined in Calcutta, around the time of Saumen's retirement, but had worked closely with Parul for over two years. Saumen was a short man, of average built, with salt-and-pepper hair. He had a small face with beady eyes that astutely looked through gold-rimmed glasses, balanced on the bridge of his petite nose. After the concert, walking squarely down the exit way with his shoulders pulled back, chest out, head held high, as always, giving his otherwise understated physique a regal bearing, he checked the missed call on his mobile-phone. The call, as he had expected, was from Shipra, who had also left a text message after he disconnected her call.

Looking around him cautiously, Saumen noticed Parul was still quite a few steps behind him, due to the crowd pouring out of the hall ahead of her. Thus, hidden from her view, Saumen read the

 Shuvashree Chowdhury

text message from Shipra as he walked amidst the sea of people.

"Didn't hear from you all day," it read. "I had been waiting for your call."

"Silly girl," he muttered to himself, smiling with the familiar glint in his eyes that came from thinking of her glowing face, as he spontaneously deleted it. Then, after deleting the record of her missed call, he turned around to ensure there was a safe distance between him and Parul for her not to have noticed him doing so. Outside of the exit gate, he waited for Parul to catch up with him. Their driver, who had been standing there, as people started to pour out, on seeing Saumen, signalled for him to wait, and then dashed off to get their car from the parking.

Looking out for Parul amidst the crowd, Saumen noticed the peaceful, smiling faces trooping out of the Mahajati Sadan auditorium, the effect of the enchanting music. He smiled to himself, but more from an inner enchantment than that prompted by the melodious evening. On the drive back home, the discussion, as expected, was about the concert. Saumen, conscious of Parul's presence, tried to pull the reins of his surreptitious exhilaration. After crossing the driveway of their complex, barely had their car parked in front of their building, when Saumen leaped out.

"Parul, you carry on up," he said briskly. "I'll be back in a while."

"But where are you off to so late? It is already past eight," she exclaimed. Then, in an even tone, she asked, "Do you have to go now? Can't you go in the morning?"

"I'll be back soon … even before you realise it," he insisted, ignoring his wife's dismal expression and the drops of rain that had burst out of the dark, cloud filled sky, onto his lined face. "I'll quickly just get myself a packet of cigarettes."

The driver could have got the cigarettes, Parul thought, getting off the car. She stood sadly watching Saumen's receding form in an olive-green, collared T-shirt and beige trousers, till he was out of sight. She then proceeded towards the lift, headed for their tenth-floor apartment. A tall woman with a slender frame and smooth skin, which, in addition to good genes, was the result of regularly practising yoga, Parul, at sixty-two years, looked a decade younger. She had an attractive face with slight features, the proud expression and intelligent eyes giving her an aura of poise always. Now in a pink and white floral-printed chiffon *saree*, with a pink sleeveless-blouse, a string of pearls around her neck and pearl drop earrings, she carried herself with elegance. The music concert had lifted her spirits, but Soumen's indiscretions, his walking off in spite of her restraint, was like the sudden emergency landing of her aircraft of happiness.

As Parul put the key into their apartment's door lock, the familiar pang of loneliness hit her. It felt almost like an ache in her chest, scaring her, as always, of a probable cardiac dysfunction. Though her echocardiogram results always gave her heart a clean chit, she knew that with women her age, often heart disease went undetected and then suddenly one died silently of a heart attack. The shooting pain Parul often felt on her back, the sudden clamming of the muscles around her heart, intensified when Saumen was out on his own, like now. The condition as detected by their family doctor was from an anxiety bout syndrome. Parul knew Saumen had dashed off to meet the woman, the one who had driven a sword into their decades of marriage like never before. Though she had acted oblivious, Parul knew well the cigarettes were only an alibi. Just as she knew Saumen's long morning and evening walks lately, or increased visits to the grocers, were all alibis to his rendezvous with Shipra.

The overwhelming power Shipra had over Saumen, never ceased to astonish Parul, though she was too tired to fight it anymore. She had been aware of Shipra's inclusion in Saumen's life for the last two years. At first, unusual to her demeanour, Parul had reacted viciously, uncompromisingly, with revulsion. After all the threats and endearments had failed to keep Saumen away from Shipra, Parul had relegated herself to a feeling of calm emptiness. She was not sure now, which would be more painful after years of marriage – losing her husband to death, or completely to a much younger woman. So she just maintained a status quo, pretending all was well. Why did this have to happen to them now at the far end of their lives, she wondered dejectedly? They should have been spending the rest of their years in warm companionship and tranquillity.

Just as Saumen stepped out of their complex's main gate to

                    Shuvashree Chowdhury

the road outside, walking through the drizzle, he quickly dialled Shipra's number. Parul had rightly assumed he had been rushing to meet her, though Saumen had no clue of that, as he thought he had long convinced her of not seeing Shipra anymore.

"Parul and I were at a musical concert, so I could not take your call," he said softly, as soon as he heard Shipra's voice at the other end. Then somewhat sharply he added, "I told you not to call me. Didn't I say I would call whenever possible? Parul was with me all the time today, so I could not call you earlier."

"I just wanted to hear your voice," Shipra replied tenderly, "though I was actually looking forward to meeting you, over your evening walk."

"Hmmm … Come now, come quickly to the regular place then," he said in a patronising tone, delighted at her yearning. "I can meet you for a short while."

It was Shipra's guileless, utterly feminine utterances that made Saumen so crazy about her. He adored the verbal admittances to her dependence on his calls and their meetings, also the grateful attitude she projected to his presence in her life. What more could a man want at his age, than to be truly needed by a beautiful young woman, given that the world at large no longer had much use of his presence in it? Parul had never admitted to needing him in all their life together, possibly too proud for that. Moreover, after his retirement from service, his life had lacked any purpose, till he met Shipra. After hanging up, smiling to himself Saumen hurried in the increasing intensity of the rain, to the small café at the end of the lane on the main road. Just before he reached the café, in the corner was a small shop selling knickknacks. Saumen bought a packet of cigarettes before stepping inside the café, walking towards their regular table.

After he was seated, Saumen lit a cigarette, watching intently as he slowly blew the smoke in a ring above him. Shipra walked in just then, and approached him in view of his ring of smoke. He looked thrilled as a teenaged boy, she noticed, smiling to herself at his ability to still do it at his age. Suddenly noticing Shipra, Saumen took a deep breath sheepishly, gulping the rest of the smoke quickly. As he swallowed, he was unsure what made him gulp so spontaneously, was it his juvenile act that she had just viewed, or the sight of her sheer beauty. Shipra had a pretty oval face, with large brown eyes that sparkled delightfully when she spoke animatedly, batting her long eyelashes. With a petite nose, a generous mouth that pouted in annoyance or formed light dimples on her fair cheeks when she smiled, there was something endearingly childlike about her even at thirty years.

As Shipra stood now, tall, slim, her brown hair falling to the back of her waist, in an aqua-blue chiffon *saree* – damp from the rain, emphasising her full form, Saumen could not help having mixed feelings towards this child-woman. She invoked a protective fatherly streak in him, perhaps due to the over thirty years of age difference, as well as, paradoxically, a fiercely passionate one.

"I just wanted to see you briefly," she started, sitting across him with that dimpled smile that always stirred his emotions. "Since you didn't mention earlier we would not be meeting today, I looked forward to it all day." Then lightly brushing the drops of water from her hair and *saree*, oblivious to the impact she had on him, abruptly she added: "Just look outside, the weather is so beautiful."

"You look so gorgeous, Shipra," Saumen whispered in response, looking meaningfully into her eyes. "The beauty outside is a meek contender to yours."

"Now c'mon," Shipra giggled. "That is very poetic, even for you. So tell me what kept you so busy all day that you are now attempting to make up with verse."

"Parul told me of the concert passes she had picked up only late this morning, so I was unable to inform you earlier," he said. "Though, I was certain, I would make time out to meet you, so I didn't text."

This café was close to both their homes and a decent and convenient place where they met often, in addition to sitting by the lake after they finished their morning or evening walks around it. A young waiter, who knew them well by now, approached, smiling broadly as usual. Saumen wondered whether the man smiled in amusement, at someone his age dating a woman so young. However, he dismissed the idea, curtly asking him to get their regular cappuccinos. He had enough to worry about Parul as it is, to allow a waiter to disturb his contentment.

It had been early one morning on his regular walk at the Lake Gardens, two years back, that Saumen had first met Shipra. She had been sitting quietly, staring at the ducks in the lake, in a navy-blue track pant and a pink sweatshirt, her long hair held high on her head in a ponytail. Walking briskly as usual, he had noticed her from behind. It was on his second round, walking very close behind her still staring ahead into the water, that he thought he heard a sob. When he passed her a third time, she chanced to look back briskly, with the sound of a stray dog close to her abruptly barking. Thus, he got a glimpse of her face, which had made him curious. Her eyes were red, tears streaming down her face that she briskly brushed off but not before he noticed. It was a strikingly beautiful face, but it was the tears streaming down her cheeks, gleaming in the sun's early morning rays, that had caught his attention.

This image remained with Saumen, till he was again right behind her on completion of another round of the huge lake. Overcome with concern for the distraught face that lingered with him, he walked up to her seated on the bench on the grass, off the metal road.

"Is something wrong?" he asked very tenderly from behind. "Can I help you please?"

Shaking her head, she replied in a shaky voice, "No, nothing, I'm fine."

"Talking to a stranger may lighten your burden, you know," he insisted, and then affectionately, as if talking to a child, he added, "What can possibly be so wrong in the life of a beautiful young woman like you?"

Turning sideways to face him squarely, her eyes red and swollen like the rest of her face, in a low muffled voice, she retorted: "Everything is wrong."

He sat down beside her, his age giving him the liberty, which luckily wasn't denied to him.

Saumen was to remain sitting here for long, talking to her, laying the foundation to their friendship. This was at the time before Parul's retirement, so she would have left for work, and he didn't have to hurry back home. Shipra had opened up to him, trusting his age, glad to talk to someone as attentive as him about the cause of her misery. She had not slept all of the previous night, she confessed, distraught after returning late evening from a work assignment. In the departure lounge at the Bangalore airport, she had come face to face with her ex-husband, Anirban, along with his fiancée. The pain of seeing him so suddenly, just months after their divorce, that too with another woman, had been excruciating. However, the acuteness of the pain had been anaesthetizing at the time, enabling her to hold her composure and exchange pleasantries with them. It was only on the flight that she had felt the shooting pain, with the recall of the last few years of their married life in Bangalore, as software professionals, in different companies.

After that morning, Saumen and Shipra had often met by the lake, where they both came for morning walks, till it was now a ritual. Shipra was drawn to Saumen for his maturity and compassion, out of her need for moral and emotional support. Being a single mother to a four-year-old boy was not easy, and in spite of her parents pitching in, she needed a friend who she could talk to. On his part, Saumen, who after his retirement had suddenly felt his life had lost focus, once again felt useful and needed, in guiding and mentoring her. They slowly started spending more time together, as well as talking on the phone. With time, they started meeting in the evenings too, on her way back from work, after his evening walks. Saumen's interactions with Shipra brought back the zing in his life. It took him back to when he was her age, making him feel young, energised and enthused, all this also from being newly in love.

To Shipra, Saumen was her confidant, advisor, and she began to depend on him emotionally. He was sensitive, caring, responsible, also made her laugh with his steady wit. But above all this, he was very compromising and made no demands on her in any way. In enjoying each other's company they did not realise how time flew, and soon, by the end of two years, Parul retired from her job. With Parul home most of the time now, it became increasingly difficult for Saumen to go out. Parul would want to accompany him on his morning and evening walks. Even the times when he made some excuse or the other and went out, he had to return soon. He seemed much happier lately, and often Parul caught him smiling to himself. With his prolonged absences following brief phone calls, his carrying his cell phone in person from one room

          Shuvashree Chowdhury

to the other, even to the bathroom, Parul became suspicious. It was not long before she concluded something was amiss.

Parul recalled these signs had been there for the last two years, but she had been tied up with work to spare much thought and importance then. In spite of her doubts, Parul did not want to alert Saumen yet, thereby giving him a chance to cover his tracks, if there was anything he was hiding. But above that, she did not want him to think of her as paranoid. Under these circumstances, it was going to be difficult for Parul to find out anything, let alone, get proof. It was at this juncture, much against her wishes that she decided to seek my help, thereby confiding in me. Parul had been the human resources manager, and I, the service quality coordinator, in the airline, and thus we had interacted closely. Saumen had retired as the head of finance. With her seniority, I had looked upon Parul as my mentor and had great respect for her expertise and professionalism. Even after her retirement, I preferred to get her opinion on any difficult matters pertaining to my work and thus we had become very close.

One evening, after I returned from work, Parul called me sounding very distressed, "Only you can help me," she said abruptly, to my utter bewilderment. "It's Saumen, he's having an affair."

"An affair, what do you mean, Parul. Are you sure?" I blurted, sounding amused, then recalling her desperate tone, I asked, "But how did you learn of it, and with whom?"

"With whom, I don't know yet," she retorted. "This morning, I happened to see an incoming text message on his cell phone, as he had forgotten to carry it along with him to the bathroom. It read: 'I need to meet you urgently. Please come to our usual place.' On reading it, he left the house in such a hurry as though it was a fire alarm, though I tried to question him to stop him from leaving."

"Are you sure, Parul, about the affair?" I asked sounding concerned now. "An affair at this age … moreover, he doesn't seem to me like the type to have one, the short time that I've known him at work. Maybe you are overreacting and Saumen will have a justifiable explanation for his association with any woman."

"No, it's not just this one time," Parul replied astutely. "I've been watching him for some time now, noting the apparent signs of someone much in love. But I didn't want to believe my own perceptions. After today, seeing the message, then his defiance in going out in spite of my protests, I have no doubts at all."

"What are you planning on doing, Parul?" I asked, feeling really sorry for her misery. "And how can I possibly help you? Do you think I should get involved, after all both of you have been my seniors? In addition to my friendship with you, I have a deep regard for Saumen. He's always been warm and kind to me."

"I'm ashamed to even tell you all this, let alone ask you to help me," she said, "And I would never have if there were anyone else I could trust or confide in. I know you are mature and smart. I really must find out who this woman is, and you can help me decide on terminating our redundant marriage or not."

"Parul, please don't think so far, I'm sure it's nothing serious," I replied dismally "You can't seriously be thinking of leaving him. It's got to be one big misunderstanding, which you can perhaps talk through. However, in order to put your doubts to rest, I'll be happy to help you."

"I'm not worried about his leaving me, perhaps for a much younger woman," she replied, adding forcefully, "In fact, I'll leave him, if I confirm anything."

"I don't think you really mean it, Parul," I said. "Now, you really are overreacting."

"No, I'm not. It's my pride that is at stake here the most," she replied intensely. "Saumen is foolish in assuming I won't take a drastic step, out of fear of disgracing ourselves, to our families and friends, at this age. He possibly assumes I'd not risk our lifetime's professional and personal reputations, but I'm not going to allow his impertinence at the cost of what people think."

"Okay, I quite get it," I replied. "I'll help you find out who the woman is."

The next evening after work, just as we had planned, I dropped in to meet Parul at home, on the pretext of discussing some work related problem.

"Hi, it's so good to see you. What a pleasant surprise," Saumen said cheerily on opening the door, leading me inside. "It's been some time since we met, right?"

     Shuvashree Chowdhury

After a few minutes of general conversation, Saumen left the house on the pretext of fetching cigarettes, as Parul had expected. As soon as he was out of the door, I waited for him to get into the lift, and then followed him. Taking the other lift, I trailed him from a safe distance down the road. I saw him walk into the café at the end of the road. I waited, hovering outside, at a position from where I could see Saumen through the window. After he was seated, a rather good-looking young woman, in a magenta-coloured chiffon *saree*, joined him.

I waited just long enough to take in the physical attributes of the woman, along with the dynamics between her and Saumen, so I could take it back to Parul. I walked back to their apartment with anger and revulsion towards Saumen.

"Did you see her?" Parul asked at the door. "Is she very beautiful?"

Simply nodding in assent, unable to meet her eyes, I asked curiously: "Why couldn't you go and see her for yourself, instead of sending me?"

"I could not bear to see her, that too with him," Parul replied, her eyes brimming.

Then she composed herself. She seemed suddenly reconciled to the situation, after my having confirmed it. Perhaps to save her pride, even from me.

"What are you going to do now?" I asked worried, seeing her steely expression.

"I really don't know," she said distractedly, as though to herself. "Thirty-five years of my life gone up in smoke. And what can I possibly do to get it back?"

On sensing Parul needed the time alone before Saumen returned, I left. She and Soumen had led a good life, Parul thought now, flashes of their times together, even recently, came flooding upon her. Having consciously decided not to have children after the loss of one who was stillborn, they had concentrated on their careers instead. They had also had a good circle of friends, taking several holidays with the free tickets they received on most international airlines. Yes, they had had their share of arguments and differences, but which couple did not? In spite of knowing Saumen had a roving eye, Parul had never taken it seriously. The other women in his life had meant little to him, or so she always thought. The aviation industry is full of good-looking, smart women. They had come and they had gone from his life. It was for the first time now that Parul saw Saumen so different. The way he acted was absolutely like a teenager in love. How could someone behave like this at his age, forgetting his position in society? It was very humiliating and infuriating to her.

Parul had assumed, having worked hard all their lives, they would spend the rest of their lives in a warm companionship, travelling the world, and doing things they had not had the time for so far. How could this be happening to them then, she thought desperately? They were, since she had retired, learning music, having always wanted to do so, but not finding the time before. Saumen was learning to play the guitar and Parul the sitar as well as classical singing. Their respective teachers came home a few times each week. After all these years of marriage, they were also best friends she had thought, but how wrong she had been. Could beauty and youth be so powerful, for him to forget all that they had shared together over a lifetime, including the loss of both their parents and their child? Parul remained sitting on their bed, staring out of the window, distraught by her thoughts, in a dilemma over what should be her next course of action.

After what seemed like a very long time, Parul heard the key turning in the lock on the front door. She heard the familiar sound of Saumen's footsteps walking inside, and then it stopped right in front of her.

"Where's your friend?" he asked casually. "I thought you might ask her to stay for dinner. It's been a long time since I've had a real chat with her, to catch up on all the gossip, on what's going on at the office lately."

Parul remained silent, still staring out of the window.

"What happened? Is something wrong?" Saumen asked, coming up closer to Parul, then sitting down on the bed, laughing, he added "Did you women quarrel?"

"Why don't you just leave, go away," Parul suddenly screamed, hysterically, much to Saumen's shock. "Just get the hell out and go live with that woman."

"What are you talking about? I don't want to go anywhere,"

 Shuvashree Chowdhury

Saumen replied innocently, sounding aghast, although his face contorted in guilt.

Parul looked at him squarely, scornfully, and then blurted "You think I am such a big fool, do you? Stop acting so innocent. I saw her with you in the café."

"So you women followed me! Did you?" he replied taken aback, then seeing the rage in her eyes, he added "Parul, it's not what you think, really. She is just a troubled woman who looks up to me for support, and I've been helping her."

"What a wretched liar you are," Parul retorted sharply, viciously, looking at him wide-eyed in horror, her eyes filled with tears threatening to burst forth.

"I promise you, Parul," he said in a placating tone, alarmed, unable to bear her crushed appearance. "I will stop interacting with her if that is what you wish."

He had never meant to hurt Parul, he thought desperately. Looking at her beaten and defeated, he was filled with tenderness. She had stuck by him, and God knows he had given her numerous reasons to call their marriage quits.

Saumen knew he still loved Parul and how could he possibly not? She had never been anything but good to him, though perhaps not the way he had hoped for or expected. Theirs was a love that had lasted almost their whole lives, having met in their early twenties, right after college. How could he desert her now at this age? More than that, how would he possibly live without her? He needed Parul in his life, Saumen concluded desperately. Just then, involuntarily, Shipra's cute face sprang up in front of him, so alluring and yet so vulnerable. He realised that he was in love with her, rather madly in love, and this was so different and special. Just being with Shipra gave him a high. To feel this way at his age, to have a beautiful woman half his age in love with him, was thrilling and he considered himself blessed. Saumen knew both the women loved him, Parul providing the stability, the habit, the security, while Shipra, along with her son, the thrill, the mad rush of hormones and the laughter.

Suddenly the loud noise of a door clanging shut brought Saumen back from his trance. Looking around, he noticed Parul was not there. She had just walked out of their bedroom, as if to put distance between them. To him, knowing Parul so well, it was like she had mentally and emotionally shut him out. He was in such a predicament. How could he possibly leave either woman, as he loved one dearly and was madly in love with the other? What choice did he have now, but to carry on leading the dual life? He would have to sort it all out soon, he thought wretchedly, but not now. For now, he had to comfort Parul, beg her forgiveness and pray that she did not throw him out. The apartment was in her name. Moreover, he would never be able to forgive himself if he deserted her.

6. *Wings of Tyranny*

One morning, as I rarely did, when still working for the airline, I visited the gym in the morning before work, instead of in the evening. After my usual hourly workout that I wrapped up with the butterfly arm press while chatting with the instructor, I hurriedly collected my bag from the locker room and rushed out. I was one of the last ones to leave that morning and was going to rush home – nearby, and then drive down to the airport about 12 km away through office-hour traffic. Other than the instructor, to whom I always chatted liberally, I did not talk to any of the all-male members who used the gym. Other women used it during the day.

As I stepped out on the road, I hurriedly unlocked my car with the remote key and chucking my bag on the adjacent seat, positioned myself at the steering wheel. It was only when I was about to release the accelerator after turning the ignition on distractedly, that I looked up at the windshield. To my shock and immense horror, something that resembled a large grey rat was plastered on it. I turned off the ignition and jumping out, walked over in front, to be struck by revulsion. A dead pigeon, perhaps run over by a car, or electrocuted on the wires above, was positioned on my windshield, with both the wings spread well out. It was actually smothered on the glass and there was muck all around.

I ran back into the gym in immense fear, as I had an intuitive sense of being targeted and perhaps attacked further in a nastier way. I felt vulnerable as one might during a riot. I breathlessly narrated the situation to the instructor, who was also just leaving. He rushed out with me and looking exasperated, guilty, and somewhat ashamed even, from the obvious sexism hurled at me for no apparent reason, removed the poor creature. He had to turn his face away from the horrid, decaying smell that hit his senses. He assured me that there was nothing more to worry about and I could go home now. He advised me to get the car washed before leaving for work.

This part time gym instructor, much older than me, incidentally a Facebook friend now, was actually a cop in service, even as he currently is - from the intelligence wing of the Calcutta police. And yet, right in front of him, even while I was in conversation with him, someone had implanted that rotting sense of sexist and perverse humour in wings, on me.

The next day I went back to the gym in the evening as usual, but I never tried to find out who had done the dastardly act, or bother with an apology or seek punishment. It never struck me even for a moment that my reserved behaviour or by my merely being a woman, I had incited this perpetrator. Sexists, stalkers, molesters, rapists – it's them who are to blame, not those who they victimise. Why would I give him further perverse pleasure, having watched my reaction to his nasty prank for sure, of having got my attention – with his vile psyche for which he chartered the rotten wings of a dead creature, perhaps even squashed it himself!

     Shuvashree Chowdhury

7. *What You Wear to Work Matters*

That morning, as usual, I walked into the swanky reception lounge of the multinational company headquartered in Toronto, Canada. It was one of my valued clients as an international sales executive with a top ranking travel company of the time. This was a few months since I had joined them after a brief stint at an institute, Computer Point, which was to shut shop in the years to come, just as this travel agency would. Smiling at the receptionist, I briskly walked into the administrative office, as it was my slotted time for a visit. The three of us top travel agents the MNC had enlisted, had a designated time of half an hour twice daily for our visits. I did not have to seek permission or wait at the reception to meet the travel desk officers if I came at my designated time of 11am and 4pm.

This MNC occupied numerous floors of the impressive Jeevan Deep building on Middleton Street, at the intersection of the arterial Chowringhee Road, running through central Calcutta. It was a time when the city was still years away from being renamed Kolkata. I visited this office at both my allotted times daily, due to their immense business potential, to enable me to make a mark in my new job in meeting my sales targets. This was from a steady and rather large part of this company's workforce travelling domestically to their various factories and offices throughout the country. But much over that, my dual visits were in the hope of attracting the steady flow of international travel of their senior executives. As being new in the trade, it would otherwise take me a while to win their confidence into earning the slice of the business rightfully mine, which currently went to the two other travel agents. Their executives were much established in the travel business and thus trusted. But I had the confidence, that with sincerity to my work and clients, I would be able to gain and stand my own steady ground.

The administrative manager, Sujoy Ghosh, a senior and much-respected man in this engineering company, noticed me, over the head of a visitor sitting across him at his desk. Sujoy-da, as everyone referred to him, was a tall, handsome man with a steely athletic frame, chiselled facial features with sharp piercing eyes and a hawkish nose. His salt and pepper hair, along with the way he held his head and shoulders erect, whether sitting or standing, added to his stately bearing. After a few moments of my standing awkwardly even as his junior, a Tamilian man older than him, tried to engage me with small talk, Sujoy-da looked up at me squarely.

"Have you brought the ABC (travel guide) I asked you to?" he asked rather curtly, as was usual with him – which I had become used to by now.

"Yes, Sujoy-da, here it is," I replied, proffering the large, heavy ABC I had walked the ten minutes stretch from my office on Camac Street with.

"No, I don't need it! You take it with you to meet Amit Chatterjee, who is to travel to the US shortly. Walk down this side corridor, his cabin is behind mine, towards the end of this floor."

I soon found myself seated in front of Amit Chatterjee. In his late twenties – as I deduced from his appearance, he was of average height and built, with a fleshy oval face and wavy black hair, and wore gold-rimmed spectacles. He was barely able to speak coherently, from sporadic involuntary blushing, while repeatedly looking over and then much beyond my head. I found his attitude distracting and annoying. In curiosity over who might be sharing his joke, perhaps even at my expense, I abruptly turned around. To my surprise, I found about half a dozen men at desks grouped together in a cubicle, smirking at Amit Chatterjee, with their heads raised above the half walls. Then, as I looked back at the man himself, justifiably irritated now, he promptly looked away. I had no doubts left that the smirking men were indeed seeking to entertain themselves at my expense.

These men, must have in the last few months that I was visiting their office twice a day, seen me coming in and out. I might have passed them at the reception lounge on their floor or any other – to a senior executive's cabin to plan his international itinerary, or even in the lift and corridors. They might have discussed me with Amit, who being senior had perhaps taken the initiative to call

     Shuvashree Chowdhury

me over to rag me, when the opportunity arose. Then there was also the possibility that Amit had blurted out to these men that he fancied me, thus they now teased him for it. And so, when I was seated in from of him, he had become conscious, as they were all watching and animatedly teasing him from behind. With these plausible causes of my humiliation coursing through my mind, whatever his provocation might me – I was immensely annoyed. I promptly stood up.

"Please leave your requirements at the travel desk, Mr Amit Chatterjee," I said sharply. "I will get back to you with a proposed itinerary."

Then passing between the men now looking at each other in amused curiosity across the narrow lane, I marched back to the administration room. The heavy ABC (travel guide) lending my walk more moral and physical gravity than I felt in having to get past my perceived perpetrators in my flustered state. I was determined to let the men here know I meant business, and only business. So I walked into the travel manager's cubicle and relayed the incident to Sujoy Ghosh and his assistant crisply, without any preamble. They merely looked down silently.

However, that evening, I returned to this MNC's administrative office as usual. This was after a brief stop at the British Airways office across the street, also the KLM office below. I tended to include similar stops often on my visits here, as they helped me build a rapport with the various airlines down the same road to get the best deals for my clients. As soon as I stepped out of the lift in the Jeevan Deep building and into the lounge, the receptionist named Sandra beckoned to me over tending to her phones, to come over. She was a middle aged, dusky but luminous complexioned, plain-looking Anglo-Indian woman, with beady eyes and curly hair, usually well dressed in smart suit-dresses. Her overall makeup and grooming was immaculate, and this included her well-manicured and red polished hand nails and her trendily stilettoed feet. I stood beside her for a while, as she finished talking and then transferring the calls that beeped on her EPABX to designated desks. Then she looked up at me with a warm gleam in her eyes.

"Amit Chatterjee requested me to give this note to you," Sandra said, proffering a folded chit of paper, stressing Amit's name with pride and fondness, as she continued to look into my eyes earnestly.

"Thanks, Sandra," I briskly replied in taking the note.

Then I quietly listened to her attempts to warm me up, by recounting Amit's popularity, in seeking of me to be receptive of his note. Sandra's desk was about four to five steps away from the administration office, where I was headed to the travel desk. In the time since leaving her desk, I quickly read Amit's note, written with a fountain pen, in neat handwriting.

"Dear Sujata," it read, "May I take you out for coffee? We could discuss my travel plans over it."

The morning's incident – Amit's face blushing in front of me at his desk, and over the smirking men behind, promptly flashed to mind. And with it, I was uncontrollably annoyed again.

"See this, *Dada*," I erupted, proffering the note to Sujoy Ghosh, dropping my usual inhibitions of his crisply reserved manner, more so in risking my business prospects here. Then, as he took the note and read it, I continued: "*Dada*, what is going on here …? You ask me to meet Amit Chatterjee … now Sandra gives me this note along with trying to convince me how really nice and popular he is at the office, in addition to having the brightest future from his current achievements, over that to being an IIT, IIM pass-out."

Sujoy-da did not respond, but he looked down avoiding my gaze, even as he handed me a list of domestic bookings for the day. His look was grim, sympathetic even I thought, and slightly perturbed – all quite contrary to his usually stern, fathomless expression. This gave me an indication not to pursue the matter further, as my reaction had made its mark on him after all. So, checking the list of domestic travel itineraries he gave me, I walked back with it to my office. I marched determinedly, unlike other evenings when I strolled back to the office or to another client, now scanning the issue over – scene by scene, in my head. By the time I took the lift and landed outside the imposing glass door of my third-floor office – through which was visible our receptionist Judy, a tall and slender lady in her fifties, I was determined to take my job more seriously than I had as yet.

The next morning, I was back in Jeevan Deep building – at the same MNC's office, as usual, but mentally fortified to be more

     Shuvashree Chowdhury

professional. I cordially greeted the receptionist – incidentally it was Sandra again on duty on the third floor where I always first visited. This company had a number of receptionists, whose duty allocations altered day to day. Sometimes it shifted on the same day, too – such that there might be one receptionist at a floor's front desk in the morning and another in the afternoon.

At the travel office, I cheerily wished the manager, Sujoy Ghosh, and his junior sitting at the adjacent desk, a good morning, in fact with more alacrity than usual. They both looked at me and nodded benignly, quite unlike Sujoy-da who did not usually acknowledge my presence. He would rather hold his head up sternly when I entered and greeted him, moving on after an exaggerated silence to what he had to say with regard to work.

I took their mutual nods as a cue to sit down across Sujoy-da. But I remained silent. I was not about to mention the incidents of the day before – just as I had planned, acting cool and composed instead. There was, however, a big change I had embraced this morning: My long hair, almost waist length, was pulled off my face and held back with a clip, rather than left open as usual. Also, I had worn a *salwar kameez* rather than wear a *saree* as I had preferred to in the last few months. From now on, this is how I would present myself at that office, wearing a loose-fitting *salwar kameez*, and my hair tied back tight, with bare makeup – of eyeliner and lipstick.

But it's quite a different matter that Amit Chatterjee, through his friend Sandra – the sophisticated receptionist, was relentless in his exertions to take me out, even if only once – for a cup of coffee. His persistence and haste, that was actually putting me off him even more, was as he was moving to Toronto where he had been transferred. He mentally sought to ensure he was not leaving here with any slight chance of our being a couple, even if it might have been a long-distance one for some time. This was, of course, after getting his travel plans confirmed through another of us three travel agents.

It might seem by now, that I'm rather arrogant, foolish even. This is, considering that two of my close friends then, had insisted Amit was the perfect 'match' or 'catch' as they preferred to use the term, for any young woman. But then, how was I to like a man who would humiliate me in public, the way I perceived Amit had

– in the past few weeks? So what if he's now settled in the US and a high ranking official, just as Sandra had predicted, along with counselling me – not to lose the golden opportunity of winning myself the benefits of being the wife of.

* * *

After I went on to join a premier airline a year later, I wore their smart uniform of an A-line dress. In another year or so, it would change to either wearing a skirt or a pair of trousers along with a bright silk blouse. After a couple of years, I moved to being a service quality coordinator for the airline's network, and did not require wearing a uniform anymore. However, I was never to return to wearing a *saree* habitually. On the rare occasions I did turn up at work in a *saree* – on Saraswati Puja or Vishwakarma Puja, I was, in addition to being the recipient of plenty of admiring glances, also the victim of snide remarks. This maliciousness, among other things on my attire, was even from senior personnel, whose job my job was now to audit. These spiteful comments were conveyed to me by loyal friends I still had from my early years of working with the airline.

One comment, I recall, as being: "She comes in a *saree* to make the men fall in love with her ... so she can have them eating out of her hands."

It was only much later, on joining a reputed jewellery chain as a manager in 2003 that I would return to wearing striking *sarees* and dressing up stylishly to work. Now it helped me fit into the cultural mould and positioning of the company, as being a jewellery house for the emerging Indian woman who uses tradition rather than being used by it. Over that, it helped me connect with the staff and clients, in both appreciating my personal taste and relying on it. Thus, the staff felt assured in my judgement on the high-value stocking at the store, and in developing the confidence to sell it astutely. The clients trusted our stocking and my personal consultation on their prospective big purchases, especially during weddings and festivals. My appearance was in line with the image of the company, and I also wore the brand of jewellery myself. Thus propping me as its regional brand ambassador – as all frontline staff and management ought to be. Overall, wearing a *saree* now and the attention to my dressing helped my career.

What we wear, how we dress and project ourselves, especially as women, plays a vital role in how we are perceived in the workplace. Though our choice of clothes is an expression of personal taste, at work we represent the employer's choice in selecting employees. Our appearance makes an impact right from whether we land the job, to influencing the next steps in our career. As how we look says a lot about us, it projects whether we are serious about our work, organised, lazy, creative and fashion-forward. Style and image have played and continue to play a crucial role, especially in the career strategies and trajectories of high-powered executives. We may like to think that focusing on appearance, as part of career strategy, sounds superficial – that we should be judged for our intelligence and experience, and not our style. Sure, it's what's on the inside that counts, but sadly that's not how the career graph's progression works.

8. Till Love Do Us Apart

Over coffee with a friend at a resto-café one evening, he soulfully narrated to me the story of the opposition to his current romantic liaison. He had lost his wife – a decade younger than him, after a prolonged battle with cancer, a couple of years back. Now the tough resistance to his desire to remarry, to be happy and live a full life over again – ironically, came from his daughter. An ex-journalist having worked in Delhi where the family lived then, she is currently a publishing professional in London since the last decade. She married her British colleague two years back, and the couple has no plans to live in India. The married son lives with his wife and children in another city.

My friend, Mr Boruah – over 75 years of age, still handsome and as fit and agile as a man of not more than 60 apparently, lives alone in Guwahati, but still travels widely. Once a successful businessman, he had sold all his ventures to take care of his ailing wife. He still plays Golf regularly at his club, in spite of a weakening elbow, has his two pegs of premium Scotch daily before dinner, and as much as possible tries to fill his life with intellectually gregarious and artistic company.

I had first met Mr Boruah in an official capacity while working at the Calcutta airport, and we eventually became friends over our varied interactions. I find I tend to strike friendships easily with men and women even decades older, as I relate to them as well as I do with those my age or younger. This is because mutual respect, admiration, and above all, empathy, are the requisites and crux of any relationship. And I find that people who are much older are usually more respectful in friendships, as they are confident of who they are, thus of their views and opinions, and their place in the world. Personal and professional jealousy and resultant aggressive and rude condescension resulting out of insecurity, in my view, are the most effective deterrents even to long friendships. I like to respect friends for whom they inherently are, and over that – how

     Shuvashree Chowdhury

they treat me, irrespective of their success or failure, financial or social status and I am rarely judgemental.

It was over our second cup of coffee – his with 'Sugar-free', that Mr Boruah had gone on to share with me the cause of his sad and forlorn look, this only on my prodding.

"There is a woman, about my daughter's age, also yours, whom, like you, I have known since my earlier years in business," Mr Boruah said, almost blushing now as he continued. "She was apparently much in love with me since a long time, as I was to learn quite recently. I'd been friends with her for long, but I'd never taken her mildly romantic gestures seriously, rather had been amused by it. But after my wife's death, this woman, who also knows my daughter well, has been pestering me to marry her. She is professionally successful, financially well off, and though over forty years, refuses to marry anyone other than me."

"What does it matter if you are over seventy-five years?" the young lady had quipped when Mr Boruah had tried to reason with her on the futility of their relationship. "Even spending a few years with you is better than decades with someone I could never love."

"So then, why don't you marry her, Mr Boruah?" I had blurted excitedly, rather pleased he would have a companion in his sunset years, as I was fond of him and tended to feel sorry for his lonely life.

"No, I can't!" he replied stiffly.

"But why … why not?" I insisted, and then, smiling teasingly, I added: "You'll get a new lease of life, you'll see … trust me! All those heart ailments you have, will all be resolved … as you'll have a new heart – won't you?"

He could not help blushing red like a boy, looking pleased with my approval as he replied, "I wish my daughter were as cool as you!"

"Ah! So it's your daughter who has the problem with it, has she … Well, it is truly only her problem then, not yours, Mr Boruah!" I replied emphatically. "She is blissfully far away and does not bother as to how you're going to live alone here. Doesn't she realise how lonely you are and how difficult it's increasingly getting for you to live by yourself, so what if you have a fleet of butlers and chauffeurs at your service?"

"My daughter dislikes this woman, and will not allow her to take her mother's place she insists," Mr Boruah stated regretfully. "Every time I've tried to broach this topic, even of remarrying anyone else, she gets furious, and then won't talk to me for months. Then even I don't call her for a while, and thus, now our relationship is rather strained."

"That's rather selfish of your daughter, Mr Boruah, isn't it?" I insisted, and then added hopefully, "Would you like me to talk to her? I'm sure I can convince her ... Well, I could try at least, though I don't know her. She needs to understand you are lucky to find genuine love and another chance to live a wholesome life again. Why would she wish to steal your happiness from you? That, too, when she will not have you live with her in London, or come here and live with you?"

"But who will make her see that! Moreover, if you call her, she will be furious that I even told anyone of this. What upsets me most is with regard to this young lady. She refuses to get married to anyone else, but me. I've coaxed her for the last ten years, but she is just as adamant as my daughter, to only marry me or no one else."

"If it's your daughter's insecurity and fear over this new woman's claim to your money and properties, over your affections, then you could make a will, dividing everything between your daughter and son, isn't it? In that way, your daughter won't have a problem with you remarrying."

"My daughter knows well that this woman is affluent herself, and she comes from an illustrious family ... so doesn't need my money."

"Then, it is her sheer self-centeredness and vanity, Mr Boruah, what else can I say. The greatest self-imprisonment we live in is the fear of what people will think, isn't it?"

Mr Boruah remained silent, looking at his empty coffee cup for a while, and then looking up, he said sullenly, "I am so overwrought with agony from the strained relationship with my daughter. But if it were only about me, I would never suggest getting married now. But I do care about this young woman, too, who sacrificed her marital prospects only for me."

"Please don't justify, you owe it to yourself, Mr Boruah, to be

 Shuvashree Chowdhury

happy … till the last moment of your life. More that God has given you a new lease of life so late that only a few get."

"I know. But God gives with one hand, and takes away with another," he grinned sheepishly, his mood elevated now after talking.

"So ironic, you know, since my father's passing, I've always hoped my mother would meet a companion again, since both her daughters live in different cities," I said thoughtfully. "But then, you've met her, what a difficult woman she is in some ways – the very idea is unthinkable for her. I've even secretly considered various elderly widowed and divorced matches in my neighbourhood (I laughed) … but she thinks I am just joking and when I persist she says she will beat me and throw me out of the house for suggesting such a horrendous thing."

Mr Boruah laughed aloud, "Well, knowing your mother, it is quite expected, even though she is younger than me."

"You see, Mr Boruah, for all my broad mindedness about wishing my mother would remarry, I'd never allow anyone to take my father's place – neither in my heart and life, nor do I wish to replace him in my mother's. I just wish upon her to have a friend, a companion, and lead a full life again. You know how in the last years of my father's life, Ma was so focussed on his illness and seeing him through it, she had no friends or life of her own left. She has no one else to call her own, except for my sister and me, and ironically we live in other cities. I truly wish she were not alone this way."

"My dear, how I wish my daughter would also think like you," Mr Boruah blurted, even as he patted my hand, and then asked the waiter for the check. As we got up to leave, he added sadly: "You see, for my daughter's sake, I can give up anyone and anything, as I will this young woman. I must part with her for my daughter's love, I owe it to her. My own happiness is not more important than her happiness, is it?"

9. An Eternal Presence

She was not in love with Amit, she was certain, even after days of pouring her heart to him. How could she possibly love him, she mentally asserted, when she was much married to Ritesh? It was barely a year into her marriage when Amit had waltzed into Rupali's life. In that first year, as yet trying to put her marriage into perspective, she had hardly discerned whether she was happy or unhappy in it. Amit had appeared like a strong, big wave, threatening to wash her off the secure shore of her marriage. She had merely gone with the flow, in agreeing to meet him that first time, too weak to resist. One's destiny is chalked at birth or so, Rupali had always believed. Then not intending the affair to happen, inexplicably drawn into the tide, why did she feel guilty ever since?

Looking through the glass window of the superfast train now, everything seemed to fly past outside, the landscape a blur. Despite that the sun was nice and bright in view, Rupali did not feel its warmth. Sitting in the air-conditioned coach, she did not feel the chill outside either. Through the blur, she recognised the contours of trees, chalets, water bodies and vast meadows – with black and white-spotted cattle meandering. In the distance, she could see the soft rise and fall of green hills, though people and animals closer up were barely discernible. The picturesque scenery was in various shades of yellow, green and brown, the apparently still water-bodies in a dash of blue-green, the obvious ripples in them not visible.

The view outside dashed past Rupali in a blur, simultaneous to snatches of her life, which raced in her mind's eye, as in a slideshow. Incidents and memories of long ago flashed to mind, taking her by surprise. She had barely had a chance to allow the experiences to sink in and register them consciously to mind in living them, she thought. Seated around her on the four-seater cluster of seats of the train's compartment were Mira and

Sangita, her closest friends since college. The women were on this trip to Europe in June, without their families, travelling by Euro Rail through most part, to Britain, Scotland, Ireland and on to France and Italy. Settled in different Indian cities now, it was a much-deserved break together, after years of marriage, raising children and all but never making time for themselves. Now with the children all well settled, they were able to afford both time and money for a trip like this, having worked hard all their lives.

Rupali Sharma had been my senior at my first job at the leading travel company before I joined the airline. She headed the international outbound-tour division and was due to retire in six months when I joined. In coaching and mentoring me, we became very close in spite of our immense age difference. However, I was able to put my interactions with her into perspective only much later. The airline stint opened my eyes to the world, increased my exposure immensely to relationships.

"Why don't you take a holiday with your family or friends before you retire, Rupali?" I had suggested to her over coffee one morning at work, "You've spent a lifetime sending people on tours, never taking one yourself, except for accompanying large groups as a guide."

She had taken me up on my suggestion, and their train was now rushing from London to Edinburgh in Scotland. It had pulled out of Kings Cross at 8am. The three friends had spent the night at a 'Bed and Breakfast' place across the station. On the train for over an hour now, silently looking outside, Mira and Sangita felt the need to connect again. Mira was vice president – human resources, of a multinational bank in Mumbai and also due to retire shortly. With her short crop of hair streaked in various shades of brown and the rimless glasses, she had an air of professionalism and authority about her.

Sangita, a chartered accountant, was head of finance in a large nationalised company in Bangalore, and due to retire in another two years. Her oval, plump face, emphasised by her shoulder length, blunt-cut black hair and soft round eyes, gave her a homely, matronly appearance. They leisurely sipped tea out of the large covered paper glasses they had bought from the attendant carting refreshments down the aisle. It washed down the large baguettes they had just consumed.

"Rupali, why don't you colour your hair as we do?" asked Sangita, abruptly tapping her hand to draw her attention. Rupali had been lost in thought, oblivious to her friends discussing her.

"Hmmm … did you girls say something?" she distractedly muttered, forcing herself out of the motion picture in her mind and the view rushing outside that she was unseeingly looking at.

"What is it with all this grey hair you're sporting?" Mira repeated, smiling, "We were wondering why you don't colour your hair like us?"

"Ah! That, well … it doesn't matter anymore, does it?" She replied, and then with a mischievous twinkle in her eye, added: "I'm not looking to be attractive to men anymore, not younger ones at least, and those my age and more should like me this way."

Rupali knew she would have looked much younger than her fifty-nine years, without the all-grey hair. Always having looked younger than her age in addition to being pretty, she had been the recipient of plenty of male attention in her youth, even speeding into old age. With time, the attention had begun to bore her, or at least was of no interest, preferring to be inconspicuous now. She wore simple light coloured *sarees* or suits, as compared to fashionable western outfits, designer *sarees* and *salwar* suits she once adorned and filled her wardrobe with. Like her friends, she had never been professionally ambitious, thus not as successful as them. Her family took precedence over her career, and she had not been very open to travelling for work or spending late hours in the office.

Rupali returned to looking outside again, with the lurking of a faint smile on her light pink glossed lips. Her smile, still her best feature, enhanced her face and its current shine, from her pair of solitaire diamond-earrings reflecting sunlight through the window in snatches. She wore a floral printed blouse under a sky-blue cardigan, over a pair of light blue jeans and white sneakers, her long hair held in a casual chignon. Amit's words from decades back rang distinctly in her ears now, her smile widening involuntarily in recall of him.

 Shuvashree Chowdhury

"You are the most remarkable woman in the world," he had said, looking into her wide brown eyes highlighted with black kohl, enhancing her lucent complexion, "I've never known anyone more beautiful."

She had believed him then. How could she have not? His words, the way he looked at her with the warm glow in his eyes, hanging on to her words, had swept her off her feet. Why and how had she ever agreed to go on that first drive with him all those years back, she wondered, making her feel guilty ever since? The first time Rupali met Amit was in front of the bookstore close to her house at Alipore over twenty-five years back, where she still lived to this day. They had planned to meet there and then walk over to an adjacent café. Standing in front of the bookshop at 4pm, the designated time, she looked around, but no one resembling him remotely had been in sight. Having seen a picture of his he had sent with one of his letters, though one taken when he was much younger, she was sure to recognise him.

As she waited anxiously, Rupali wondered how Amit would be in person, what he would look like in real life? Would they be able to connect the way they had through the numerous letters and in the telephonic conversations so far? They had chatted ceaselessly in the past months, from office and home, exchanged letters a month before they started to talk. In the last two months, Rupali had opened her heart to him like to no one ever before, telling him all about herself, of her fears, aspirations and disappointments. A good listener, adept at the art of probing, with accompanying empathy and sensitivity, Amit had encouraged and enabled her to spill her heart to him.

Comfortable as Rupali had felt with Amit, she had even confided in him incidents leading to the abrupt end of her disastrous engagement, leading to the sudden marriage to another man. The day-to-day events after her wedding had needed little prying on his part for her to spill. There was no one with whom she could discuss what was happening in her life, till Amit had suddenly walked into it. Her husband, Ritesh, a nice, easygoing, kind person, charming when the mood arose, was usually aloof with her. He was certainly not in love with her she had concluded, as she had believed at the time of marrying him hurriedly. Rupali had decided early in life, that she would only marry for love and now she felt trapped in a loveless marriage.

Ritesh was emotionally elusive and in his own world usually. She was not sure whether his love she had been certain of initially had vanished after the wedding or had she done something to trigger its going. Maybe, he still truly loved her, who knows, just not the way she had envisioned love to be? Was she not beautiful, intelligent and desirous as she had always been told? Men had sought her most of her life till she married at twenty-seven years, then why did her husband a renowned cardiologist, show so much interest in every other woman? His outrageous flirtations, which he declared were harmless, hurt her deep. How could a barely married man find so much interest in other women if he loved his wife, she wondered dejectedly? Why could she not hold his interest? The problem perhaps was in being the romantic that she always was, she concluded, and expecting much from marriage.

Amit Nair's office had once been in the same building as Rupali's, in a high-rise in Colaba overlooking the sea on Marine Drive, in Mumbai. This was much before they met at the bookshop near her house in Calcutta for the first time. After work, Amit had often seen Rupali walk out of the building. She would cross the road to the beach, stand looking at the sea for a few minutes, her hair flying in the sea breeze, then hail a cab and go home for the day. He had been tempted to follow her a few times, if for nothing else than to catch a few more glimpses of her striking beauty. She carried herself so well, he thought, with her thick brown hair usually left loose, cascading below her waist. However, he never followed her, certain that someday he would ask her out for coffee at the least. He could wait till then, he decided, merely watching her from a distance.

Amit knew nothing about Rupali yet, except the company she worked for. On several occasions he had seen her press the 'seven' button on the lift wall, or say 'seven' to the lift man, on her way up in the morning or after lunch. He knew the sixth and seventh floors were rented by one of the reputed worldwide travel and tourism companies. She did not seem married, or at least had no visible indicators that she was. Even if she were, it would not deter Amit from befriending her, he had determined. It was only when he had not seen Rupali for over a month since his tracking her that Amit decided to ask someone from her office. Luckily he knew her name, ever since someone had called out to her in the lift once. He learnt much to his exasperation that Rupali had just got married, and taken a transfer to the Calcutta office of the same company.

He had felt an initial stab of dejection in his chest, but numbness taking over thereafter he could not fathom the intensity of the wound. It merged with the numbness caused by his wife's going away. Renu had left him three years back to live with her parents in Pune, taking their then school going daughter with her. Initially, he had thought it would be another of the many times she had left after a fight. It had taken him three months to discern she was gone for good this time and never coming back. The longest duration she had left before had been a month. Each time before, she had returned of her own accord, even if having left due to his fault, knowing his ego well. Amit's pride, as always, prevented his going over, bringing her back even the last time. Moreover, much time had elapsed in assuming Renu would return for him to shirk off his now hardened ego and go after her.

His wife's leaving him had hit Amit badly; he had felt dead for over a year and numb since. At forty-five years when his wife left, Amit was handsome, charming and intelligent. Above that, he had a distinguished career in Mumbai, as the political editor of a reputed newspaper. There were a lot of women who had come into his life thereafter, but not one held his interest long enough. It had been Rupali's intelligent face with the stubborn set of her jaw line and the big mysterious eyes with a lurking sadness that had caught his attention in the lift one day. Carrying herself with elegance and poise, a touch of snobbishness even, perhaps from being introverted and reserved, she had intrigued him.

Rupali's abruptly leaving town, when Amit learnt of it, strangely seemed to reinstate within him the familiar hurt of his wife's going away. There was a shadowy resemblance Rupali had to Renu and possibly the reason he had been so fiercely drawn to her. It was something about both their eyes that he found himself drawn to and that also haunted him. Amit tried to put Rupali out of his mind like he had his marriage, but without much success on both accounts. Renu, his wife, was a journalist with a fashion magazine in Pune. Their daughter, now in college, spent her vacations with him, the rest of her days with Renu. Amit was sorely lonely, though luckily his job took up most of his days and there were his colleagues he hung out with in the evenings. The weekends he spent reading and working on his next book.

It was more than a year after Rupali had left Mumbai that Amit was head-hunted. He took up an assignment as the resident editor of another newspaper and moved to Calcutta. It was suddenly one evening six months after he had moved, settled into his new job and the city now, that while nursing a drink after work he thought of Rupali. He had consciously blocked images of her out of his mind, and now, abruptly he recalled that she was in Calcutta, too. Even though he knew she was recently married, the compelling need to connect with her overcame him. Rupali had taken a transfer to the same company in Calcutta, he recalled, so it would not be difficult for him to find her. He decided on writing a letter to her at her office address. He was not sure what he wanted from her, considering she was now married, except for an acute desire to connect with her somehow. Rupali's disappearance had come as a shock just as his wife's unexpected departure.

Still staring outside the train window, en route to Scotland, smiling to herself again, oblivious to her friends, Rupali vividly recalled receiving Amit's first letter. It was one afternoon at her office desk, a year after she had moved to Calcutta, that she received a call from the reception, informing her of a registered letter for her. It was from her bank she assumed, as she walked towards the front desk, having given this address for all communications. After signing, returning the deliveryman's receipt list, she scrutinised the envelope curiously, since it was not from her bank. In a neat and stylish handwriting, the envelope was addressed to her from an Amit Nair. She had opened it on her walk back to her desk. The writer introduced himself as a journalist, a newspaper editor. He then detailed his first seeing her in Mumbai at their common office building and his interest in meeting her over coffee, till her sudden disappearance. He signed off after stating his desire to be friends with her now that he was in Calcutta as well.

What had caught Rupali's attention, in addition to his

   Shuvashree Chowdhury

impeccable writing, was Amit's openness. He had written how his move to Calcutta, subsequent to her, after working in the same building in Mumbai, meant they were destined to be friends. He also mentioned that he was the divorced father of a college going girl. Then added that he hoped Rupali would consider his friendship request and he would wait while she considered it. She had smiled to herself, flattered that someone in his position, and in all probability, much older than her, should take an interest in befriending her. What could possibly interest him about her, she wondered. It was after much deliberation, curiosity getting the better of her, that she had replied to his letter a few weeks later.

Amit's face, in recall now, seemed to be looking at Rupali tenderly through the train's window from outside, keeping pace with her at an elevated level. He seemed to be smiling down at her with the familiar shine in his eyes like when they had first met. Would he still like her with her grey hair and the wrinkles, if they were to meet now? Would he still find her beautiful, she wondered, though she knew she had aged gracefully. He must be pretty old himself, over fifteen years older that he was to her, she recalled fondly. She smiled at how he might look now, as she went back in time to their first meeting. Rupali had waited in front of that bookstore, now over twenty-five years since, beginning to get restless, looking this way and that, before she had spotted a car in the parking at a distance.

Amit had been parked for some time, watching her discreetly from inside the car. Suddenly Rupali had noticed the headlight of the car flicker, like the driver was using the dipper to signal to someone. Assuming it was for someone who had just walked out of the bookstore, Rupali looked behind towards its entrance. By the time she turned back, the man behind the wheel had got off the car and started walking towards her. She noticed at first his black silk shirt with light-blue jeans and black shoes he was wearing. His wavy black hair faintly streaked with grey was pushed back neatly, and he wore a French beard that accentuated his prominent nose and the firm set of his jaw line. The eyes were light brown and piercing, as they bore into her. He did not appear very tall, an inch perhaps over her five feet seven inches.

As Rupali looked into the man's eyes, she detected the

humour in them as they crinkled at the sides, and then noticed his face break into a smile. She squinted, ensuring she was not imagining him smiling, but by which time he was grinning widely, clearing any doubt she had.

"Hello, I'm Amit Nair," he said, coming up close, offering her his hand to shake, "and you must be Rupali."

Nodding silently, she shook his hand, still staring at his face in bewilderment. Suddenly she became very angry. Why had he been sitting in the car watching her, instead of walking across right away, when all the while, waiting for him to show up, she had been so tensed. Her anger was further propelled by the immense anxiety she was in, over whether she was doing the right thing in meeting him at all.

"If looks could kill, I would be dead," he laughed. "In fact, I've been watching the emotions flitting through your face for a while now."

"Very funny," she replied mockingly, "to keep me waiting here, while you sit and watch me tormenting and fuming over your delay in showing up. I was just about to go back home."

Her apprehension, in addition to the anger, made her suddenly feel very vulnerable. This man knew her so well, as she had revealed so much over their conversations and letters not really planning on meeting him. Now facing him, Rupali felt exposed, like he could see right into her soul and there was no hiding from him. She turned to go into the coffee shop adjacent to the bookshop like they had planned to.

"Rupali, let's go for a drive first," Amit blurted from behind her.

Turning back to face him, she replied determinedly, "No, let's just have coffee here, Amit, and then we can go wherever you want."

She intended to go nowhere from there but back home, after the cup of coffee she had agreed to. How did she ever allow him to convince her to meet him in the first place, she wondered?

"Don't worry Rupali, we will certainly have coffee as I promised and get on back to our lives," he replied smiling, sensing her nervousness. "But we can have it somewhere else, can't we?"

Rupali nodded. In any case, why was she afraid of him now?

     Shuvashree Chowdhury

After all, they knew each other so well already. What harm could possibly come from going for a short drive and then coffee later?

It was on a Saturday, when she worked half-day, that she had met Amit after work. She had told her husband she was going out with colleagues, so he would not expect her to be home until late. In any case, he would not be home himself till late at night. Walking together to Amit's car, he got in behind the wheels and she beside him. Driving for a distance, acutely aware of the silence between them, Amit turned on the car stereo, playing old country songs. After the closeness they had shared, through their conversations and letters so far, it was weird they felt like complete strangers now. Rupali was trying to bridge the gap in her mind between the men – the one she was mentally close to versus the complete stranger she was physically meeting for the first time now.

"Do you want anything, some water or a cold drink perhaps?" Amit asked in breaking the silence, dejectedly sensing her discomfiture.

"A cold drink is a good idea," she replied, her mouth felt dry.

Swirling the car to the left, pulling off the road, Amit got down. He walked over to a small roadside shop, got a cold drink and a big bar of chocolate. Rupali accepted both through the window, taking the opportunity to assess him physically for the first time now. He was athletic for his fifty-four years, she noted, and carried himself lithely. After waiting for Rupali to finish the drink, sitting beside her in the car, he handed the empty bottle to the shopkeeper through his side of the window. Then they drove some distance before speaking again.

"You seem disappointed in seeing me," he said, looking ahead at the road, noticing her sidelong glances at him.

"No, no, it's not like that at all," she replied promptly, "I've talked to you for long, now I'm trying to acquaint myself with your physical presence, to match it to the person I know mentally."

After a moment's silence, Amit said theatrically, looking at her: "I'm Amit Nair, a journalist. I'm very pleased to meet you, ma'am."

Rupali looked at him quizzically at first, and then broke into a grin. Though trying to put her at ease, Amit was himself uptight from thinking Rupali had not liked him in person. Perhaps she was disappointed at his appearance, he thought, or he looked older than she had expected. This might just be the last time he saw her. And now that they had met, they could not go back to merely being pen friends or telephonic friends again. There was only one way out from here, and that was in going back to being strangers. The thought of it made him very sad. He wondered whether he should have met her at all, then they could have remained friends for longer. Driving a while longer, Amit abruptly pulled into a gravel pathway that led to a huge open iron gate. They drove through it on to a path amidst a beautiful garden.

"Where are we going, Amit?" Rupali asked, alarmed.

"Don't worry, ma'am, you are safe with me," he replied in a placating tone, in response to her frightened voice. "This is my favourite hangout, a garden café. I'm sure you will love it here, too."

They parked and walked through the low entrance into the quaint café. Looking about her curiously, Rupali noticed at first the huge terracotta lamps that hung from the ceiling. They threw multi-coloured light, along with shadows in varying shapes and sizes, on the ceiling and the walls. The place resonated with the sound of numerous wind chimes swaying in the breeze through the two large windows on either side. The breeze was cool now and heavy with the flowery smell of the adjoining garden. Led by Amit, Rupali walked through the café and into the lawn behind, on which were set a number of tables amidst a vast array of potted plants. A few of the tables were occupied.

Amit drew out a chair at a vacant table, indicating for Rupali to sit down. By now, dusk having set in, each table was lit by a candle held upright within a glass chimney. They sat facing each other across the round table with the red and white checked cover. The candlelight flickered against the wall of the chimney. Amit looked tenderly at Rupali, her face aglow from the candlelight, cheeks flushed as much from the heat, as perhaps the anxiety of meeting him. She looked beautiful and radiant in the light pink, boat-neck top she wore over blue jeans. Her long hair left loose, blew incessantly over her face in the strong breeze, even as she tried desperately to hold it away behind her. Amit noticed the beads of sweat glistening on her forehead and on the tip of her nose that was accentuated by the candlelight.

    Shuvashree Chowdhury

"Here, wipe your face with this," he said, handing her a paper napkin from the holder in the centre of the table.

Rupali took the napkin with one hand, the other clutching her hair behind her head. She dabbed the napkin over her face, noticing Amit viewing her intimately. The way he continued to gaze at her appreciatively with his big brown eyes, smiling affectionately, Rupali slowly relaxed. She suddenly felt sure of herself like she had not in a long while. The surge of excitement she felt at Amit's attention, took Rupali by surprise; her apprehension over meeting him slowly waning. She had never noticed anyone look at her with as much admiration, least of all her husband, Ritesh. It was the kind of look she had searched for longingly in Ritesh's eyes, but never found.

When a man truly appreciates a woman, finds her desirable, is in love with her, it is visible in his eyes. Why do women look for mere words to assure them of love then, she wondered, or believe in words that can ring hollow? Rupali placed the napkin she held on the table, distractedly, after a waiter brought them the menu card. To her surprise, Amit picked it up, folded and tucked it into his chest pocket.

"Why did you do that?" she blurted in embarrassment.

"I want to keep a token of you, with me, if that is all I have," he replied, smiling indulgently at her, "I'm not sure we will meet again."

Rupali looked down, averting his gaze, suddenly petrified. She realised with panic that she was afraid more of herself, her own flustered emotions than of him. Was she falling in love with him?

But how could she help falling in love with him. He was sweeping her off her feet with his words, gestures, the penetrating look that seemed to look into her soul, and the boyish smile that lit his face.

"You look like you've seen a ghost, shivering like that," Amit laughed, and then reading her discomfiture, he added sombrely, "Now come here, give me your hands."

She obeyed him as a child, placing both her hands palm down on the table. He placed his own protectively over hers, then smiling he said: "Don't be afraid Rupali, I'm the same guy, your friend, whom you have been talking to so freely. Nothing can change that.

Even if we were never to meet again, I'll still be your friend and your secrets will be safe with me. You are going to be fine hereafter and so am I, whether or not we're in each other's lives."

Rupali nodded, then looking into Amit's eyes, said: "I wish it were that simple, to leave from here and go back to our respective lives."

"Have faith in God's will. He will see you through your trials, show you direction, even from here," Amit said, in a placating tone.

He felt sorry for her. She had gone through much emotionally in her twenty-eight years and most of it for what – the quest for love?

"You are beautiful, intelligent, feminine, and above that, a warm and special person, Rupali," Amit said, patting her hand on the table. "I'm more convinced of that after meeting you today. What kind of an idiot is your husband, I wonder, not to see the diamond he has found, instead frivolously going after every other woman he comes across?"

Rupali slowly relaxed, happy now after a long time. Thus the evening laid the foundation to the next phase of their relationship.

After that, meeting regularly at coffee shops or restaurants, going on long drives, Amit and Rupali spent considerable time together. She decided to throw caution to the wind. After all, she had the right to happiness, didn't she? Ritesh was happy, at least so he seemed, with the women who dropped into their house every now and then. He insisted they were good friends only. Rupali was now able to entertain them calmly as he expected her to. Through this time, Amit, recognising her talents, encouraged her to develop new interests, form new friendships, introducing her to a new set of people in the city. With the positive energy she now exuded, the favourable impact she had on all, her confidence grew. Amit's seniority in age and profession, added to life's experiences, naturally made him her mentor and guide.

Above all this, his sense of humour was infectious, making Rupali laugh a lot. She felt relaxed and self-assured now, looked younger, more beautiful. In the course of her interactions with Amit, she underwent remarkable changes, so that people she knew

 Shuvashree Chowdhury

for long noticed and commented; only they did not know what to attribute it to.

"See what love and appreciation can do to a woman," Amit said to her often, pleased with the results of his effortless existence in her life. "I don't think you are yourself aware of the changes you've undergone."

She would just smile back at him, feeling insulated in his love and admiration. Having finally found love, her quest had ended, and the world was now a beautiful place. Nothing could take away her happiness and sense of well-being. Amit, on his part, only wanted Rupali to be happy, as he believed she truly deserved it. Nothing made him happier than seeing her happy.

Loving Rupali was the best thing that could have happened to Amit, and he felt fulfilled, in watching her blossom in his company. When he had first met her, she was steeped in sadness, low self-esteem brought on by the neglect of her husband, but now she seemed confident, ready to take on the world. In a way, he owed all this to himself, as not having done enough in his marriage for it to have ended so abruptly, this was a way to compensate for it. Amit, too, came out of his earlier angry, depressed state since his wife had left, coming to terms with it now. He became the gregarious person he actually was. However, Amit knew how much Rupali wanted her marriage to work. He would have to disappear from her life, he knew, for her to return to her husband emotionally. He respected her values on marriage though afraid she would hurt herself again. But he hoped with her enhanced strength and confidence she would never be devastated from it again.

It was after an insignificant tiff that Amit and Rupali completely stopped talking to each other, after two years of companionship. Rupali, plagued by a nagging sense of guilt about their relationship, had decided to end it to get back into the groove of her marriage. But it was the most difficult decision she made in her life, not to call him after their tiff, knowing his pride would prevent him from ever calling her. But by now she was certain whether they ever talked or met she would continue to love him. He would be in her mind every step of the way in life. She fervently hoped he would understand her reasons for letting him go from her life so abruptly. He had to know, after all, he knew her so well.

Over the years, Rupali thought of Amit often, but in order to check her temptation of reuniting with him overwhelming her, she never tried contacting him. As expected, her relationship with Ritesh improved considerably as a result of her own internal changes and self-assuredness. Ritesh started to respect her for whom she now was and stopped taking her for granted as he had earlier. When they had a son in a few years, followed by a daughter, she was the best mother one could possibly be. Rupali often prayed that Amit's life had been alright after her, that he had moved on well. The connection between them was so strong, that in spite of his absence, Rupali still felt his presence a lot, after decades, like she had in the years just after their friendship.

"Hey, wake up, Rupali … we are at the Waverly station already," Mira said excitedly, shaking Rupali gently by the shoulder.

Rupali opened her eyes abruptly, blinking at her friends looking down at her worriedly, wondering when she had dozed off.

"Are you feeling alright?" Sangita asked tenderly. "We have been trying to wake you up for a while. Is something wrong, Rupali?"

Shaking her head in denial, Rupali looked outside the window, relieved to know she could still see Amit, waving at her with his charming grin and the familiar twinkle in his eyes whenever he looked at her. He seemed as young and handsome as he did all those years back, she noticed. They were in Edinburgh together now, just as he went along with her everywhere. As long as in her mind she had Amit's company and his love, she would always be happy wherever she was.

Standing up, pulling off her stroller bag from the rack above, Rupali walked to the exit in a trance, behind her friends. Stepping off the train, she mentally took Amit's hand, as she had so often in the years gone by, in good times and in bad. Ironically, she did not even know whether he was still alive, considering he had been much older than her. But it didn't really matter, as in her heart, Amit would always and forever live. In spite of the guilt she still felt over her affair, Amit's love had been the support on which she had lived her life, insulated from its trials and tribulations. Walking out of the station, waiting in queue for a taxi to take them to their hotel, Rupali felt the cosiness of the sun's warmth through the biting chill. Or was it the warmth of love's eternal presence in her life?

		Shuvashree Chowdhury

10. *Walking Through Vulnerability*

If you're afraid of vulnerability you'll never cross over to strength. This is in love and all things else.

I've evolved into the position of courage, from being one of the most timid girls you might have ever met. This is from a lifetime of never shirking a series of risks, both personal and professional.

After a year of working with an airline, after more than a year of working as a sales executive for a premium travel agency of the time, when I thought there was no scope of growth for me, I went and applied to a bank. This was to prove to myself that in spite of my grave fear of numbers and apparent weakness in Maths, even though I was a commerce graduate, I could get the job.

At the final interview with the vice president, I was asked some tough mathematical questions, which I obviously felt challenged in answering spontaneously.

So I bravely replied, somewhat like this (I don't recall the exact question): "You add this to that, multiply that with this, and then divide with this, then you subtract that."

I looked at the VP confidently through the process, even as he looked at me curiously. I assumed he was going to show me the door right thereafter. But to my sheer amazement, he was charmed and immediately confirmed my appointment at the reputed multinational bank, at its rather large and extremely busy, only branch in Calcutta at J.N Road.

I looked at him in shock and he said to me: "I like your confidence … and we have calculators to get to the final figures anyway. I liked your presence of mind."

I then worked at the bank for six months before returning to the airline, as over and above getting bored at the bank, there was a bigger opportunity I was offered at the airline. The VP at the bank gave me a month to think over whether I'd like to return, but I didn't, I stayed with the airline.

But those six months changed my life forever. It took away my fear of numbers, and gave me so much confidence. This is just one of a series of impulsive things I've done, and each time I did them, I could jump a higher hurdle next time. It's like lifting weights, as you build strength and garner courage with the lifting of every increase in weight.

   Shuvashree Chowdhury

11. *The Loss of My Face*

I thought I had lost my face, the end of my life.

It was early December, about a decade ago. We had just come out of Mocambo, the restaurant off Park Street, after dinner. It was 10.30pm and our next destination was a discotheque nearby. The car was parked at a distance and on our way, my friend stopped at one of the cubbyhole shops to buy cigarettes. I like to have a *paan* sometimes from these shops, but only after an Indian meal, and right now, I had had continental, which Mocambo specialises in.

As he bought the cigarettes, I stood a few steps behind my friend on the pavement, looking around. I soaked in the delightful weather, smug about the meal that I had just had: baked fish over a bed of spinach and white sauce with garlic bread, followed by tutti-frutti ice cream. Also, the headiness of the two Bloody Marys I had started the meal with.

My friend was taking longer than I expected because the shopkeeper was preparing a series of *paans* before attending to him. I suddenly began to feel conscious about my being overdressed for the roadside: a chocolate brown, full-sleeve ankle-length dress and my waist-length hair then that I usually wore open. I stepped forward to ask the shopkeeper to hurry up when I felt a sudden hot flush hitting the right side of my face. It hit me with such force that I froze to the ground.

Instinctively, I touched my right cheek to feel a hot liquid, just as hot as the sting on my cheek. I looked at my hand and it was blood red, I looked up to see my friend staring at me, fear written large on his face. The red was now dripping all over my hair and my dress, but there was something else now that I felt stronger than the sting: the hammering beating of my heart, from the fear of no longer having a face because of the acid bulb thrown at me. With every drip of the liquid from my face, I felt my face charring, melting away.

Only when my friend started to run behind the bike whose two riders had committed this dastardly act, did I react. I called out to him, "Please don't go … don't leave me here."

If he went chasing them, what if the rest of the gang took me away in a car? Such things are not unheard of in Calcutta.

My friend, hearing my desperate cries, stopped right there on his run. His face, as he turned around, was of one caught between raging anger — to go get the hooligans — versus the need of the moment, which was to save me from further abuse. He ran back to me and scrutinised my face. He was scared to see what had become of the face he had always complimented. Then he realised my face was intact, even though red all over with the thick fluid still dripping. The fluid, he deduced, was nothing but the juice of chewed *paan*. So that guy on the bike had used my face as a spittoon.

My friend bought a water bottle, poured it all over my face, and then we walked to the car. By now I was calm, really calm. I didn't care whether I had a face, I was just happy to be alive and safe. On the drive back home, our plans spoiled due to the muck I was in, I went over the incident in my head.

All I could recall accurately was how I felt in the moments when I thought I had lost my face forever. This was an invaluable lesson, to know how it feels to lose my face, even if only for a few moments, without actually having lost it. The first thing that would happen perhaps, I had thought then, would be that I would lose my job with the airline I worked for, with no marriage prospects ever. After this experience, how could I ever take my looks seriously? I was determined thereon that I had to have an identity far superior than what my face would ever give me, and marry someone who liked me over and above my physical looks. So if ever I really lost my face, I would survive — and still not be faceless.

     Shuvashree Chowdhury

12. *In Search of My Friend*

"**M**a'am, the old lady on that sofa," he said, pointing to her, "wants a third cup of coffee. Should I give it to her?"

"Why are you asking me such a silly question, Ramesh?" I asked. "Have I ever told you to account for the cups of tea or coffee you make?"

"No ma'am, but please ... please say no for now," Ramesh pleaded, sounding rattled, "or I will be making coffee for her the rest of the day. She comes here every afternoon, never buys a thing, but requests the staff for one cup of coffee after another. I am kept busy making it."

"Never mind, Ramesh," I smiled in a bid to placate him, "give her another cup. I will go out and meet her after that."

As he walked away to make the coffee, I looked in the direction of the beige-coloured sofa in the centre of the plush showroom. An empty coffee-cup on a tray lay on the side table. The silver haired, elegant looking lady, Ramesh had pointed to, flipped the pages of a magazine.

It was an afternoon barely a week after I had joined as manager at a flagship store of a branded jewellery-chain. This was after the rewarding airline stint of seven years, followed by the brisk, disappointing, yet instructive luxury hotel one. I was in my office, trying to figure out a strategy to make profits for the company, thus also ensuring good sales-incentives for us employees. Our salaries had a large incentive component. The resources I had at hand were – merchandise worth about twenty crore rupees in gold and diamond jewellery, an ornate, plush showroom in central Calcutta, fifteen sales staff, three cashiers, an accountant, six security and three housekeeping staff. The optimum use of these assets, simultaneous to keeping the over-head costs low, is what I was graphically plotting on my computer when Ramesh interrupted me.

My office door had been ajar as I preferred it. So, from

behind my desk, I got a view of the shop-floor where the lady, with straight, shoulder length hair, sat with her back to me on the sofa. After Ramesh left, I tried to get back to what I was doing, but curiosity nudged me out to meet the lady, even as she awaited the next cup of coffee. She could perhaps give me some practical indications on what I was trying to figure out at a computer, I thought. I had already chatted with a number of regular customers since joining. The feedback had enabled me to chalk out a plan of action for the coming months. I was also in constant dialogue with the staff for they would have to be the key to the changes I had in mind to bring about. In the past two years, the store had logged incredible losses. This had catapulted with the termination of the previous manager, along with most of his team, due to integrity issues. The current staff, except for four who had worked with the previous manager towards the end of his stint, was recruited in phases and relatively new. Before meeting the lady on the sofa, I first walked over to a senior staff, to verify Ramesh's claims.

"Who is the lady sitting on the sofa, Sonali?" I enquired.

"Oh! Her," she grinned looking in the direction of the sofa, "She is Mrs Viswanathan."

"So, is she a long time regular customer?"

"Well! I've been seeing her since I joined two years back. She comes almost every afternoon, around 2pm." Sonali replied.

"Would you say she is a high-value customer?"

"No, she buys only sometimes, brings a few friends. But mostly she looks around intently at the jewellery on display, asks questions. At times she asks us to take out some pieces which she scrutinises."

"Oh, I see!" I said, in surprise, "Could she be an external auditor?"

"No, no," Sonali stated. Then looking amused, she continued, "Mrs Viswanathan just has all the time in the world. At every visit, after briskly browsing the store, she sits on the sofa requesting for a cup of coffee. It is not before having at least two to three cups of coffee that she quietly leaves. We never refuse her."

My curiosity peaked. Why would an elderly lady visit a branded jewellery store regularly, with no intention of buying? What could

     Shuvashree Chowdhury

possibly bring her here repeatedly? She certainly didn't look like someone who would come only for free coffee – or maybe she did, perhaps she liked the coffee here. I walked over to the sofa.

"Hello, Mrs Viswanathan," I said, bending slightly, extending to her my hand to shake, "I'm the new manager here."

She looked up squarely at me, her face lighting up. Then promptly she extended her hand to shake mine.

I asked, "Are you are a regular customer here?"

"You can call me a regular visitor, not a regular customer," she replied, smiling uncomfortably. "I love jewellery, especially that which you have here. But I can purchase only a bit now and then, when my retired husband is in the mood for generosity."

"Ah! That's nice," I replied, taking a seat next to her on the sofa.

Ramesh walked over to us carrying a tray with a cup of coffee and a plate of biscuits. He gave me an exasperated look, as he set the tray down on the front table, and removed the tray from the side table.

"It's not only the jewellery I come here for, honestly," Mrs Viswanathan continued, softly, slowly, peering at me through her black-rimmed glasses. "I love the warm, enthusiastic bunch of people you have here. I enjoy spending a little time amongst these young people. The coffee here is also excellent," she stated and then, bursting into peals of laughter with the sound of tiny bells ringing, she added, "Most places serve the machine-made variety of coffee, in paper cups, which I don't like."

I registered her views. The strength of this store was the staff, the personal touch they provided, the hand-made coffee being an example. I noted I would try to retain the warm, friendly atmosphere, by not being rigid with the staff. After all, happy people make happy employees, and in turn, create happy customers.

"I'm glad you like coming here, Mrs Viswanathan," I smiled, "Perhaps you would like to help me by giving me critical feedback on the store, so I can improve things. The senior management has given me six months, in which to make this place profitable."

"I would love that," Mrs Viswanathan replied, almost getting up from the sofa in excitement, and then slowly settling down, she continued, "Jewellery fascinates me, you know, especially the traditional and antique variety. I have done a lot of research on the traditional design types of various regions and their origin."

"That must have been really interesting," I said.

"Yes, it was. I have reviewed a coffee table book titled – 'Indian Jewellery – Dance of the Peacock.' It is about the jewellery traditions of India. I have also written about jewellery for leading dailies."

"I would love to see your work, Mrs Viswanathan, read your reviews, if you still have the copies," I said.

"Sure, I will bring them over on my next visit," she replied, beaming with pride, and then placing a fair, wrinkled, yet well-kept hand on mine, she added, "You know, I have been coming to this store since its inception."

"That must be much over ten years now," I stated.

"I suppose so. I seem to lose track of the years now. At my age – I'm seventy-six you know, I count by the day," she chuckled, drawing my attention to her gorgeous smile – over a set of exquisite, pearl-white teeth. On her earlobes shone a pair of solitaire diamond earrings. Her large, light-brown eyes, complimented by the honey coloured floral printed georgette saree she wore, shone gold in the light of the chandeliers above – even through her thick glasses. She must have been quite a beauty in her youth, I mused, noting the deep-set laugh lines and wrinkles all over her fair and still luminous face.

Thus was formed a friendship between Mrs Viswanathan and me. I only knew her by this name. She never divulged her first name, and I never asked. This was perhaps a concession the forty-five years of difference in our ages called for. She came to the store almost every alternate afternoon. A slender built, slightly stooped woman, barely over five feet now, she strode from one counter to another, sure-footed. She spoke to the staff passionately on the design range, history of the design types, advising them on the displays – grouping jewellery under various themes, colours, based on their place of origin. The staff obliged her when asked to shift stock or displays. She was as diligent as if appointed a jewellery consultant. I was impressed by her sincerity, involvement, and very grateful, hovering around her, noting her suggestions.

Ramesh and the other two peons' brought Mrs Viswanathan coffee, even before her asking. She displayed a verve contradicting

 Shuvashree Chowdhury

her years. What drove her thus, I wondered? Could it be her need to feel useful? Was she helping me for taking an interest in her, showing her respect, acknowledging her knowledge and experience? I recognised her sincerity in friendship and was very grateful for it. But I concluded it was her need to be needed at this age, more than my need for help that propelled her. Her husband, I had learnt, hardly had a few words to exchange with her anymore. He preferred to stay home and live a retired, lonely existence. But she had a passion for life and was still in the throes of it. They had two sons. One settled in the US. The other worked and lived in Delhi. She proudly showed me their photographs along with their wives and children. She narrated anecdotes of their lives or pranks of the grandchildren that they narrated to her over the telephone.

One afternoon, Mrs Viswanathan abruptly proffered to me her heavy golden *tali*, from inside her blouse. I had never seen anything like it yet, so was taken aback at someone carrying all that weight in gold on her person always. She explained it was the Tamil version of the *mangalsutra* – an insignia that proclaims to the world the wearer is married.

"Can you get one made exactly like this?" she enquired. "I would like one for my grand-daughter in America."

"Yes, Mrs Viswanathan," I replied, "but for that, you will have to leave it with us as a sample."

"No, no, I could never do that," she blurted, shaking her head vehemently. "I've never ever removed it since I got married at eighteen years. There is no way I'll remove it now, at this age. I cannot take a chance. *Tali* is the guardian of the wearer; to every woman, *tali* is precious, as precious as her loving husband."

"I'll see what I can do," I stated, taken aback by her emotive outburst, "perhaps we could take a close shot picture of your *tali*."

At her age, anxiety over death, her own or her husband's was justified. It could knock on their door, whisking away either anytime. Her husband was older to her by six years. It is in old age that one needs a companion the most, having discharged responsibilities towards children and the world. Wretchedly, it is then, that one lives in constant fear of death separating them from their partner.

Every afternoon Mrs Viswanathan had the car and a part time driver at her disposal. Her husband did not want to go out. But she made it a point to get out of the house. Thus, her afternoon gallivants. What was she supposed to do? Sit at home and rot? She refused to be defined by age, did not allow societal margins of her age restrict her from as active a life as possible. Not one to sit around complaining of ailments, arthritic limbs, fatigue, breathlessness, all usual for people her age. Her husband's illnesses, also her own that had caught up with her, would not keep her down.

However, with time and the frequent visits to our showroom, Mrs Viswanathan got unnerving and pushy with the staff. She now treated the place almost like her home, overboard in her attempt at improving it. The patience the staff had shown her due to my support, gradually wore thin. They took to pretending not to hear or notice her when she spoke to them, even when standing right beside them. They just walked away, ignoring her. When attending to customers, they snubbed her outright. When I pointed out their behaviour would give out wrong signals to other customers, they justified they had targets to achieve.

Mrs Viswanathan, still certain of my support, was undeterred from her mission in life. When one staff ignored her, she proceeded to the next, muttering aloud to herself, "She is busy today."

She instructed the gardener on the plants, both in and around the store. The housekeeping attendants, especially Ramesh, were recipients to her instructions on serving tea and coffee to guests. She even went into the pantry, to observe and then counsel the attendants on how to prepare tea and coffee, which was still manually made. Over and above it was me she advised. It could be on anything that came to her mind, not just on the development of the store. At times she gave me skincare and hair-care tips, at other times, guidance on *sarees* and makeup. By now, she was truly a test on my patience as well, but like the staff, I could not be overtly rude to her.

I continued bearing Mrs Viswanathan's every visit, empathising with her latent loneliness, her desperate need to find friends among strangers. I found it awkward to detract from a friendship I had myself initiated, knowing she now depended on it. She insisted

                    Shuvashree Chowdhury

on taking me to other reputed jewellery stores of Calcutta to show me designs. She had lived here, since coming from Chennai along with her husband after marriage. He had been appointed a finance professional by a reputed organisation, headquartered in Calcutta.

"It will help you understand customer taste in jewellery," she stated, in persuading me to go along with her on the so-called 'market visits'.

At times she suggested we go to handloom houses, at others to furniture auctions or handicraft exhibitions, to find new and improved decorations for the store. I went along with her a few times. But thereafter I would find polite ways to turn her down. Mrs Viswanathan now cost me dearly in terms of working hours. I often had to complete my tasks working late. Yet, I could not summon the spirit or the nerve to take the excitement and sparkle out of her eyes. How was I to tell her we had had enough feedback and help? Or make her aware that she had overstayed our hospitality way too long?

The afternoons that she did not visit our store, she visited art exhibitions, libraries, other jewellers or antique stores. One afternoon, having already turned her down several times, I agreed to go along to a jewellery exhibition. We had to get off the car at a distance, walk to the hall. Mrs Viswanathan suddenly felt ill. On the crowded Camac Street pavement, suddenly slouching over, she leaned on the trunk of a tree with one hand. I was alarmed.

"Let's go back, Mrs Viswanathan," I said, noting her sick pallor. "I'll call the driver for you to go home. I'll take a taxi back myself."

"No, no I am alright. Let's carry on," she insisted, straightening with effort, embarrassed, "It's just the flu I'm recovering from."

"It's alright to feel tired at your age, Mrs Viswanathan," I stated.

"No, it's not. I got you to come out after long. I don't want to miss the exhibition," she countered, "God knows when you will be able to make it again. Moreover, the exhibition will be over in a day or two."

It was pointless arguing with someone as strong willed as Mrs Viswanathan. We slowly resumed walking to the exhibition.

The arrival of the festive season of Durga Puja, Diwali and Dhanteras – meant an incredible rise in work pressure at the store. In spite of a centralised indenting system, additional stocks had to be indented for locally, keeping regional tastes and the local market in mind. Then there was the festival-specific display, visual merchandising, counter re-allocations and accounting of incoming stocks and additional staffing to be looked into. With all the planning and multi-tasking required, I barely could say "Hello!" to Mrs Viswanathan. I now found it impossible to make time for her when she visited. So, I stayed in my office on learning of her arrival. The staff ignored her completely. The showroom was now buzzing with customers they had to attend to, with a view to meeting the enhanced festive season targets. Mrs Viswanathan now insisted on chatting with the security staff, gardener, attendants, who also pretended not to notice or hear her.

At times she would telephone me, on her return home.

"I was not able to meet you today," she would start and then add excitedly, "I had brought this *saree* I wanted to show you," or "I wanted to tell you about that great exhibition I went to yesterday. I wish you could have come along."

"I'm sorry to have missed you too, Mrs Viswanathan," I would reply politely. "I was caught up in a meeting when you came."

She would, to my chagrin, visit the store the next day or the day after, hoping to meet me again. At the peak of the festive season, I stopped taking her calls. It had been my fault, I realised, for not discouraging her overtures earlier. After a few unanswered calls from her, Mrs Viswanathan stopped coming to the store. Then abruptly there was no call from her. I had too many things to worry about simultaneously. Yet, a sense of guilt, for snubbing her out the way I did, would pervade my conscious from time to time and linger.

We surpassed our festive season targets. After that, the workload reduced along with customer walk-in. It would remain low till the next high season of Christmas and New Year. It was now that I missed Mrs Viswanathan. I could not help thinking of her contribution to the positive changes, our target achievement and the high sales-incentives we earned. Her sincerity had been unmistakable, whatever her motivation.

 Shuvashree Chowdhury

"Has any of you seen Mrs Viswanathan?" I asked at a morning meeting. "It's been a long time that she visited us."

"No, we haven't. Thank God!" was the spontaneous response. "Please ... please don't call her, Ma'am," the staff pleaded in unison.

"Perhaps she has a son for whom she is considering you a prospective bride," someone joked, while another added, "She asked us if you were married and we said 'no'."

"Yeah, I'm sure she's looking for a bride," I grinned, though my heart felt heavy.

"Can you imagine a mother-in-law like her?" one staff mocked, "A nightmare, I tell you," another staff rejoined.

There was roaring laughter, but I remained silent. My joining in the hilarity would mean a breach of loyalty to my friend.

Mrs Viswanathan's absence was a relief to everyone at the store. But for me, she had become an integral part of us since my joining. Her not visiting again, not even calling me, meant we had hurt her deeply, I concluded. So I called her on her mobile phone. There was no response. I dialled several times, but still, there was no response. She must be really upset, not to take my calls or call back later if busy, in spite of my several attempts to connect with her, I thought. I decided on visiting her at home. We had her address in our sales records, from old bills. It was a few days before Christmas that I drove down to her residence in Ballygunge. I carried a large box of cookies and a Christmas fruitcake I had organised for regular, loyal customers. In the elevator to her tenth-floor apartment, I mentally smiled at her initial anger, which I was sure would be followed by her warm smile that would light up her eyes.

I rang the bell. An old man with a head of silver hair answered it. He opened the door a couple of inches wide, peering out. Then after scrutinising me head to toe, he opened it wider.

"I'm here to meet Mrs Viswanathan," I said, "I'm her friend."

He looked at me curiously, squinting hard. Then his eyes lit up in slow recognition, as though we had met a long time back. His deeply wrinkled face broke into a nearly toothless smile.

"Please come in," he replied, opening the door wide now. "You are her young manager friend, aren't you?"

I nodded, smiling back. He led me inside. He was a tall man with broad shoulders – slouched with age now, also, as though, dejectedly. He bent forward wearily as he walked, his head stooping low.

"Please sit down, make yourself comfortable," he said, in a soft mellow voice, once inside the drawing room. "I will be right back."

He went into an adjoining room, perhaps to call my friend. I sat down on the olive-green sofa, placing the parcel of cookies and cake on the glass centre-table. It was a beautifully furnished room, I noticed, everything elegantly matched. I would not have expected any less of Mrs Viswanathan with her sense of style. Looking around me, I suddenly felt her eyes staring at me through her black-framed spectacles. I was about to get up to greet her, when I noticed it was her eyes from a life-sized portrait, which was intently viewing me, smiling warmly at me. I smiled back involuntarily. Then shifting my gaze from her lifelike eyes, I suddenly noticed the huge garland of yellow marigold flowers around the picture.

I stood up rapidly. Then as I remained rooted to the floor, staring at Mrs Viswanathan's smiling life-like face, the tears sprung to my eyes. Her husband was watching me closely.

"Meera always told me you would come in search of your friend, once you had the time," he said softly. "But I did not believe her. She told anyone who cared to listen that she had made a young, new friend. The excitement would ring in her voice, recounting you."

"What happened?" I stuttered.

"She died of a heart-failure in her sleep," he replied, "always had a weak heart, you know. The doctor had declared a year at most, last Christmas. She never wanted anyone to know."

                    Shuvashree Chowdhury

13. *Love Like an Indian*

I briskly swirled into my neighbourhood petrol bunk to a high-pitched, heartrending yelp of *Kancha, Kancha* (boy in Nepali).

Bringing the car to an abrupt halt, I peered outside the left side window toward the origin of the sound. Two women were squatting on the ground, sobbing. They were shabbily dressed and in a state of disarray, like they had just woken up from sleep or had not slept at all. One was an average looking, swarthy complexioned, *saree*-clad Indian woman, with dark black eyes and oiled hair held back in a bun. The other, squatting on the road exactly in the manner of local slum dwellers, was, to my surprise, a westerner with a short crop of blonde hair, blue-grey eyes, wearing a cotton *kurti* teamed with cargo trousers, a *dupatta* casually thrown about her neck.

They had grabbed my curiosity – the way they were wailing, with the Indian woman, in archetypal style, also lovingly stroking the hair and hands of the western woman to console her. But I felt uneasy about interfering. A part of me wanted to get off the car and offer my help, but the other decided to watch a few minutes from the sidelines, before plunging into what could be a very personal affair. Moreover, in the meantime, a few men had gathered around them, looking at the women – especially the western one, as she was young and pretty, even though slightly overweight – like they were two monkeys in a circus. This further augmented my protective streak towards those of my sex. However, I proceeded towards the tanker and after filling my car's fuel tank to capacity, paying up, I slowly manoeuvred the car towards the air-check gauge, parking very close to where the two women were still squatting with intermittent shrill cries of "*kancha … kancha ….*"

I got off while the attendant was checking my car's tyre pressure, and walked over to where the women squatted. A Maruti Omni van was now parked nearby and a gentleman, with a stethoscope in hand, stood in between the squatting women and the van. It was not unusual to find a doctor or two around here, as this petrol bunk in Salt Lake, Calcutta, is adjacent to three hospitals. I did not know about the cause of the grief of the two women, but the sound and sight of their pain had infiltrated into my psyche and I could almost feel their pain by now. I noticed that I was the only woman there, in the by now large group of people that had collected around the two anguished women, other than one sitting equally morosely in the van.

On enquiring of the doctor with the stethoscope, he burst forth with the story of the two women, like his emotions were waiting to be rescued, from the prison they had been held in till now. He seemed to need telling the story more that I needed to hear it. I was in sympathy of the women without even knowing their grief, while he had been with them through their whole journey leading up to it. The western woman squatting on the ground, I learnt to my amazement, was a German doctor, an endocrinologist, who had come as part of a group of health workers to work with an NGO in Calcutta. While here, she had fallen in love with a Nepali NGO employee and had extended her stay month on month, till she had been here for over two years by now. During this time, she had even taken the Nepali man home to Germany, thinking they could settle down there. But somehow they had returned and gone back to working with the NGO, perhaps because the man was unable to adjust to life there or she missed her life at the NGO and amongst the slum dwellers in Calcutta.

A couple of days back, after a severe attack of Tuberculosis, the Nepali man had been admitted to the adjacent hospital. He had succumbed to his illness the previous night. Now the women were waiting to take his body to the crematorium. By the time the doctor came to the end of his brief narration, he was as emotional as I was – in reliving the sincere, deep love of a woman who perhaps had it good in life. Then gave it all up for the love of her life – to be with her man and those he was comfortable with. I could as yet hear the German woman hysterically rocking back and forth, beating her chest sporadically, amid calling out to her *Kancha.*

What struck me deep, is how she had adapted to the culture and surroundings, dress, language, living and behavioural attributes of her slum dweller Nepali boyfriend. She was now reacting to her grief

     Shuvashree Chowdhury

at his loss in a primal way, like someone born into a slum dwelling and without pretentions, propriety or care for the world. The woman was squatting on the road in public view, hysterically wailing like the people she had perhaps become used to interacting with, through her poor boyfriend and the other benefactors of the NGO she worked for. She had adapted totally to the ways of her lover and to his culture.

On suddenly noticing the two women being escorted to the waiting van by their co-workers, I interrupted the doctor I was talking to: "Who is the Indian woman with the German doctor?" I asked.

Before he could reply, I distractedly looked in the direction of the two women for a few brief moments, with a newfound admiration and respect for the German lady doctor, adding to my existing empathy for her loss. It was after the women were seated in the van that I returned my attention to the male doctor standing with me, for the answer to my question.

"She is the Nepali man's wife," he replied sombrely.

Then he looked me in the eye, waiting for me to register the implication of his disclosure. I blinked, blinked yet again, before swallowing the lump in my throat, with the fluid shock of this revelation.

I had been on my way to work that morning, at the jewellery store I managed. I drove out of the petrol bunk, my mind reeling from having been fuelled by the power of true love. But I was enthused – I was going to share with my mostly women staff at the daily morning meeting I was now late for – the lesson I had learned, of love's gigantic capacity to adapt, over and above to share.

14. *What a Woman Wants*

It was a warm, sunny, April afternoon. We got off the bus, on the pavement overlooking Pattaya beach, having driven from Bangkok in a little over two hours. The sea was a beautiful aqua-green. This was an excursion twenty-five of us from the jewellery company I worked with had taken after the business associates meet, held in Bangkok that year of 2006. Incidentally, this was two weeks prior to my wedding in Calcutta, after which I was to resign and move to Chennai to live with my husband. As we stood facing the sea, the midday rays of the harsh sun made it difficult to look into the shimmering water with bare eyes. In order to ascertain the accurate hue of the gorgeous sea, I removed the pair of sunglasses I had worn through the drive, placing them over my head. Each time I gazed, the water appeared a different shade of blue or green. The warm breeze struck my face harshly after the air-conditioned bus ride, blowing my shoulder-length hair wildly over my eyes, and face.

I tried to hold the hair strands away, but the intensity of the wind interrupted my desire to feast my eyes on the view. The waves lashed noisily on the infinite sandy shore, liberally strewn with multi-coloured beach-chairs and umbrellas. There were men and women of varied skin colours representing diverse nationalities, in flashy swimming trunks, glitzy bikinis and sarongs, on the beach. They either lounged on the beach-chairs or stood by the water's edge waiting to ride the next big wave or submerge in the smaller playful ones. Behind us on the road, bicycles and motorbikes whizzed past, their riders wearing colourful shirts and Bermudas. A number of people strolled on the pavement around us, as well as on the other side of the road, lined by shops selling knick-knacks and a variety of merchandise, from beachwear to party wear.

We had spent a good part of the last three days at the conference in Bangkok, the evenings we utilised exploring the city and its nightlife. Today, the fourth and last day was a bonus for us employees to spend it the way we liked. The retail associates or franchisees had three more free days at the cost of the company. A visit to Pattaya then, considering its popularity and proximity to Bangkok, had seemed logical. So my friend and roommate at the luxurious five-star hotel in Bangkok and I had promptly registered our names for this excursion, the expense of which was to be borne by us respectively. Ashima and I had become close over the last four years that we had managed flagship stores of the company, having joined about the same time, she in Delhi and I in Calcutta. A slim, sprightly woman of thirty-two now, Ashima was beautiful – with a luminous complexion, large light-brown eyes, high-cheek bones and a wide sensuous mouth. Her long straight hair, the same shade as her eyes, enhanced her beauty.

Though Ashima and I shared the room, we spent only the mornings together. I was usually fast asleep long before she crept in very late at night. She would leave right after the conference ended in the evening, while I joined colleagues from other departments from across India. It was in the mornings over breakfast, before the conference began, or during the tea and lunch breaks, that Ashima and I exchanged notes on how we had spent the previous evening. Her boyfriend had travelled to Bangkok, just to spend the evenings with her, though he was staying at another hotel. At the Pattaya beach now, we were waiting to board the speedboat that would take us across the sea, to Coral Island. According to the itinerary, we would complete that tour, and then spend the rest of the evening shopping and sightseeing in Pattaya. We would head back to Bangkok late, after a popular concert by transsexuals who dressed up gorgeously as women, at this hall known as Tiffany's, and finally a Thai dinner.

Since we had some time before our boat was ready to leave, Ashima and I strolled across the road to the shops behind, along with a few others. We viewed the merchandise sold out of shacks lining the road. Then coming across an indoor market, we stepped inside to freshen up at the rest room, and then returned to wait by the promenade. The speedboat, when it arrived, was big enough to accommodate our large group and more, if need be. We trooped inside, assisted by hand by the stout Thai lady operator and her two male assistants. Once we were settled in on the seats lining both the sides, the lady took her place at the helm and revved up the engine. The boat instantly breezed through the now perceptibly clear-green water. It spurt jets of water all around, some of which fell like a light drizzle on us who were leaning over the boat's sides. The view of the sea embraced by tiny islands and settlements was spectacular, in a medley of unidentifiable shades of blue and green. Beyond where the blue-green sea merged with the blue sky at a distance was our destination.

As we approached Coral Island, one of the attendants urged us to peer below, through the small transparent window at the base of the boat. A shoal of fish had enclosed the base of the boat. By the time we took turns gazing at the silvery-green creatures, the boat had been anchored. Ashima and I stepped onto the whitish-sand, liberally strewn with tiny corals. A man wearing an aqua-blue fish printed shirt over a pair of faded blue jeans and sandals, walked up to us. He was tall, burly, with a short crop of salt-and-pepper hair combed back slickly. With a hooked-nose, deep-set brown eyes and a wide jaw line, he was handsome.

"Good that you are here already," Ashima said to the man cheerfully.

"Is there anywhere else I'd rather be?" he asked her, smiling indulgently. Then, pointing at a distance, he added, "I've set up two beach chairs under that umbrella there. Chilled beer is awaiting us."

I looked from one to the other in surprise.

"This is Sunil Mehra," Ashima said, as if on cue. "You know all about him."

"Ah yes! Yes, of course!" I exclaimed, and then turning to Sunil added, "Nice to meet you, Sunil. I've heard so much about you, it feels as though we've met."

"I hope it was all good that you heard," Sunil replied, laughing, looking much younger in spite of the crows-feet that became very pronounced as he did.

"Well, yes, mostly good," I said, and then turning to Ashima, I added, "But you didn't tell me that Sunil was coming here to Pattaya, and to Coral Island."

     Shuvashree Chowdhury

"I meant to tell you," she replied sheepishly, "Then decided to surprise you."

I tried to hide my disappointment as I disapproved of Sunil's coming here, since we were with our work group. Ashima's having a much older boyfriend though she was married and had a four-year-old son was entirely her choice, but bringing him along on this trip was, in my opinion, unprofessional and foolish. Sunil's coming to Bangkok on the pretext of business, and Ashima's spending evenings discreetly with him, was one thing, his coming here amidst everyone, was quite another. I looked around, the rest of our group had moved ahead by now. The owners of the tiny shacks down the road were approaching us, with chilled beer and cold drink bottles in hand, to entice them into their respective shanties. They thrived from batches of visitors patronising their shops.

"I'll leave you two," I said, taking a step to go and join the rest of the group.

"No, please stay," Sunil replied persuasively, "I'll get us another chair."

I wanted to leave them alone, but it would look odd to the rest of the group if Ashima stayed back alone with a stranger, so I agreed to stay with them a while, and then wander off to join the rest of the group. Led by Sunil, Ashima and I walked towards a large deck umbrella, hoisted in front of a tiny shop.

An oriental-looking man added another of the blue, red and yellow striped deckchairs, to the two already set. The three of us then settled down on them, reclining comfortably, facing the sea. Another man brought three bottles of beer, along with plates of fried-fish and roasted-shrimps. In our view, a large number of people were jumping over the high waves, swimming, or engaged in various water-sports organised by the agents there. After a brief exchange with me, Sunil and Ashima were engrossed in a conversation. They laughed heartily, and I noticed how comfortable and happy they were in each other's company. In spite of my initial reservations, I could not, but be happy for Ashima. As I lay back, staring at the sea, my mind wandered to her husband Rajesh, and their marital life, about which she had shared with me on previous official trips together. She and I had first met three years back, by when she already had a year old son.

* * *

It had been a regular day, when after work, Ashima had driven to the gym near her parent's house at Greater Kailash in Delhi. It was 7.30pm. She had quickly changed into her workout clothes and then proceeded to the treadmill, where she routinely ran for half an hour daily. After another fifteen minutes of cycling, she had barely settled on the floor-mat to do a round of abdomen-crunches, preferring it to the machine, when she felt a shadow over her face from behind. Involuntarily, she looked at the floor to ceiling mirror in front of her. Through its reflection, Ashima saw a young man, in a bright aqua-blue t-shirt, standing close, almost over her head. He was lifting a barbell that looked at least sixty kilos, if not more. On appraising the situation, she briskly jumped up to stand in bewilderment. The fear of the barbell crashing on her head looming menacingly on her mind, she barely saw the man.

"What the hell are you doing, can't you see?" she interjected sharply, and then looking ahead at his reflection in the mirror, indicating the barbell with her eyes, she added, "What if that falls on my head?"

"How and why should it fall on your head?" he quipped, in mock surprise, then added, "Can't you see my developed biceps and triceps?"

"Biceps … triceps … my foot," she retorted. "All I can see is that huge weight with which you were standing over my head. Put it down now, will you?"

Slowly, with effort, he placed the barbell on the floor. Ashima was still glaring at his reflection in the mirror in horror, without really noticing him. As he lifted his head to look at her squarely, she noticed, at first, his lopsided grin. The roguish smile drawing her attention to his lean face, she noticed it's well-defined features, the sharp hooked nose, broad forehead, the piercing light-brown eyes twinkling in amusement, and finally, the sharp fall of his jaw line. Then, as she turned around to face him, she almost bumped into his sculpted torso, accentuated by the tight t-shirt he wore.

Now, she noticed his bulging biceps and triceps, under the short sleeves of his t-shirt, and gauged his muscular chest through its stretched fabric, as he towered over her with his imposing height.

"You are really insulting me now," the man said in a mockingly hurt tone, then smiling, added, "But, at least fear made you talk to me, considering you never speak to anyone here, I've noticed."

Abruptly looking away, flushed from realising she had been staring at him, Ashima replied sternly, "You left me no choice, did you, standing over my head with that weight."

Then with sudden comprehension, looking him in the eye, she added, smiling, "I get it now. This was a ploy to get my attention, wasn't it? Well … never mind that now, let's just get back to what we were doing, shall we?"

"I'm Rajesh Nath," the man said abruptly, proffering his hand to shake, before she could turn away, "I'm a software professional."

"I'm Ashima Mathur," she replied, shaking his hand, "Nice to meet you."

Then, after the exchange, they went back to finishing their workouts.

The next evening, after their workouts, Ashima and Rajesh exchanged pleasantries. Then with Rajesh's pursuance, they changed out of their gym wear into regular clothes, driving in their respective cars to a coffee shop down the road. Over cups of café lattes and sandwiches, they discussed their work, their lives.

"You need someone to really care for you, Ashima," Rajesh said, abruptly.

"Don't we all?" Ashima replied, trying to comprehend his words, and then, after a pause, she amusedly added, "You know, you look more like a rock star than a software professional, the type women would swoon over, not the type a woman would be seriously interested in, for fear of too much competition."

"Yeah, perhaps you're right," he replied, "Never quite looked at it that way. No wonder I don't meet intelligent women. You're the first girl I want to listen to." Then, abruptly, he asked, "By the way, what is your opinion on men, in general?"

"Well, for starters, they never grow up," Ashima replied, chuckling. "Men I've known, both personally and professionally, came across as mature initially, but with time, whether twenty-three or sixty-three, they all act like boys."

"See, that's your problem … you take life too damn seriously," he said, "What's it about age, really? It's only a state of mind, isn't it? I'd feel like I'm twenty, even at sixty years. And you, too, should stop taking your age so seriously. Think you're twenty-three from now and here, and you'll always feel that way."

Ashima laughed, thinking, at twenty-eight years, whether she looked it or not, she definitely felt a decade older. Rajesh, she was to learn later, was the same age as her. Their coffee over, by now comfortable in each other's company, they walked to a Chinese restaurant nearby. Their lively conversation continued through dinner. They left the restaurant holding hands. It seemed like the most natural thing to Ashima. A few steps ahead, Rajesh lightly put his arm around her shoulder, and she did not stop him. They walked together like that, to her car, like two people who had known each other for years.

Just as Ashima opened her car door with the remote key, Rajesh abruptly took her hand in his, looking into her eyes sincerely.

"Close your eyes, Ashima," he said, abruptly.

She complied with a mischievous smile, her hand outstretched, assuming he would put something onto her palms. With her eyes closed, Ashima suddenly felt something warm on her lips, felt the warm breath on her face. With the comprehension of Rajesh's lips taking hers softly, as she gasped, abruptly opening her eyes, he pulled away.

She was standing rooted to the ground in shock, when Rajesh whispered into her ear, "Ashima, you are a very special person, and I say it again, you need someone to love and care for you unconditionally. Consider allowing me."

Rajesh abruptly turned, retreating in the direction of his car. Ashima, in a daze, got behind the steering of hers, then started the engine, slowly accelerating.

Ashima's eyes welled with tears from the emotions, the longing Rajesh's words stirred in the depths of her heart, blurring her view. Was it not what she had always wanted in her relationships with men, to be truly loved for the person she was, not merely for her beauty? There had been a couple of boyfriends in her life so

     Shuvashree Chowdhury

far, but she had felt by the end of each relationship, the men had liked her only for her good looks. Perhaps she was too serious, boring even, she thought, and came across as distant due to her inherent shyness. But somehow, she believed, Rajesh having figured her out, still liked the person she was, over and above her good looks. Thus, she decided to give love and Rajesh another chance. They met the next day at the gym, initially awkward. But by the time they drove to the nearby coffee shop again, they were cosy. After that, they met almost every day. After a whirlwind courtship, Rajesh wooing Ashima relentlessly, convinced no one could ever love her more than him, she consented to marry him.

When I first met Ashima, she came across as happily married. But with the stories she told me, I concluded, she yearned for her husband's love and attention. Beautiful as she still was at thirty, Ashima had no dearth of male attention, from colleagues, as well as strangers. But all she cared for was the love and attention of her husband. Still much in love, she spoke a lot about Rajesh, more about how he was not around much, and didn't care about her like before. On our official outstation trips, every time he telephoned, I heard her cribbing, either about his not calling earlier or his not taking her incessant calls.

"See, he calls me only for his needs," Ashima would then justify to me, in our room. "He'll either call to figure out where something is or about our son."

"But doesn't it feel good to be needed in a relationship?" I asked once.

"Well, perhaps, but what about when I need him?" she retorted. "He is not available then. He's either out of the country or tied up with business. Even at home, he seems mentally preoccupied and distant with me."

"He's just started a new business, it can be very difficult, you know," I had reasoned. "After all, isn't he doing it for you, for a better life for the three of you?"

"But money's not what I want," she replied sadly. "I don't need a better life; I only want him to love me like he did when we got married, before the baby. Now even when he is home, he hardly notices what I wear, how I look, least of all he listens to what I say.

He comes back from work, and the first thing he does is switch on the television. I'd like to talk about my day, our son, but he is so distracted."

"But watching TV may be to unwind after the day's stresses," I said. "Perhaps you could sit quietly in front of the TV, then, in a while, he'll be ready for a conversation, though, probably, not a run-up of your day right away. Now that you're married awhile, things are bound to be different; it's another new phase."

"You don't get it," she retorted. "But how can you? You're not married yet."

"I hope I won't have such high expectations of my husband then," I smiled. "I'll take life as it comes. We'll figure each other out anew, after the wedding."

"All I'm asking is for Rajesh to care for me, and make me feel special, like he used to when we were dating," Ashima had continued, and my heart went out to her. "Now he treats me as the wife ... the one who keeps the home for him. He takes no responsibility for household chores, or in parenting. All he thinks of is his business."

"But he really loves you, that's for sure," I stated, to cheer her. "In fact, I distinctly recall you telling me the details of how you guys first met, so romantic."

"Yes, he loves me, only not in the way I expected him to," she sighed. "He loves me like one would love a family member, one's parents or siblings perhaps. But I want more. He was so different when we met. Why didn't I see through all that talk of my being special and all that? What a fool I was, he's like every other guy."

"Ashima, what is it that you want most from Rajesh, from your marriage, your life together?" I once asked, curiously, to get a better insight.

"Well, what I want is little things that keep reminding me he still cares. I want Rajesh to bring me flowers, or surprise gifts from his foreign trips, rather than giving me plenty of money to buy whatever I want," she replied, smiling bashfully at the thought. "I'd love for him to make surprise dinners or holiday reservations for the two of us, instead of expecting me to organise everything, while he concentrates on his work. I want candlelight and wine

     Shuvashree Chowdhury

dinners, long drives and romantic getaways … stuff he did when he wooed me initially."

"Have you ever spoken to Rajesh about what you truly want?" I asked.

"Obviously not, if I have to tell him, then what's the point?" she retorted. "He should understand, know what I want, and be spontaneous and sincere."

Still staring unseeingly at the sea on Coral Island, Ashima's merry laughter ringing in my ears, simultaneous to her boyfriend Sunil's animated voice, I recalled Ashima's list of what she craved. What a woman wants then, I thought, are simple things really, yet marriages fail for want of trivial things. I took a large swig from the bottle of chilled beer in my hand, swallowed hard, along with the irony of the circumstance I was closely observing. After munching on a couple of sautéed prawns, I looked from Ashima to Sunil. I could not help noting the resemblance between Sunil and Ashima's husband, Rajesh, whom I had met a couple of times. Sunil, in his younger days, might have looked a lot more like what Rajesh looked now. Ashima was perhaps recreating with Sunil, a life she had envisioned with Rajesh, I thought.

I could not help wondering whether Sunil would make Ashima feel truly like a woman, lifelong, the way she wanted. But seeing the contentment in Ashima's eyes, the lilt in her voice, their light-hearted banter, their chemistry despite the twenty-five years of age difference, I realised he did treat her right. They laughed a lot and seemed really happy together. From the tender look in Sunil's eyes, the way he doted on Ashima, I could envisage that he was grateful for the opportunity of loving her. They had first met on a flight to London from Delhi, she had told me. Sitting on adjacent seats, they had opened their hearts to each other, on their lives, their families, it being easier sometimes to talk to a stranger. Sunil was a top-rung corporate executive, at fifty-five years, nearing the end of his career. His wife was no more, having died in a car accident a couple of years back, leaving behind a daughter who presently studied journalism in London.

Perhaps it was his wife's untimely death, I thought, that taught Sunil to value the person he loved, demonstrate his love, before it was too late. The lines on his face, the soft understanding glow in his eyes as he looked lovingly at Ashima, reflected a maturity that only experience brings. Meeting and loving Ashima had given his perhaps lonely years, a new meaning. However, he didn't expect much from her in return, in terms of seeking a hurried security for their relationship. He was happy to support Ashima, be there for her and her son, who by now he was close to, only when she needed him. This had enabled Ashima to maintain the harmony in her married life so far. Rajesh did not know of Sunil yet.

Ashima had said to me only the day before, over breakfast, with a sparkle in her eyes, "Sunil really knows how to make a woman feel special."

"Now how does he manage that?" I had asked, with a mischievous grin.

"Well, he makes me feel good about myself, bringing out the best in me. I feel secure now and more confident," she had replied ingenuously. "I am comfortable in his presence, so I can be myself. Also, I have discovered new aspects of my personality, like my love for poetry, painting, etc. He always listens to me, encourages me, and makes me laugh like I never have before. I am now a better wife, daughter, mother, and also, manager. Perhaps carrying my enhanced self-worth into my relationships, I am able to nurture them better." Then, after a pause, she dramatically concluded, "He's really been good for me."

I had to agree, having noticed the changes. Ashima was now more relaxed, laughed more, and professionally, too, she was more productive from the improved sales figures and overall ratings of the large format store she managed in Delhi.

When a woman values herself, the world also values her. Does a woman have the right then, to go after happiness where she finds it? Ashima had decided on getting a divorce from Rajesh, keeping her son. We had discussed this on our drive to Pattaya in the morning. Was she justified in doing so?

"A penny for your thoughts, ma'am," Sunil said aloud to me, waving.

Startled out of my reverie, I looked at him bending across Ashima, who was sitting between us. He had a quizzical expression, which promptly broke into a smile.

"Ashima is very lucky to have found you, is what I've been thinking," I said, smiling back at him. "And you're a lucky man, too."

Sunil and Ashima smiled at me simultaneously. My beer bottle now empty, I stood up, and then excused myself to go for a walk. I planned on catching up with our other colleagues and on spending some time with them.

As I took purposeful strides over the sand and the corals, I felt blessed for this reality check on love and marriage I had just had. This lesson seemed like my wedding gift from the universe, two weeks before my wedding to a man I had loved for two months yet. I was convinced in marrying him, from our daylong, long distance telephone chats and a two-week visit to Chennai where he lived. I was in agreement with Ashima that we women want to be loved, to be listened to, desired, respected, needed, trusted and sometimes just to be held. But men often don't understand that, or are unable to match our emotional needs, bogged as they may be by the pressures of career and life. The reverse is also often true, of men feeling misunderstood, their needs ignored. Thus, for a sustaining marriage and life, in addition to love, we need to strike a balance in our expectations from and duties to our partners. I decided I would start my new life on this adage.

15. A Reckless Life

"The day our debts go over our head we will commit suicide," Sanjay stated, his tone nonchalant.

I looked at him aghast. If not for the preceding conversation, I might have thought this was another of his mindless attempts at impressing me.

"Ma'am, could you lend me some money, please?" he had asked me over coffee at the staff room, right after the morning meeting.

"Sure, but how much do you need?" I asked.

"About six thousand rupees," he replied.

I looked at him surprised. I had expected him to ask for a few hundred.

"Well, I don't have that much right now," I stated, and then unable to hold my curiosity, I asked, "Sanjay, we received our salary only last week, so why do you need this kind of money, so soon?"

"To pay the house rent. The landlord has given us an ultimatum to vacate," he replied with a casual shrug. Then, noticing the questioning look on my face, he added sombrely, "I get delayed in paying the rent most months."

"But why don't you pay it the first thing after you get your salary?"

Sanjay remained silent. As usual, there was no sign of remorse on his lean face. He looked at me cheekily with his beady eyes. His arched bony nose stuck out with the insolent sideward tilt of his head, his chin pointed downward, thin lips curling almost into a grin. It was obvious he had no justifiable response to my query. He had adopted his usual offensive stance for whenever I reprimanded him. He suddenly assumed a pleading look now, realising that I could rescue him from his financial crisis.

I had known Sanjay for over a year. He was in charge of the financial operations at the department store I now managed.

    Shuvashree Chowdhury

This was in Chennai, where I had moved after my marriage. One would expect someone accountable for the finance of a large format store to act responsibly, but in Sanjay's case it was not so.

"Ma'am, he never has money for rent," Sudha, an assistant manager interrupted. She was looking at Sanjay menacingly. "He squanders his salary even before he gets it."

I briskly turned in the direction of Sudha's voice. Sitting at an adjacent table, she had been privy to our conversation. Sanjay's conduct and inability to manage his finances judiciously had resulted in his borrowing from many in the store, including the security staff. Left with no option, since others refused to lend him more money due to his inability to repay, he had approached me.

Sudha's interest in our conversation had been more than a fleeting one. She had known Sanjay would ask me for money, after she had recently turned him down. Designing on thwarting his plans as well as bringing his conduct to my notice, she sat at an adjacent table at the staff room. I preferred having my lunch or coffee, there, in the staff room, to my cabin. It helped me connect with the staff. Sudha had lent Sanjay money several times before, with no hope left of his returning it. His reckless attitude towards money and life in general infuriated her. After all, she worked so hard, only for the money, for a better life for her family. She got up from her table, teacup in hand, and walked over to ours. Standing alongside, she took an impatient sip from her cup, and then placed it on our table.

"Get a grip on your life, Sanjay," she said looking Sanjay in the eye, then wanting me to hear the story, continued: "You bought a pair of jeans for yourself, yesterday, with so many new clothes for your wife. Didn't you? Was the splurge more important than paying the house rent? Also you owe so many of us money."

Sanjay glared at Sudha, eyes wide in horror. It took him a few seconds to compose himself.

"You don't have to worry about me, Sudha," he shot back, holding her gaze. Then, with a derisive grin, he added scornfully: "The day our debts go over our heads we will commit suicide."

Sudha and I looked at him in shock, outraged at his brazenness. He had not considered Sudha would divulge his ways. He supposed that all the lady staff was under his spell. This was not totally untrue of most at the store, for he was indeed a ladies man. Sanjay was of medium height with a slender, athletic built. His eyes were light brown, deep set and piercing. The sharp nose was set on a chiselled jaw line. In addition, the bright and clear complexion did make him a good-looking man. His real charm, however, in addition to the boyish good looks and smile that gave him an aura of vulnerability, lay in his being a smooth talker. Sudha, however, was not one to be impressed with a reckless, insolent man, whatsoever his charms.

"Ma'am, just look at his attitude," she said in an exasperated tone, turning to face me, "He has not an iota of repentance. All the banks are chasing him over credit card dues, and also he is living off borrowed money. Then he talks of suicide as if it were bungee jumping."

"But whatever I bought was on my new credit card," Sanjay stated, giving Sudha a contemptuous look. "I still have credit-balance on it. Moreover, everything was on sale. I got the stuff at excellent prices."

"Sanjay, you always have a handy excuse for everything. Your splurging is inexcusable in your current financial situation," Sudha shot back, walking away in anger. She left her unfinished teacup at our table, along with leaving me to deal with Sanjay.

Sanjay had married Nirupama soon after he graduated with a Bachelor of Commerce degree. She was his junior by two years. It was only a registry marriage then, which was to remain a secret between their families. It was after Sanjay took up a job that they had a wedding ceremony announcing their union. It had been love at first-sight for Sanjay on viewing Nirupama's *Kathak* dance recital, at their college festival. But it had taken a lot of time and persuasion on his part, for Nirupama to respond to him. By the time she did, his tall claims of undying love had to be substantiated by a promise to marry her. She came from a middle class Tamil family, wherein the presence of a boy in a girl's life, her being seen in his company, indicated that she would be his for a lifetime.

In Nirupama's case, this societal imperative was steadfast, also since Sanjay's family was much lower in the economic rungs as compared to hers. Sanjay's father held a clerical position in a government organisation, while Nirupama's successfully ran

     Shuvashree Chowdhury

a pharmaceutical business. Her parents, as expected, did not approve of Sanjay from the minute he walked into their T Nagar residence, introduced as her friend. The way he was dressed, his lack of confidence and refinement, the accented English – denoting his Tamil medium schooling, in spite of his good looks, met with their instant disdain. But Nirupama had mentally braced herself for this. Smart as she was, she had planted the idea of his moving in with them, in their minds. She impressed upon them that Sanjay, loving her as sincerely as he did, would not mind moving in with them. He would consider living in the comfort of her house till he could provide her similar or better conditions. Her parents believing that he never could, were thrilled at the idea of their only child living with them for a lifetime. Nirupama's father perhaps mentally also nurtured the idea of Sanjay joining his business one day.

Sanjay's parents, on the other hand, approved of Nirupama from the start. She was pretty and came from a good family. In their trusting opinion, what more could be necessary? Little did they envision they might lose their only son to the connivance of an affluent family. However, as with a male child, Sanjay's parents were not in any hurry their son legalise his liaisons with a girl. He had little to lose in way of his reputation, in hanging out with one as pretty and classy as Nirupama. His parents impressed upon him to complete his education, get a good job, only then take on the financial and emotional duty of a wife. But being the economically weaker of the two set of contending parents, Sanjay's had to give in to the pressure of Nirupama's – on the couple having a registry marriage quickly, if not a social one, just to be sure. It was however mutually decided the newly-weds would live in their respective houses, till Nirupama finished her studies, and Sanjay got a job.

It had been Sanjay's dream to pursue a chartered accountancy course, after graduating in commerce. It would have been the right thing to do, providing the gateway – provided he could clear the tough course, to a good career and uplifting his economic and social standing. But Nirupama and her family dissuaded him. They urged him to take up a job instead, so he could assume responsibility as a husband soon. Moving in with them was primary in their agenda, though he didn't comprehend their motives. They insisted, that Nirupama's not being socially married, now that she was well over age, was raising questions from relatives and friends. Thus, in order to expedite his bearing the palanquin of his marital life, to set it in motion, Sanjay gave up his dream, to take up a regular accountant's job. Moreover, his father by now having retired from government service at a position that drew a negligible pension left Sanjay little choice.

The accountant's job, which Sanjay, a fresher without proficient English communication skills could attract with his qualifications, was limited in terms of earnings. So he managed to stall the social marriage, till his earnings improved. In a short time, to augment his earnings, by way of moving up the corporate ladder, however adjoining the succeeding rung, Sanjay switched jobs. It was at the panel-interview of his third job, that I first encountered the ambitious, bright Sanjay. His insufficient English language skills, resultant awkwardness and stuttering, overridden by his job knowledge, experience, communication skills in Tamil and dynamism, clinched him the job. He joined the lifestyle retail outlet I managed, within a month, in the position of commercial officer. After a short induction at the company's head office in Mumbai, followed by a longer stint at the regional office in Chennai, he seemed confident to take on his responsibilities.

In Sanjay's first week on the job, I encountered a conscientious, diligent, efficacious man. To my amazement, thereafter, he gradually started coming in late to work. He would reach beyond 11am, by which time the morning meeting was well under way. Since the cashiers at the store all reported to him, it was difficult to coordinate and discuss issues pertaining to them at the meeting, if he was missing. The morning meeting was very crucial to keeping the wheels of the retail store on track and running smoothly. Moreover, Sanjay was in charge of the stock and in possession of the vault keys where the cash boxes were deposited at night. So, until he came to work, the multiple cash desks could not be functional even though the store was open to customers at 10.30am.

Every time I asked Sanjay the cause of his delay, he would come up with excuses like – he had to pay the electricity bill, the cooking gas had run out, or that he had woken with a splitting headache. There were days when he would not turn up without any information, till late in the day, while we waited for him. Then he would call to make frivolous excuses. In spite of all this, he was a technically efficient worker. He was the last person to leave the store every night. Making sure he completed his work before leaving, knowing he was going to be late the next morning. There was little scope to find fault with the quality of his work for he was meticulous. It was that he did not follow rules, had scant respect for time and discipline. He believed as long as he completed his work he was on the right track. Others were inconvenienced due to him. The security and some other staff had to wait till late at night along with him. Our store thus incurred higher overhead costs – through staff overtime, their conveyance, and higher electric consumption. All this impacted the store's performance as well as mine, making me very angry.

What irked me in addition to his attitude to work was also his attitude towards me. He would be very friendly and charming most of the time and yet not follow the rules of the place. I could not help thinking it was his chauvinistic streak that caused his disdainful attitude to working under a lady boss. I was also concerned about the bad example he set on new and existing staff. The four assistant managers, including Sudha, as well as other senior staff affected by his work, were also peeved at his attitude. But in spite of the stress I encountered in dealing with Sanjay I decided to not write him off yet. A few times when he came late, I firmly asked him to leave for the day, and marked him absent. I also sent him a couple of times to the regional HR head, on disciplinary issues. But his attitude still persisted. So, I began to ignore his indiscipline, as long as both stock and funds was well under control.

After much thought, in my bid to improve him, I planned on talking to Sanjay on a personal level. I realised I had to understand his psyche, before I could initiate any change in him. His was a severe attitude problem, which is very difficult to reform, if at all possible. It is simpler to sack an employee with poor attitude, or learn to live with it, as compared to coaching him to improve. I knew it was a steep road I had chosen. My seniors were aware of the problem, due to the appraisal system. I did not hesitate to rate Sanjay very low on discipline and to even put on record his misdemeanours. I was not about to pretend all was well just to prove my capability as a manager. With suggestions from seniors, I was tempted to insist on Sanjay's termination, but did not succumb.

I started having coffee more often at the staff room, with an eye out for Sanjay to get him into a conversation. Initially, he would not talk much, other than about work. But soon he opened up. Our conversations gradually became informal. We discussed his wedding less than a year back, five years since the registry marriage. It was expectantly a lavish affair organised by Nirupama's affluent father. In order to match the social status of his bride's family, for the reception organised by his parents, Sanjay had taken a personal loan from a bank. I had attended the reception along with other staff from the store. It was indeed a grand affair. Nirupama moved to Sanjay's house after the wedding.

Adjusting to her in-laws old-fashioned ways, in a humble house with limited resources, was a struggle from the start. They were conservative as compared to her parents, did not approve of her westernised clothes, drinking, smoking and late nights, even along with her husband. Their financial differences as compared to her parents perhaps impacted their outlook in life. It was not long before Nirupama began to put her foot down to the dictates of her marital home. It became difficult for Sanjay to handle the ever-increasing differences and ensuing arguments between his parents and wife. After much internal-debate, Sanjay decided to move out to another apartment with Nirupama. However, he would not abide by Nirupama's design to move in along with her to her parent's house.

Both their parents were devastated. Sanjay's on learning about their only child choosing his wife over them. Nirupama's on their dreams for her being crashed by their foolish daughter marrying a headstrong fellow, below her class.

"Please don't leave us at this age, son," Sanjay's father implored, clutching his hand, his face a mask of pain, as he and Nirupama were packing their belongings.

His mother sobbed inconsolably, adding, "We will make all adjustments to make your wife comfortable here. Please stay with us, don't go."

"Don't worry, *Appa, Amma*," Sanjay replied, as he hugged his parents one at a time. "I will support you forever. Have no doubts on that. Niru and I are going to be living nearby and I will visit you regularly, you will see."

Moving to another apartment with Nirupama was a huge financial strain on Sanjay. Now he had two rents to pay and two households to run. This burden, his limited earnings could have well done without. The loan he had taken for their wedding was, as it is looming large over his head. It was not merely the financial strain that was in excess of his ability, it was also the physiological load of running two households along with a demanding job. The emotional demands of the most important people in his life as if seated on either ends of a seesaw, with him as the fulcrum, took its toll on his psyche. Unable to cope with the stresses of his existence, Sanjay resorted to coming late to work, and taking uninformed leave. It brought on his mood swings, disoriented bearing and above all the defensive stance to anyone who expected anything more out of him than he was able to cope with.

But to my surprise, with time, he showed some signs of an internal change. One morning he walked in late for yet another morning meeting. We were planning a major store-event before Diwali. On seeing him, I lost my temper that had been brewing since noticing he was not present at the meeting.

"Aren't you ashamed at being pulled up every second day Sanjay?" I said vehemently, "You really need to look at disciplining your life, you know."

Sanjay did not reply. He merely looked down. This, along with the stress of the discussion at hand, infuriated me further.

"What is it with you, I just don't understand," I snapped in the face of his silence. I added in a very firm but steady voice. "Sanjay, please leave the store right now. Go home to where your priorities lie. You will be marked absent today."

"Sorry, Ma'am, I'm really sorry," he blurted, to my amazement. I gave him a quizzical look, least expecting his apology, as he added, "I just cannot wake up in the morning. I try hard, I honestly do. Please believe me, Ma'am. I wake up as tired in the morning, as when I go to sleep."

I was taken aback by this sudden outburst of apology, so was everyone else. But I could not out-rule the possibility of this being his ploy to gain my sympathy and win the rest of the team over. However, I noticed that this time, unlike times earlier, he looked genuinely apologetic and repentant. Perhaps my personal attention and conversations with him had made a difference to him after all. I cooled down, but was not going to allow the team to think I had softened my stance on him

"I believe you, Sanjay," I said firmly, then added, "But you really have to change your lifestyle. You need to plan, organise and prioritise your time, making it more productive. I quite understand that both work and family are very important. The key to success is in balancing the two."

He did not reply, and we continued the meeting. I empathised with Sanjay, but could not allow his indiscipline at work to impact the rest.

His varied responsibilities aside, Sanjay also wanted to have a good time, like most twenty-five year olds, especially since he was recently married. He wanted to give his wife a good life and the comforts she was used to. Nirupama often came to the store at closing time, all dressed up to go out with her husband. She was tall, slender and very attractive, with big kohl rimmed eyes and a generous mouth set on a honey complexioned face. She had the most attractive smile and her silky straight hair fell to the back of her waist. With his confidence enhanced since he started working, Sanjay now carried himself better, dressed well, his communication in English having improved, too.

The couple loved eating at good restaurants, were regular visitors to cine-multiplexes and discotheques. Most nights after his work, Sanjay and Nirupama had dinner in restaurants and then went to a nightclub or to a night show movie. They returned home late and slept when it was near morning. Little wonder Sanjay could not wake up timely in the morning for work. Moreover, erratic eating and sleeping patterns tell on one's physical and mental agility. Often, late in the evening, sometimes beyond 9pm, Nirupama waited outside the store while Sanjay finished work. When I learnt of this, I asked her to wait inside. In time, Nirupama became friends with everyone at the store, including me. She joined us for coffee, snacks and conversations, while we

     Shuvashree Chowdhury

finished work. It was watching the counter sales women at work, perhaps also with their initiation, that she decided to take up a job herself. They could well do with an extra source of income, to fund their lavish lifestyle. Nirupama took up appointment at a stand-alone retail outlet close to ours. Though the salary was meagre, it was something to start with.

Sanjay always noticed the rich, beautiful and well-dressed customers who came to the store. He became increasingly enamoured by them, desiring to lead his life similarly. The strains of his aspirational lifestyle after running two households, his meagre salary could ill afford. But working for a reputed company now, enabled him to get a number of premium bank credit cards. I later regretted validating his application-forms and salary-slips. Banks overlook the fact that competing banks are simultaneously making credit available to a person based on the same salary. A person could thus own four to five credit cards, with a combined credit limit perhaps three to four times his earnings. In fact, the bank representatives walked into our store, wooing young employees, like a spider to a fly. They were very persuasive, offering credit cards with minimal paperwork, also a host of benefits and freebies. Sanjay was soon the proud owner of four credit cards. The thrill of spending, much over ones means, even having a nil bank balance, which salary-account holders are allowed, can be exhilarating. It gives one a pseudo sense of power and prestige, instigating one to live much beyond ones means. Credit cards can take to the brink of ecstasy, people like Sanjay, then plunge them into a precipice of insurmountable despair when unable to repay. They suck uninitiated young people into a mental and emotional whirlpool that shakes their very soul.

It was not long before all of Sanjay's cards were used over their credit limits. He found it difficult to pay the required minimum amounts on each card. The respective banks debt-collection centres started telephoning him for minimum payments. If bank sales-representatives are so target driven and aggressive, little is left to the imagination of their debt-collectors. That which started as a one-off phone call, turned to incessant calling. Sanjay found creative ways to procrastinate payment.

"I am in hospital with a severe bout of food-poising," he would say to one debt-collector. Then to another he would say, "I'm at my grand-mother's funeral."

By now the banks had blocked the usage of his cards. This was followed by men landing up at his house as well as our store for his credit card payments. He would stay inside the office, or at home in the bedroom – asking Nirupama to find a way to disperse them. She too had little money, spending just as recklessly as him, so there was nothing she could do to help. By not moving in with her parents, due to Sanjay's refusal, she had alienated them and now could not go to them for help.

The only option Sanjay had left was to borrow money from friends and colleagues who luckily were fond of him due to his congeniality. They were fond of Nirupama, too. When unable to return their money, if the person did not lend him again, Sanjay asked a second person, and then a third. Sanjay's apologetic elucidations of his inability to return the money were accepted. His boyish looks, inherent simplicity and vulnerability may also have had something to do with it. But soon people stopped lending him more money.

After Sudha left the staff room, introducing me to facets of Sanjay's recklessness he had kept hidden from me so far, I called him into my office. I grilled him on the details. I was shocked to learn of his total outstanding debts to people. I felt responsible having aided his availing of the credit cards.

"Sanjay, I've made up my mind. I'm not giving you the money," I stated firmly, "There has to be an end to this borrowing."

Sanjay remained quiet, looking down, thoughtful – as if planning an alternate move. I looked at him squarely, trying to gauge his thoughts. He averted my gaze.

"Does Nirupama know how much in debt you really are?" I continued.

He shook his head sideways, slowly.

"You have to tell her, Sanjay," I said firmly. "Move back in with your parents. It makes no sense for you to run two households when you can ill afford it."

Sanjay looked up at me sheepishly, as he pleaded – "Ma'am, please give me the money, just this one time."

"No, Sanjay," I replied emphatically, "You have to vacate your

 Shuvashree Chowdhury

apartment and move back with your parents. I'm not giving you the money."

I saw disappointment etched on his face. He had been sure he could count on me to give him the money, bail him out of the biggest crisis of his life.

"Please, please don't do this. I really am desperate," Sanjay pleaded again, "I promise you … I will return the money after I get my next salary."

"How many people are you going to repay after you get your next salary, Sanjay?" I retorted. "How much is your salary to repay from? Then what about the credit card dues and the household expenditures for the month. Borrowing is a vicious cycle."

"I know, I totally agree with you," he replied morosely, then as if a brilliant idea struck him, he blurted excitedly: "But Nirupama is expecting a huge sales-incentive next month. So we can pay a lot of our dues."

"Sanjay, honestly, I don't believe you can or that you will," I said impatiently, "Moreover, it is not repaying me that I'm worried about. If I were convinced my giving you money would solve your problem, I would give it without your needing to repay me. My giving you money will only propel you to continue misusing it."

"I'm promising you, Ma'am, I will not go out this month, or buy any more clothes," Sanjay insisted.

"Sanjay, no way," I said, shaking my head firmly. "I'm not convinced. If you move back with your parents for now, you won't need the money for the rent. Once you're in control of your finances, you can decide what to do."

I got up and briskly walked out, leaving him in my office. I could not help wondering whether I should give him the money, let him worry about his problems for the long run. Sanjay went about his work with a sullen face the rest of the day.

In a week, unable to pay the rent, Sanjay was forced to vacate his apartment. Nirupama and he moved back with his parents. In the coming days, they went straight home after work. They ate the simple meals Sanjay's mother cooked – *sambar* and rice. Nirupama now realised the value of a hot cup of coffee when they returned home, a warm meal without the bother of cooking herself. Relationships started to improve in that household. The older couple, happy their son had returned, were cautious not to upset his wife. They realised their son's happiness lay in his wife's. Nirupama was grateful now for the effort her in-laws made to make her feel comfortable. Since working she had started to feel the strain of managing the house herself. She reciprocated warmly, also realising their worth in her husband's life. She cooked on her weekly off, whether or not Sanjay was off on the same day.

With his next salary, Sanjay started returning the money he had borrowed from people in small amounts. But his credit-card dues were still very high. The debt-collection calls from banks continued to stalk him. Sanjay was still a harassed man.

"Ma'am, I need a break," Sanjay said to me one morning, over coffee, "Just to get away from everything for a while."

"That's a good idea," I replied, feeling sorry for him, "Perhaps you and Nirupama could take a holiday, go to a nearby hill-station, maybe. Getting away helps to relax, think afresh. I'll take care of the leave, don't worry about that."

Sanjay nodded, visibly cheering up at the thought. I was happy he had taken the first steps to getting his life back on track. Moving back with his parents, reducing their outings, repaying some of his debts, was definitely a good start.

"Don't splurge, and take some money from me for the trip," I added smiling, "Consider it your wedding anniversary gift. Isn't it just coming up?"

Sanjay nodded, smiling gratefully, his eyes misting.

Nirupama was ecstatic when she heard of the trip. They had not gone on a honeymoon after the wedding, since Sanjay did not have any leave left. In a few days, Sanjay and Nirupama left for Ooty. They made reservations on a three-tier compartment of an overnight train to Coimbatore. Their plan was to spend a day there with a friend, who had agreed to lend them his car. Then drive up to Ooty. It was two mornings after they had left that I got a call on my mobile phone from Sanjay's mobile. We had just completed the morning meeting. As I said his name aloud, everyone looked at me expectantly for news of them. They were perhaps calling to say they had reached Ooty safely, I thought.

I smiled to myself as I said, "Hello!" imagining their exultant faces in the chilly hill air.

          Shuvashree Chowdhury

"Yes, Sanjay! What's up?"

But it was not Sanjay but a strange male voice at the other end that responded.

"Hello! Ma'am, I'm calling from S.M Nursing Home, Ooty," he said. A shiver went down my spine, as he continued, "I got your number on Sanjay's mobile – it was titled *Aka* (elder sister), so I'm calling you."

"Is Sanjay alright?" I stuttered, "What about the girl with him?"

"Both were admitted here an hour back. They were in a car accident."

"How bad was the accident? Who was driving?" I hurriedly asked. The wildest thoughts were racing through my head.

"Sanjay was driving. The lady was beside him. Isn't her name Nirupama?"

"How are they now? Are they safe?" I persisted, fear constricting my throat.

"I am sorry, Ma'am, they were both brought in dead," was the impassioned reply, "Their car hit a tree and rolled off a cliff ..."

He continued to speak, but I did not hear him after that.

Sanjay's voice rang out loud in my ears – "The day our debts go over our head, we will commit suicide."

16. Who I Am

Istepped in through the glass door, held open by a doorman, smiling, bowing courteously. He wore the maharaja style uniform with the headgear. The aroma of fresh pastry and coffee pervaded my senses, along with the clinking of knives, forks to plates, and the buzz of muted conversations. As I looked around, a good-looking young man, perhaps the manager, in a suit and tie approached me smiling warmly. He led me to one of the few vacant tables at the far left of the popular tearoom, Flurys. I sank into a leather seat at a four-seater table facing the doorway. To my right was a floor to ceiling glass window. It had a clear view of the late afternoon traffic on Park Street in conjunction with its sidewalks – where people walked past briskly. This was amongst my favourite places, from where I loved to watch Calcutta go by. I would fondly carry this image back to my life and work in Chennai, from where I was visiting my mother here briefly.

I was to return to Chennai the day after, to managing the lifestyle departmental store and had felt compelled to take one last stroll on the sidewalks of Park Street, before stepping in here. The string of doors, windows opening into popular shops and restaurants, the numerous peddlers of books and an array of merchandise flanking the street, visible now from my seat, held an appeal since I was a child. Some of the shops and restaurants had changed completely over the years, some, only the ownership.

The tearoom where I was seated was very different now after a mammoth overhaul, since its last change in ownership. But it was the nostalgia of coming here as a child, then through college, that brought me back here on every trip to Calcutta. A waiter in a brown uniform with Flurys appliquéd in pink above his left chest pocket brought the menu – its cover in the same pink. I opened it and cursorily skimmed it, noting the familiar items along with a number of new ones. Then I ordered my all-time-favourite chicken-patty, a rum-ball-pastry, along with Darjeeling tea.

After I returned the menu to the waiter, he retreated. I noticed a person – not sure man or woman, standing near the entrance along with two women. They awaited a table to be allotted to them. A number of people were turning in their direction, staring at them curiously. The man – I ascertained this after sizing him up, looked very feminine, in a striking green silk *kurta* with strings of multicoloured beads around his neck. The colours accentuated his fair glowing complexion and shoulder length brown hair, streaked in gold and green. He was of average height, a lean built, with stooped shoulders. His chiselled face – with large brown eyes and a generous mouth, could best be defined as pretty. The women with chiselled physiques wore the distinct air of ramp models, dressed in halter-neck tube tops, short-skirts, stilettos, their long permed hair streaked in shades of burgundy. As the man led by a waiter sauntered in my direction, I recognised his familiar swagger, and the exaggeratedly feminine facial and hand gestures in talking to the waiter.

This was Ritik. I had once worked with him closely while managing the branded jewellery store in Calcutta, till I married and moved to Chennai. I noticed he looked more effeminate now, his mannerisms and dressing more overstated, perhaps the reason for my not recognising him earlier. His shoes were of a blue-newsprint material that curled inward at the toes like those wizards wear. Ritik had teamed his green close-fitting *kurta* with a beige *churidar*. A long dangler-earring hung from his left earlobe, three studs lined the other. As he came closer to my table, he abruptly stopped, then looked at me in surprise, with recognition.

"Ritik, it's so good to see you," I exclaimed cheerily, standing up.

"Good to see you, too," he gushed, flickering his eyes exaggeratedly, almost hopping over to my table in excitement. Then giving me a dramatic bear hug, he added, "You look as gorgeous as always. It's been ages since we last met, right?"

I extricated myself from his hug, then viewing him appreciatively, warmly said, "And you look much better Ritik, more glamorous, and mature. I like your shoes."

His gestures and mannerisms once a source of embarrassment

to me, did not bother me now that I understood him well. I was genuinely happy to see him.

"Really," he gushed. "And do you like my outfit?"

"Yeah, it's nice and striking," I smiled, recalling how he was touchy about his appearance, over which he took great care, also how flattered when appreciated.

"Nice to meet you," the two women said, simultaneously extending their hands that I shook warmly, after Ritik introduced me as a close friend.

"I'll join you soon …" he said to the women. "I'd like to catch up with her."

The women moved to an adjacent table the waiter was standing by, waiting for them to settle down at. Ritik sat down enthusiastically across me at my table.

A waiter brought my order on a large tray. After he set it all on the table, Ritik asked for a cup of black coffee and a plate of chicken-sandwiches for himself.

"I've barely slept in days," he said, after the waiter left. "I had a big-budget fashion show last evening, followed by a party that went on till early this morning. I badly need the coffee now, to keep awake."

"Well, not unusual for you, is it?" I smiled, "The late nights and odd hours?"

He nodded, smiling, "And who knows that better than you."

I had first met Ritik, when he had come over to the jewellery store I managed in Calcutta, introducing himself and his services to me. He was a model and event-coordinator, who owned an agency. At twenty-five years at the time, he was sincere, talented, and good at his work, so already recognised in relevant circles. It was in the course of working with him that we became friends.

Looking at Ritik now, as I took a sip of my cup of Darjeeling tea – of the pot he declined to share, preferring to wait for his coffee, I recalled my first meeting with him. It had been a regular afternoon at the jewellery store I managed on Camac Street, just off Park Street. There were only a few customers then. I was seated on the sofa on the shop-floor overlooking the entrance, talking to the staff, planning an upcoming celebrity product launch and press meet. Each time the door opened, the armed doorman holding it

   Shuvashree Chowdhury

to allow customers in or out, I looked in the direction. This time, I noticed a young man in an oversized shirt hung outside his jeans, striding in my direction purposefully. He sashayed femininely, as he pushed his longish hair behind his ears with his head tilted upwards. I looked at him curiously mid-sentence, to ascertain his being male or female. Though physically he seemed to look male, his mannerisms were exaggeratedly feminine. However, he was a strikingly good-looking person whatever his sexual identity.

"I would like to speak to the manager please," he announced firmly, to a male staff at the diamond necklace counter right in front of me.

The voice was male but high-pitched and somewhat feminine. It sounded more like a man imitating a woman's voice or something like an adolescent boy's.

"May I know what this is about?" the staff asked, appraising him curiously.

"It's personal," he replied very curtly.

"She is our manager," the staff replied, gesturing to me with his hand.

The man walked over to me, then said: "Ma'am, I would like to talk to you."

"Yes, how may I help you?" I replied gingerly, still in bewilderment of him. The staff standing around me was in splits of laughter. Even I found it a struggle not to laugh, to hold a straight face, as amused as I was of him, and his comical demeanour.

"Ma'am, I would like to talk to you only," he asserted with dramatically feminine facial and hand gestures, his eyes indicating the laughing staff. "I mean, could we please move into your office or someplace more private?"

"We can speak here," I replied, in dread of a private discussion with him.

In fact, I had been noticing that the laughter and attention he generated propelled him to heightened absurdities. There was no way I was going to allow him to make a mockery of me as he was of himself. I had an image to upkeep here at work, in order for the staff to continue respecting me.

"Ma'am, I'm Ritik Dutt. I'm an event coordinator," he said,

abruptly standing in an attention position, as if in elocution or a mono-act on stage.

He handed me his business card and before I realised he slipped on to the sofa beside me, and made himself comfortable, as though I had invited him to. The lady assistant manager seated on my other side promptly stood, looking at him impatiently, suspiciously. The other staff, who I had been talking to before his interruption, remained standing, watching him curiously and giggling.

Ritik drew open the string of his multicoloured, sequined ladies handbag and retrieved a photo-album. He flipped it open and then thrust it over to me.

"These are the pictures of the events I've hosted," he said.

Compelled to look at his album, I took it from him. Slowly, deliberately, I turned the pages, impressed at what I saw. The pictures illustrated professionalism – detailing in the layout of stage, ramp, decorations, and models. His work was meticulous, far from amateurish as I had expected on seeing him.

After turning all the pages of his album, I concluded that Ritik's work was indeed proficient. But I did not foresee myself working with someone as peculiar as him, even if I were to consider giving his work a chance.

"It's very good," I said, handing back his album to him. "But you see we already have an event manager. He's been commissioned by our head office."

"Maybe you could just try me out once, please Ma'am," Ritik pleaded, and then with an air of confidence, in an even tone, he added, "Just to see the difference in my work and pricing, as compared to his. I assure you, you will not regret it."

"It's not in my hands," I replied, and then stood up to suggest the end of this conversation. "You see, our company spends a lot on marketing, on promotions, product launches, and events, etcetera. My seniors will not agree to take a chance on a new manager at this point, since we are satisfied with the current one."

"I quite understand, Ma'am," Ritik said, following me in standing up. "But please give me one chance. Maybe even for a small customer meet or something."

"I'll keep you in mind," I said, walking to the door. "I have your business card."

                          Shuvashree Chowdhury

The doorman holding the door open gaped at him, as we approached. He retained his composure, unlike others in splits of laughter, audible behind us.

After this meeting, it took several months for me to be convinced on using Ritik's services. It was for a fashion show he choreographed and coordinated at the Saturday Club that I agreed on our participating as the jewellery sponsor. In the time leading up to this, he landed up at my store every now and then. At times, he brought *sandesh* or *rossogolla* for the staff, at others, he insisted on taking them out for lunch. Thus befriending everyone and making himself at home with us, while acquainting with the organisation. I accepted his proposal to participate at the fashion show after necessary clearance from the regional office. Ritik, I was to learn, was a strict taskmaster with a sharp eye for detail, evident from every aspect of his work. When it came to the models – otherwise difficult to handle, he was firm and demanded discipline. He was a totally different person backstage at the show, and during rehearsals leading up to it, compared to his usual penchant for frivolity. I was impressed by his ingenuity, thereby allowing him a free hand.

The fashion event turned out to be a success and resulted in a number of new customers to our store – which was near to the club. After this, on Ritik's initiation, we participated in events at Calcutta and Tollygunge clubs and both helped us in terms of the visibility of our brand, and increase in footfall and sales in all the three stores in the city. By now, Ritik had begun to coordinate most events for us, and we worked well together. During this time, I noticed things about him that made me very curious. Initially certain he was a homosexual male I became unsure, due to his attitude towards me, and women in general. That he flirted with me outrageously, made me decide that he must certainly be bisexual. There were so many queries in my mind. It is one thing, knowing about the gender crises existent in the world, but actually interacting with someone closely is quite another. I had never met anyone like him before, and he still shocked me.

I often wondered about Ritik's birth gender – was he born male or was he a transgender? Was he now male or female or did he belong to the third sex? The apparently feminine side to his male personality mystified me to no end. I noticed he always observed what I wore, right down to my shoes and bag, always interested in feminine stuff. This, perhaps, I could attribute to his interest in fashion. But what of his asking to borrow my lip-gloss? Then heading to the ladies restroom along with me to apply the same? His wearing feminine clothes was strange, but more so, was his wearing a bra he didn't physically require.

"Were you always like this, Ritik?" I blurted one day, unable to hold my curiosity, when waiting backstage before the first sequence of a fashion show.

"Like what?" Ritik giggled, in his usual effeminate singsong way.

"Well, you know ... hmmm ... feminine ..." I replied haltingly, anxious whether I was right in asking and would he be offended? "With this outrageous dress-sense and all ... like different ... You know what I mean?"

Ritik looked at me intensely, like he was about to bare his soul. I returned his gaze in anticipation of an admission. It was in knowing he was very fond of me that I had taken the liberty to raise this sensitive issue. However, very abruptly, the opportune moment for a probable admission was interrupted by a model. Ritik just smiled at me shyly, turning instead to attend to her. I was very disappointed and never had the opportunity to bring this topic up again. It was only later I learnt from a staff at my store, whose brother studied with Ritik, that at school he had been like any boy his age. He had worn normal male clothes, played basketball, even football, with other boys of his class. It was sometime after his adolescence then, I concluded, that he would have discovered his being different, in order to proclaim to the world that he was different.

"You know Ritik likes you a lot. I mean he really likes you," is how one of the lady-staff at the store had started the conversation one day over evening tea.

"But, isn't he gay?" I had asked surprised, "And what makes you think that?"

"You know, the way he is around you," another added, "It is obvious he is in love."

"Now don't put your imagination into overdrive, all of you," I had laughed.

This conversation had triggered my curiosity on Ritik further,

                    Shuvashree Chowdhury

now that my association with him was close to two years. He often went across to our regional-office, sometimes to collect his payments or to convince the business development and commercial teams on budgets for an event. When he walked across the office area from the reception, the whole office watched him in amusement. At times his shirt was held together by strings, tie-up laces, was transparent, but always his attire was bright and ornate. The bra or camisole he wore was often clearly visible. The regional office team would call me to complain of his absurdities in behaviour and attire, asking me how I tolerated him. I would then emphasise he was very good at his work and his personal matters were no concern of mine. Though I have to admit, at public places with people staring at him, at us, he embarrassed me often with his mannerisms and flamboyant clothes.

But, with time, I was getting used to it, ignoring people who glared at him like a specimen out of a circus. In fact, I had even begun to enjoy his hilarious company and the conversations we had on various topics. Ritik was, after all, intelligent, savvy, and articulate. I learnt that his parents had divorced when he was a child and his mother ran a high-end ladies beauty parlour since then. It was in spending a lot of time there after school, as he waited for her to finish work, that Ritik had been exposed to woman's beauty and fashion trends from an early age. This exposure and awareness developed his interest in the fashion industry and set the tone for his current skills and business. But could it also have triggered his feminine bent of mind, I often wondered, more so due to lack of any close male influence in his life? He lived with his mother and grandmother, and though he went to an only boy's school, he had spent a lot of time amidst women since childhood. Could his influences have advanced Ritik's feminine psyche then?

The waiter came and placed Ritik's coffee on the table, bringing me back to the present at Flurys. I realised Ritik had been talking, but I had been lost in thought. Looking at him now, I realised I had not been wrong in once assuming his exaggerated feminine gestures were to stand out in a crowd, to identify to the world as being female. I knew now he was androgynous. It was after I encountered someone quite like him in Chennai that I learnt more about them. With my awareness came understanding and compassion for Ritik's condition – wherein he had a feminine mind trapped in a male body. An androgyne is a person psychologically, intrinsically and socially intermediate between male and female, displaying physical traits and a merging of the roles as belonging to male or female. The primary difference between people who are androgynous and other individuals is that they cannot live life fully as either men or woman because they are intrinsically both genders.

Awareness of such people gave me a newfound respect for Ritik's attempts to display his individuality, at the cost of the world ridiculing him. I now understood he dressed and acted overstatedly to display his feminine streak. It had been a revelation to me that this was a biological condition, resulting from hormonal miscues during fetal washing of the brain during gender identity development. A person with this condition merges both gender identities, displaying an assortment of both masculine and feminine qualities. People who are androgynous rarely consider themselves to be of the transgender community, though they may undergo a sex change to fit into the criteria of either gender. Androgynies do not fit cleanly into the typical gender roles of society. The condition can be either physical or psychological, and in Ritik's case, probably the latter.

"You know, Ritik," I said, looking him in the eye, after swallowing the last bite of my rum-ball-pastry and another sip of my Darjeeling tea, the chicken-patty long over. "I often wondered how you take people ridiculing you so sportingly. In fact, you seem to thrive on it, by dressing and acting shockingly. But now I do understand your need to express your unique personality."

After a short silence, while he looked away into the distance, Ritik softly replied, "I am comfortable with being who I am. It was a long search to find my true self. Though I'm male, I love many things women do, in so many ways I'm female. I realised I'm different and that doesn't make me bad or wrong, there is nothing to be ashamed of. With time people will learn to accept me like I've accepted the way I am. In fact, in my profession I can utilise the skills and talents God has given me, to groom, train and enhance the careers of young men and women who want to be in the fashion-industry. Why then should I hide who I am? I would rather flaunt it, and also show the world what I am capable of, though I may be unusual. People like me should be valued for our talents and work."

I nodded, placing a hand over his comfortingly on the table, as I said, "You are brave, Ritik, and truly special. I admire your strength in standing up to the world."

"Luckily, choosing to be self-employed, I do not have to abide by any expected, established, dress and behaviour code at work," Ritik said, laughing.

By now, Ritik having finished his coffee and sandwiches, I waived to a passing waiter, asked him to get our bill.

"No way, no, you are not paying," Ritik said assertively, after the waiter left. "This one's on me; I can treat one of my favourite ladies now, can't I?"

"Chivalry is not dead yet, Ritik?" I smiled indulgently.

He nodded. He had always been the man with me, insisting on paying wherever we went, for lunch or at the events. I found it endearing, that in spite of his feminine streak, he liked me to think of him as the man. No wonder the staff at my store, who I still visit on every trip to Calcutta, teased me about him. As we waited for the bill, I filled Ritik in on my current life and job in Chennai.

"How I wish you were there, Ritik, to help me with events," I said. "The large format lifestyle store I'm managing now includes a bookstore on one floor, a children's outlet on another, and numerous other brands, along with a lovely café. There's some event round the year, like book launches, children's events."

"Really, that's interesting," he replied. "Maybe, if it's cost effective, I'll come to Chennai very soon, work with you again."

After Ritik paid, we got up, and he waved to the models at the next table. They would be enrolled at his modelling agency, I thought. Having finished their coffee, they got up. We walked to the door together. The doorman bowed politely, holding the door open, as we stepped into the dusk, to the neon lit Park Street.

"Keep in touch," Ritik said, giving me a warm hug, as I nodded, hugging him back. "I hope you still have my number and email address. They're still the same."

17. A New Beginning

We made it to the party just before the stroke of twelve, in time to usher in the New Year. The hour's drive had taken us over two hours, in the dense Chennai traffic on New Year's Eve. The party, husband and I were invited to was at a beach-house. It was off the East Coast Road – a highway along the Bay of Bengal on the way to Pondicherry. Our car wound its way through the iron-gate of the house, up the pebbled driveway bordered by hedges entwined in tiny coloured lights. I looked at my watch; it was barely five minutes to the New Year. We got off the car at the porch of the house also decked with coloured light bulbs. The sound of loud music emanating from a distance reaching us, we followed its trail to the party. We were led through a gravel pathway, flanked by a lawn enclosed by a garden with a variety of flowers.

As we approached the source of the music, we spotted people leisurely standing around the large pea-shaped swimming pool, their drinks in hand. Closer up, we noticed some of them around a barbeque, others by the concrete bar-counter, topped with a range of liquor bottles. A few couples danced on a makeshift dance floor, on the green patch by the pool. We were nearing the pool, when suddenly we heard the crackling sound along with the smell of fumes, coming from right behind us. We turned around briskly, to see fireworks go off in the lawns we had crossed. An amazing body of tiny specks of light grew bigger, brighter, shooting up higher than the tall trees bordering the property, illuminating the dark sky with splendid multi-coloured light. This was followed by a series of fireworks that lit the horizon, marking our crossing over to the New Year.

We turned back in the direction of the poolside, the music by now soft and romantic, as couples held each other and swayed on the dance floor, or hugged and kissed. Shreds of glitter-paper and balloons showered over us, where we stood very close to the pool now. Husband and I hugged, too.

     Shuvashree Chowdhury

"Happy New Year" I said, "Glad we made it on time."

"Happy New Year," he replied, nodding sheepishly, hugging me.

Our delay in coming here, in addition to the traffic, had been due to his retuning late from work, though he had dressed quickly. I had left the department store I still managed then, well in time. The next few minutes into the New Year were a flurry of greetings, hugging friends and wishing everyone we encountered a happy New Year. As light and sound fireworks continued unabated for a while, we let ourselves absorb the happiness and bonhomie of the moment.

Our hosts, Mr and Mrs Krishnan, a striking actor couple approached us, before we could find them. The man named Ajay, tall, brawny, piercing eyes, hooked nose and a playful smile, was dressed in a printed white silk shirt with beige trousers. His wife, Jaya, wore a red satin dress below her knee, with red stilettos that accentuated her height. She was slim, pretty, with large black eyes, high cheekbones, a sharp nose and a sensuous mouth. With her long straight hair cascading way below the back of her waist, she exuded grace and warmth, as she walked towards us, arms outstretched, and then hugged me.

"So glad you could come," she said. Then she and her husband cheerfully added: "Wishing you both a very happy New Year."

"A very happy New Year to you too," husband and I replied in unison.

"Now come with me," Jaya said to me abruptly, taking my hand, "I'll introduce you to some people, they are also from Calcutta." Then turning to my husband, she added smiling, "I'm stealing your wife. Ajay will take care of you and introduce you to the others."

"I'll be right back," I said to husband, taking a step after Jaya.

A few steps ahead, a lady walked up to us as if out of the blue.

"Here you are!" Jaya exclaimed. "We were coming over to find you."

I looked at the beaming, pleasant face, curiously. The small eyes accentuated with eyeliner, mascara, and the wide cheekbones with blusher, lips in pink gloss, looked familiar.

I appraised her elegant long black georgette dress and black high-heeled sandals appreciatively, wrenching my memory in identifying her.

"*Didi*, it's you, I can't believe bumping into you like this," the lady announced, her face excited as a child's. "What a pleasant surprise."

It was her sincere wide smile, the familiar warm manner in which she looked at me, called me "*Didi*" that struck a chord from the past.

"Oh my God, it's you, Madhumita!" I said cheerily, recognising the young woman who had worked with me in Calcutta. "Look at you!"

"You know each other?" Jaya interjected, curiously looking from one to the other of us. "What a small world this really is."

Turning to me, she remarked: "I had wanted to introduce you to Madhumita, but since you already know each other, I'll leave you two to catch up while I attend to the other guests." Then, before leaving, she added: "I'll ask a waiter to fix you both drinks and bring you some nibbles."

"Madhumita, you look marvellous, so elegant, and grown up since we last met," I said keenly, taking a step forward, enclosing her in a warm hug. "It's so good to see you. What brings you to Chennai?"

"I'm here only for this weekend," she replied. Then softly, shyly looking me in the eye, gauging my reaction, she added: "I recently got married. My husband and I are on our way to Munnar for our honeymoon."

"That's wonderful," I said, my eyes suddenly misting from the recall of incidents from my past association with her. Then looking into her eyes, holding both her hands in mine, noticing the slight dash of vermilion in the parting of her well-styled shoulder length hair, I added: "I am so happy for you, Madhumita."

"It is a lot because of your support and encouragement, *Didi*," she replied, looking into my eyes earnestly, "that I've come this far, in life."

"I am so proud of you," I replied. "I want to hear all the details though."

"Sure, but I want my husband to meet you first. I've told him

     Shuvashree Chowdhury

so much about you. He'll be as excited as I am." Then, looking around, she added: "I wonder where he is though. But wait, I'll go and find him."

A uniformed waiter came over then, with a tray balancing a number of glasses of red and white wine, another behind him held a salver of a variety of kebabs. Madhumita rushed past them, unseeingly, excited at the prospect of her husband and I meeting. I took a glass of wine in one hand, and then with the other, a kebab – dislodging the warm, succulent piece from a toothpick into my mouth. The waiters moving on ahead; after swallowing the last bit of kebab in my mouth, I took a sip of the claret liquid, as I looked around me.

I noticed the beautifully dressed men and women, most now dancing to the peppy music. Along with the wine, I drank in the magical beauty of the place glittering with lights, the bonhomie all around, and yet I felt restless. With the thoughts of my past association with Madhumita coming to mind, I decided to take a brisk walk till she returned. My husband, I noticed, was with a group standing in front of the bar, as I strolled towards the iron back-gate, glass in hand. Though locked, I could see through its grills, the full moon and the shimmering sea foaming up to the sandy shore. It was quiet, except for the roar of the sea, the sound of the waves lashing noisily on the shore. Looking out towards the horizon, much above nature's din, I distinctly heard the harried voice on the telephone, as I did that morning three years back. The voices in our head usually seem the loudest, I thought, as compared to any external sound.

* * *

The voice, anxious at the other end of the line, had been Anil's. He was an accounts officer of the jewellery store I managed in Calcutta, till I married and moved to Chennai.

"Ma'am, Gautam had a heart attack," he had blurted.

I had taken his call stepping outside the conference room of our state of the art jewellery factory at Hosur, while attending a new product indent meet. My mobile phone had been in the silent mode, but Anil had texted me, urging me to take his call as it was urgent. Anil's words, as I walked the corridor listening to him intently, had shocked me. After all, the man, Gautam, who had suffered the heart attack, was twenty-seven years, seemingly healthy and fit days ago.

"Oh my God! How … and when, but isn't he too young?" I rejoined, then enquired, "How is he now and where, I mean, in which hospital?"

After a long pause, Anil softly replied: "He is no more."

I was baffled, unsure what Anil really meant. So I quizzed him, aware as I was of his limitations in the usage of the English language.

"Anil, no more – what are you talking about?" I asked impatiently, sounding as horrified as I felt at his implication, desperately hoping he meant otherwise. "Do you mean he is dead? Are you sure?"

"Yes ma'am, he is no more," he repeated in a sullen voice, at my inability to comprehend his words, also his panic at the news incapacitating his explaining better. "That is exactly what I meant. I'm here at their house now with his body, along with the family."

I was unable to return to the meeting, even after Anil hung up. I paced the long veranda on the fifth floor of the building. The sunny sky, birds chirping, a few sitting on the railing, made it impossible to conjure the image of Gautam being dead. I recalled our last meeting.

"Why don't you wait inside?" I had said, just days back, smiling at the tall, dark, burly man, with an amazingly boyish face.

It was 9pm. He had been leaning on his bike that he had parked on the pavement in front of our jewellery store. Wearing a bottle-green long *kurta* over blue jeans, open-toed sandals, he clutched two bike-helmets. He was waiting to take his wife, Madhumita, home.

"It's okay, Ma'am, I'll wait over here," he replied, smiling shyly with downcast eyes. "She will be out soon."

I nodded in assent. As I walked away to my car parked in the adjacent lane, I mentally noted his shyness, the reticence, as compared to the gregariousness of his wife.

Madhumita was a retail sales officer in my store. She was the youngest at twenty-three years, having joined a year ago. With her

    Shuvashree Chowdhury

sincerity, enthusiasm, and proficiency, she had shortly become my favourite staff. Unlike most who called me 'Ma'am', she called me *'Didi'* – elder sister. I had become fond of her husband, Gautam, too. On some days, with my insistence, he would wait inside the store, coming through the back gate, after the regular front entrance was closed to customers. He waited on the sofa in the centre of the sales floor then, while stocktaking and other closing procedures were carried out. The staff, especially the women, often bullied him good-humouredly, making him blush, while Madhumita briskly finished her work. This was the image of Gautam that I carried, as I continued to pace the balcony at the Hosur factory, after receiving the news of his death.

On the flight back to Calcutta the next morning, it was Madhumita's image that I travelled with, though my heart was already with her. It was unfair, I thought, that life should strike someone as vivacious as her so brutally, this early in life. She had been married for barely a few years now. After landing in Calcutta, on the drive home from the airport, with trepidation, I called Madhumita. I had not called from Hosur the day before on receiving the news, knowing she and the family would be busy with the funeral and meeting people. To my amazement, when Madhumita came on the line, she sounded very calm, and composed. It was a contrast to her usual exuberance, but she did not sound, in my opinion, like a young woman who had just lost her husband.

"How are you doing, Madhumita?" I asked tenderly. After a pause, wherein she remained silent, at a loss for words that would make any difference now, I simply said: "I am so sorry. I don't know what to say."

"I'm alright," she replied softly in a distant tone, after a brief silence. Then in a worried tone, she continued: "Gautam's parents are devastated. His mother had a nervous breakdown this morning and had to be hospitalised. I just returned with her from the hospital."

"That is understandable, Madhumita; she will be fine. You don't stress about his parents now. It's your loss, too. Please take care of yourself," I said emphatically, and then softly added: "I'm coming over to see you in a few hours. Though I'd like to hear the details, how all this happened, it can wait till later, when you're up to talking."

"No *Didi*, there is no need for you to take the trouble to come. I will be coming to work as it is from tomorrow," she said coolly, as though talking about coming to work after a bout of the flu.

"But why do you want to come so soon? Take some rest at home," I replied. "Don't worry about work now. In fact, why don't you go over to your mother's place for a while?"

"I've got to come to work right away," she insisted. "That's the only thing to look forward to in my life now. And I can't leave his parents; they need me. But I don't feel like staying home with them all day."

"Of course, if that's what you really want, please come," I relented, understanding her need to stay away from the lingering presence of Gautam at home. "I'll see you tomorrow, and we can talk then."

I could not help but worry about Madhumita's surface calm, her composure, which, in my opinion, was unusual. She had suffered the loss of her father as a child, but this was different. I admired her courage, her concern for Gautam's parents, for her mother, in continuing to be their support, squashing her own grief. But I was certain this was detrimental to her emotional well-being. I decided to have a chat with her, get her to deal with her own feelings to begin the healing process after the trauma she had suffered. The next morning, true to her word, Madhumita turned up for work at the usual time of 10am. She wore her uniform *saree* neatly pinned, her hair in a French-roll, and makeup in place as per grooming guidelines. I was taken aback by her professionalism in the face of her loss only two days back, having expected slackness in her punctuality and grooming.

I walked up to Madhumita, gave her a warm hug and then led her by hand to my office. Instructing an attendant to bring us coffee, I asked her if she would like to sit there, rather than join us for the morning meeting. She preferred to attend the meeting. A cup of coffee later, over generic work related conversation to put her at ease, we walked to the adjacent meeting room. On noticing us, silence descended upon the staff. Everyone looked at Madhumita in amazement. No one had expected her to be at work two days

                    Shuvashree Chowdhury

after her husband's death. I knew how proud Madhumita was; she would not like people to pity her or treat her differently. So without giving anyone a chance to ask her any questions, wishing everyone a good morning, I started the meeting.

"Maybe you'd like to remain in the back office today," I enquired of Madhumita, after the meeting, "rather than attend to customers?

"No, *Didi*," she replied firmly, much to my surprise. "I would rather be out on the floor. I'll only get bored sitting inside."

Though I did not think it was a good idea that she got back to normal work so soon, I didn't want to refute her. I was still discerning what really was going on with her. As it is, I still didn't know the details of Gautam's sudden death. So I proceeded to my office, deciding on giving her the space she needed to open up and talk in time. Moreover, there were urgent tasks that required my attention. I had barely taken my seat behind my desk, when one of the floor managers – a lady named Sumita, knocking on the open office door, stepped inside.

"You know, Ma'am," she started abruptly, softly. "Madhumita's husband, Gautam, didn't die of a usual heart attack. He was too young for that!"

I looked up at her in amazement, inquiring, "What do you mean?"

"His post mortem report said it was from a drug overdose," she replied.

"But who told you that?" I asked sharply. "This is so absurd. Gautam didn't do drugs. I mean, we all knew him."

"Madhumita told me," she replied. "The report came in last morning."

That explained his mother's sudden breakdown yesterday, I thought, also Madhumita's stony response when I called, followed by her insistence to come to work immediately.

"Please do me a favour," I said to Sumita. "Go and bring Madhumita in here. I want to talk to her. She is handling too much by herself."

Shortly, Madhumita came into my office, looking at me inquiringly. I was on a long distance telephone call, but I signalled to her to sit.

"What really happened with Gautam?" I asked her, coming straight to the point after hanging up. "I thought I would wait till you were ready, but I think talking will help, put things in perspective maybe."

Looking at me dejectedly, Madhumita started: "Gautam and I went to the same school, the same class even, and were best friends. My father had passed away while we were in school. After college, my mother, by then a heart patient, was very worried about my future. So Gautam and I decided to get married, even though he had not got a job yet. I started working immediately, not to depend on our parents, while Gautam continued his studies to build a good career."

"You've been very responsible, Madhumita," I said, placing a hand over hers, on the desk. "It was the best thing to do in the circumstance."

"The night of his death, after dinner …" she continued sombrely, "Gautam and I were sitting on our bed watching television. He suddenly started having strong convulsions and then collapsed. I awoke his parents in the adjacent room, and they called the doctor immediately. The doctor arrived shortly, but declared him dead. He said it was due to a massive heart attack. Though shocked, we believed the diagnosis, since Gautam had a high blood-cholesterol level, bordering hypertension, and more so, he loved rich fatty food. But, the next day, when I was skimming through his wardrobe drawer, the one he always kept locked, I came across bottles of medicines, prescriptions, that none of us at home had an awareness of."

"Madhumita, but you've been married a while now," I interrupted. "You never opened his cupboard or drawers, to clean them or something?"

"No, never," she replied vehemently. "I respected his space, as he did mine. After his death, I opened his cupboard and drawer, more from the need to feel his presence, rather than curiosity over what was there. When we showed the prescriptions to the family doctor, we detected they were fake. The post-mortem reports confirmed an overdose of the same drugs I found, as the primary cause of his death." Then after a brief silence she continued, "It's from the doctor I learned, most illegal drugs can have adverse

     Shuvashree Chowdhury

cardiovascular effects, ranging from abnormal heart rate to heart attacks. Injecting illegal drugs can also lead to cardiovascular problems, such as collapsed veins and bacterial infections of the blood vessels and heart valves. Many drugs affect the central nervous system and can alter a user's consciousness. In addition to addiction, the side effects and risks associated with use of these drugs include: changes in body temperature, heart rate, blood pressure, headaches, abdominal pain and nausea, impaired judgment and greater risk of sexually transmitted infections, heart attacks, seizures, and respiratory arrest."

Then, suddenly, anger over-riding her grief, her eyes and tone reflecting her annoyance, Madhumita added, "I feel so cheated, as though learning after his death, he was having an affair, and that he had died in his lover's arms. I was not good enough for him, you see, *Didi*."

"Madhumita, don't be so harsh on yourself," I chided softly. "I understand you have every reason to be angry, to feel betrayed in Gautam hiding so much from you since you were childhood friends."

"Why should I mourn over him? You tell me, *Didi* ..." Madhumita interrupted indignantly. "I realise now that he did not consider me his friend. I knew he was having problems at work, he had barely joined a few months back, but couldn't he discuss them with me if they were bothering him so much, rather than turn to drugs for solace? But he didn't trust me enough to share his problems, let alone letting me in on his taking drugs. He not only betrayed me in life, *Didi*, in death, too. He left me alone, after promising my mother to take care of me lifelong."

Madhumita sounded so rational even in her grief, in her anger, that I could not disagree. My admiration for her strength only grew.

"I know how you must feel, Madhumita," I said, also angry with Gautam now. "What kind of a foolish man, married to a remarkable, courageous woman like you, did not rely on your strength, and find a prop in you, but resorted to drugs?"

"I will not mourn the death of a coward, a deserter," she replied sternly, "One who has chosen death through drug abuse over life. I cannot even relate to him anymore, as the man I knew and loved almost my entire life. I will live my life well, not waste it mourning his death. In fact, I feel really sorry for his parents, how could he do this to them? He was their only child. They had literally begged God, I've heard, till he was born to them late in their lives. But I will take care of them, as their son should have, rather than live with my mother."

Madhumita had continued to live with Gautam's parents, trying to compensate the loss of their son, looking out for their needs over hers. It was immensely challenging, in spite of her anger at Gautam, the determination not to grieve over him. She had stopped caring about herself, what she ate, wore, how she looked outside working hours. She lost interest in everything other than her job and her in-laws, even tending to neglect her mother, who became her sister's responsibility. Gautam's parents, devastated by the sudden loss of their only son, were initially distant with Madhumita, holding her responsible for his irresponsibility. But her persistent concern for them, her living in their house rather than living with her mother, soon softened their stance, making them accept her as their daughter.

"Maybe you should stay with your mother now, Madhumita, even she needs you, doesn't she?" I suggested, after a year of Madhumita's living with her in-laws. "I recall you mentioned taking your mother to the cardiologist last week, after work. Moreover, living in Gautam's house, his family is a constant reminder of his absence. You can always drop in on his parents. You said you were going to live well, not spend it mourning, but in effect, that's what you are doing."

"You may be right, *Didi*, but I cannot desert them, you see," she replied. "It's only a year, and they still need me. How can I deprive them of their daughter, after the son has gone away irresponsibly?"

"You always place everyone's needs before your own, Madhumita," I stated. "You've been through so much, but all you can think of is your duty to everyone. You have a responsibility to yourself as well."

However, with time, once they opened their hearts to her, Gautam's parents started noting Madhumita's sullenness, in spite of her attempts at her usual vivaciousness with them.

     Shuvashree Chowdhury

So far caught up in their own misery to notice hers, they now began encouraging her to go out, spend time with her mother and friends. They insisted upon her to dress in bright clothes, wear makeup, preventing her from wearing white, dull or drab clothes, as she had started to. Also, they insisted she resume eating the non-vegetarian food she had given up. Madhumita had started following all the customs laid down for widows in our society to please them. The death of the husband is a cruel, poignant event in a women's life. Why then, does our society, along with the stigma of a widow, tie the atrocious boulder of customs to her sinking feet? I wondered. Is it so she goes totally down under?

After two years, Gautam's parents also encouraged Madhumita to get married, worried what would happen to their daughter after them.

"I cannot think of re-marrying," Madhumita had replied resolutely, when I broached the subject myself. "I cannot forget what I shared with Gautam, even though it meant little to him for him to leave me the way he did." Then, in a sad voice, she added: "I truly loved Gautam, *Didi*, I don't want anyone to replace him in my life."

"Obviously you loved, Gautam," I had said to her tenderly. "But you are still very young to spend the rest of your life alone. However, if that is what you truly want – to remain single, then let no one stop you. In my opinion, you have to get on with your life and marrying again doesn't have to mean forgetting what you shared with Gautam. Marriage is also about companionship over and above true love."

* * *

The empty wine glass in hand, as I stood by the sea across the back gate of the beach house, at the New Year party, tiny jets of seawater spurt on me intermittently. In recounting my earlier association with Madhumita, on the face of her recent marriage, I was in awe of her strength, her personality. When someone younger, there being over a decade's difference between us, inspires you, it stays with you for life. Her experiences showed me with clarity that no one has the right to take his life whatever the problems at hand. One's life is a gift not merely to its owner, but to their loved ones as well. Thus, taking one's life, above being drastically gutless, is the most selfish act one can commit. The family and the loved ones are left to a life of shame and betrayal. Life or death is not our choice to make, but rather, the choice we need to execute judiciously is how we live our lives.

I was abruptly brought to the present, by a light hand placed on my shoulder. I turned around briskly, taken aback in the darkness and the solitude. It was Madhumita, smiling at my startled look. My husband, with a man, stood behind her, both looking at me curiously.

"What are you doing here, *Didi*, all by yourself," Madhumita asked, in a concerned tone. "We've been looking for you everywhere. Luckily, one of the waiters mentioned he saw you walking out, down here."

"I came for a brisk walk," I replied smiling, "and then got lost here in the sight, smell and sound of the sea."

"I can understand. Isn't it lovely here?" Madhumita said chirpily, and then shyly added: "*Didi*, this is my husband, Rahul Dutta. He's a businessman, a merchant of the company I now work for."

I looked up at the tall, dark, bulky man with the round, youthful face, big luminous eyes, smiling shyly at me.

"It's so good to finally meet you," Rahul said to me very warmly. "Madhumita and I talk about you often. You changed your mobile number, so we were unable to contact you before our wedding. But see the will of God … meeting you here like this. Ajay, our host, and I went to engineering college together in Bangalore."

What I saw in my mind's eye was Madhumita's ex-husband, Gautam. Slowly, as I continued to look at the man in a navy blue blazer over a white polo necked T-Shirt and jeans, I actually saw him for who he was. The striking resemblance he had to Gautam didn't seem to me as odd, as I discerned how Madhumita had changed her mind on remarrying. Rahul's looks, one she was accustomed to since a child in Gautam's, might have had something to do with her marrying him.

"I'm so happy for you," I said earnestly, turning to Madhumita

     Shuvashree Chowdhury

as we walked back towards the swimming pool, the men following us. "I want to hear the details of how you met before we leave tonight."

Ajay and Jaya, our hosts, joined us by the bar counter, having seen the four of us walk back together. The party was still in full swing, people dancing with gusto on the makeshift dance floor. We decided to have a drink each, before getting on the dance floor. Each of us got our choice of drinks from the waiter at the bar counter. Madhumita, Jaya and I, asked for glasses of red wine, while our husbands, Scotch. I waited till each of us had our glasses in hand.

"To a new year, a new beginning," I said, raising my glass, looking at the newlyweds simultaneously. "And love and happiness."

"To a new beginning" all repeated, raising their glasses.

18. A Doctor

It is Saturday morning. Uma has to take her daughter to work with her, as Preeti's school is closed on weekends. Her husband leaves for his work by six and her mother-in-law, the only other member of their family, leaves right after. Uma's parents live far away, in the suburbs of Chennai, and there is no one else she can leave Preeti with and leaving her four year old child alone at home is not an option. Luckily, Uma's employers do not mind her bringing Preeti to work. Even if they did object, there was little she could do besides quitting. Over the week, Uma goes to work only after dropping Preeti off at school. The girl is later brought home by her father, in time for lunch. Her mother-in law is usually back by then too. Uma gets home in time to prepare the midday meal for the entire family. Lunch is usually a simple affair – vegetable curry and dal with some rice, or sometimes Sāmbhar and rice. There is always some curd-rice, does not take much time to prepare.

Uma just rang the doorbell at her employer's apartment in central Chennai. It is about 10am. I open the door drowsy-eyed, having just awoken from sleep. Usually an early riser, I take it easy on weekends, sometimes even napping after breakfast as I did today. Now I work as a senior consultant – in the consumer, retail and services vertical, of a multinational executive search firm. I had approached them to find me a suitable assignment, no longer finding managing the lifestyle department store in Chennai a challenge, when they offered me the role I had accepted eagerly. I work random Saturdays now, to meet time-starved high-ranking candidates, to make mandatory assessment reports for senior, urgent positions. But not today. At the door, Uma is standing dressed as usual in a timeworn *salwar-kameez*. She is tall with a sturdy athletic frame, a dusky complexion. Her thick long hair is braided, reaching behind her waist. Standing upright carrying herself in a dignified manner, the hardships of her life reflected on

Shuvashree Chowdhury

her plain scrubbed face, Uma looks much older than her 23 years.

Opening the door wider, I spontaneously lower my gaze. A pair of large black eyes, lit up with excitement, stares back up at me from a chubby face, with a small nose and a generous mouth. Preeti's small head, full of big black curly hair – tied in two neat ponytails with red satin ribbons, is tipped far behind her, in order to look at me.

"Aunty, Good Morning" she says in her singsong lisp, eyes mischievously twinkling and the face twitching in excitement.

"Good Morning Preeti" I reply cheerily, trying to match her exuberance.

I look back up, smiling at Uma. She smiles in a manner adults do over the antics of a child. Then Preeti rushes past us carrying her sling bag, sprinting through the hall, in the direction of the bedroom. She knows my husband will be there. She has to greet him too. Uma strides towards the kitchen. I shut the door and follow Preeti to the bedroom.

"Gooood mauuurning uncle" Preeti says, up close to the bed, in the singsong manner children wish teachers with as they step into the classroom.

"Good morning Preeti" he replies in a drowsy voice, lying on his side propped up on one elbow over the pillow.

He takes a sip of his morning tea, placing it on the tray at hand, before reaching for the newspaper again. The bed is strewn with glossy supplements he will browse through later at leisure. Preeti looks about her and then back at him. Having slept late at night, and barely awake, he is clearly not in the mood for a conversation with her. But Preeti undeterred, scampers on to the bed beside him, sitting on her haunches. He is still not paying her any attention, so she opens the cover of the alphabet book she has carried with her, and then flips the pages with her eyes on him.

Uma meanwhile, has set about her tasks diligently. As our domestic helper, her job entails: cleaning the house – sweeping and swabbing the floor, dusting the furniture; washing and drying clothes; as well as assisting me with sundry other household chores. Uma does not cook or wash dishes though. Ramya the cook engaged for both purposes is in the kitchen, nearing the end of her tasks, having come much earlier. She is a middle-aged stocky woman, with a pleasant round face and sparkling black eyes. The sound of her ladle against the cooking pan is heard intermittently. The smell of spicy mutton curry permeates the air, drowning the smell of the fresh jasmine flowers she is wearing on her profusely grey streaked hair. The whiff of her flowers had been wafting around the house with the gusts of wind coming in through the open kitchen window.

My husband and I like our weekend lunches to be elaborate Bengali meals, since on weekdays we make do with simple, mainly vegetarian dishes. I have taught Ramya, who is Tamilian, the intricacies of Bengali cooking. It is only on weekends that I have time to supervise both her and Uma. I go about tidying rooms, changing bed clothes and towels, calling out to Uma to assist me. The cook makes another round of tea for everyone. She keeps a cup in the kitchen for Uma to have at her convenience. As I take the tea tray for my husband and myself into the bedroom – Uma has cleared the earlier one already – I am surprised to see Preeti sitting upright on the bed beside him, on a makeshift blanket-cushion. My surprise promptly turns to irritation at the mess she is making of the sheets. A stickler for cleanliness, I tell myself I am not irritated because Preeti as the maid's child shouldn't be sitting on the bed. I am not class-biased I would like to think. But I have a strong aversion to any outsider sitting on my bed, more so a child who plays on the road, as she does sometimes.

I notice that Preeti is bending over her Hindi alphabet book. I recall asking her to bring her English and Hindi books, so that I can teach her. As I set the tea tray down on the bedside table, I brace myself to ask Preeti to get off. In doing so, I irritably face my husband first.

"How could you…." I begin in Bengali, in an exasperated tone, giving him a disparaging glance. Then in spite of my anger, I remind myself, it is Preeti's innocence which lets her treat this house and the bed like her own, as much hers as ours. So, I evenly say "Preeti, come down here. Your mother is calling you."

In order not to hurt the child's feelings I also smile, signaling her by hand to get off, and follow me out of the room. I am sensitive to her feelings, but I am not sure it is merely the

         Shuvashree Chowdhury

hygiene issue that prods me to get Preeti off my bed. If Preeti had belonged to a family like ours, would I still have minded her sitting on my bed, I ask myself? She would not then be playing on the road, would she, I think justifying my response to the situation.

Preeti continues to sit on the bed, in spite of my repeated cajoling, and my voice turns sharp from impatience. My tea is getting cold. Uma hearing my cajoling Preeti to get off the bed, perhaps also reading into my controlled annoyance, promptly walks up to us. In a strict voice, she commands Preeti to get off the bed. Preeti quietly collects her books and pencils strewn on the bed, and then, hopping off the bed, runs out of the room. At first relieved, my guilt makes me follow Preeti in an attempt to mollify her. I don't want her to get the wrong signal. We are very fond of her, even though at times I do get impatient when she runs all over the house, distracting Uma from her work.

Preeti looks forward to these visits and I am careful not to detract from the experience. Unlike her home, which she can cover with a few steps of her tiny feet, our house gives her ample space to run around. Also the colorful and fancy things here fascinate her. Preeti has not seen a house like ours, though our home is far from luxurious. Her father is an auto-rickshaw driver and her mother and grandmother work as domestic help. Their friends, relatives and even neighbors live in humble, mostly single-room homes. However, her family's lower economic and social status compared to us is not something that has dawned on Preeti yet. She has no comprehension, of the basis of this variance – the education, jobs and income. All she cares about is that Uncle and Aunty have no children, they love her and she has their undivided attention when she spends time with them.

On an earlier visit, Preeti had rushed into our house, excited as usual, along with her mother. That morning, we had a friend visiting us along with her daughter. Preeti ran into the bedroom looking for "Uncle", and then not finding him, rushed to the adjacent room – his study. Our friend's daughter of less than two years was sitting on my husband's lap atop the sofa. Preeti looked visibly surprised at the scene, and then to my astonishment, she did not wish him as she always did. Her face fell and with a hurt and shy look, she retreated with backward steps, out of the room. I promptly called to her to come back, but she looked at me desolately, then from outside, hiding behind the curtain with her face downward. I walked up to her and I led her back inside by hand.

"Take this Preeti" I said, offering her a piece of sweetmeat from the tray served to the guests, hoping to distract her from the other child.

But she did not accept the sweet, her face still bent downwards as she shook her head in refusal. I broke a piece of the sweet and fed her. With the sweet in her mouth, sulking, she abruptly turned, ran out of the room to the balcony. I followed her, cajoling her to finish the sweet in my hand, and then come back and play with the little girl. But she would not take the sweet from me, the piece in her mouth lumped to one side of her cheek. She squatted stubbornly on the balcony floor. From her expression I realized she would not heed my words, so I went back inside. I handed Uma a small box of sweets to take home. Preeti remained in the balcony, till she left with her mother.

When I returned to the room, the little girl oblivious to being the cause of Preeti's jealous sulking gurgled on my husband's lap.

"If this is how Preeti reacts on seeing another child with us" I said turning to my husband, "how will she handle having a sibling, when she does?"

"Actually I was quite taken aback by her behaviour" he replied over the child's head. "The initial reaction was expected, but I had thought she would come around and want to play with her."

"Children are very sensitive, you know" my friend adjoined, "Since this little one was born, we have had to be very delicate with the elder child. He is four now and throws tantrums, to grab our attention. But rather than dealing with him severely, my husband and I pay him the attention he seeks, involving him in caring for his sister and making him feel responsible for her."

As I follow Preeti out of our bedroom now, after she has got off the bed at her mother's behest, I say in a coaxing tone "Come now Preeti, show me your Hindi alphabet book … let's see what you have learnt."

    Shuvashree Chowdhury

But Preeti ignores me, pulls out a chair at the dining table, and climbs on to its seat. She places the Hindi alphabet book in front, on the table, and opens it. She puts a finger to an alphabet, reads it aloud, and then moves to the next one. Since she's apparently normal, I return to the bedroom, sit on the bed with my cup of tea. From where I am sitting, the dining table and Preeti are directly in my line of vision. Uma, I notice, has a contented look on her face, as she goes around the table, sweeping the floor. Preeti's education costs her dearly and she worries how she will fare in life. Uma knows she cannot teach Preeti on her own or monitor her studies much longer, having dropped out of school herself after the sixth standard. But our presence in Preeti's life, my overlooking her studies, assures Uma. She hopes I will be able to foster her daughter's academic interest, in the long run.

After a few minutes of reading aloud, trying to articulate the words slowly and with much difficulty, Preeti starts getting restless. By now I have finished my tea and am seated beside her on an adjacent chair at the dining table. I make her repeat after me, making her note my exaggerated mouth movements, so as to help her shed her strong Tamil accent while pronouncing the Hindi alphabets and words. The cook Ramya signals to me from afar, to suggest she is done with her cooking. When I nod back, she places the serving dishes of food for our lunch on the table, bringing them out from the kitchen, one at a time. She leaves soon after, pulling the gate shut behind her. I continue to read the alphabets along with Preeti, till she abruptly stops. I look at her questioningly. She sticks out her tongue grimacing, indicating she is tired, and then jumps off the chair.

I look at Preeti and smile indulgently. She is wearing a long mauve dress with frills. She always wears her best clothes to our house, as though she was coming to a party. At times it is a narrow-strap short dress, at other times it is a long pleated skirt with a lace blouse. Her favourite outfit is a pair of jeans worn with a tank top. Her short curly hair is tied in one or two ponytails on her head, with matching ribbons. She also carries a handbag like a grownup.

"Who bought you this dress?" I ask Preeti, who is facing me.

"Papa" she replies with an air of pride, and then shyly looks down as though assessing the lace dress. She has also worn eye-liner, pink lipstick and blusher, as she does on most days. Uma always dresses her up, though she herself dresses plainly. They look far from being mother and daughter, when they are dressed. Preeti looks like she belongs to an affluent family, while Uma presents a rustic working-class face to the world.

Uma has dreams and lofty ambitions for her daughter, far outside their means. This makes Uma strive hard, at the cost of neglecting herself immensely. Preeti attends an English-medium school, unlike their friends and neighbors children who attend a Tamil one.

"I want to be a doctor" Preeti always quips, in response to anyone who asks her what she wants to be when she grows up.

This ambition is her mother's, implanted in Preeti ever since she started going to school. Uma is making every effort to ingrain this goal into her daughter's psyche, as she strives to enhance her earnings through hard work, in order to support the ambition. Preeti is only in Upper KG now, but expenses will mount. Uma works in a number of houses, but is trying to secure a government job, to enhance her pay and ensure job security. Uma is determined her daughter will not live her life the one Preeti watches her toil at, from house to house.

"Akka (elder-sister), can I keep a *hundi* (piggy-bank) in your house," Uma had asked me the last time she got her Rs. 2200 salary. "I will put some money into it every month for Preeti. If I take the entire money home, it will get spent. My husband takes it away."

I had looked at the makeshift piggy bank in Uma's hand curiously. It was a simple cardboard box, with a lid. Uma shoved in Rs. 500 through a slit cut on the top. She proceeded to keep the box in the guest room cupboard, as I instructed her to. Her grit and determination, in the face of her poverty overwhelmed me. I mentally made a note to put some money into Uma's makeshift piggy-bank regularly, to support her cause. The money I got from selling old newspapers, which collected in abundance every month due to our subscribing to five papers, would go into this box. I would however not tell Uma about it, I decided, not wanting to steal her credit by my meager contributions.

      Shuvashree Chowdhury

Uma has finished her work and is washing up. I retrieve sweetmeats onto a plate from the refrigerator adjacent to the dining table.

"Take this, Preeti" I say, bending to her level, handing her the plate. On seeing the two large conch-shell shaped *sandesh* on it, Preeti turns to Uma and squeals in delight "Amma … See this." Then turning towards me, her eyes twinkling, in accepting the plate she says "thank you Aunty."

Then promptly, hands extended, Preeti offers the plate to her mother. As always, she will not have anything without sharing with her.

"That is for you, Preeti. I have another plate for your mother" I say, smiling at daughter and then her mother, as I hand over a plate of sweets to Uma too.

I usually keep sweets for Preeti's weekend visits. It's an added incentive for her to bring her books and come study with me. After Uma accepts her plate, Preeti takes a bite of a sweet from her plate. Then they sit outside the kitchen, on the floor, eating their respective portions. I watch them indulgently, sitting on our bed along with my husband. I notice how Preeti's cherubic glowing face above the expensive looking dress, is a sharp contrast to Uma's worn-out one, and her ragged clothes.

"I sincerely hope Preeti becomes a doctor" I say to my husband. "So she can take care of her mother, who gives her the best of everything, works so hard only to ensure a good future for her.

"I hope so too," my husband replies, answering from behind a magazine. "More so, I hope she recalls her mother's struggles and respects her."

"You're right" I say, pensively.

If and when Preeti becomes a doctor, I think, the naivety of her childhood lost, will she remain unbiased by status, and regard her mother as she does now? I hoped she would always remember that it was her mother who shaped her rise in society and she would not be ashamed of Uma then. Having finished eating, both mother and daughter stand up. They throw the paper plates into the kitchen dustbin, and share a glass of water. I watch them walk towards the main door, looking in my direction.

"Bye Uncle, bye Aunty" Preeti says chirpily, walking hand in hand with Uma who smiles gratefully, nods at me saying softly "Bye *Akka*."

"Bye Doctor Preeti" I reply chuckling. Then smile as I say "Bye Uma."

'A Doctor' was published in the 5th October 2016, issue of the reputed literary magazine, 'Himal Southasian.'

　　　　　　Shuvashree Chowdhury

19. Homeward Bound

The aircraft gently descended over Chennai. As he watched the twinkling city lights through the window, Raghu's heartbeat quickened. He was coming home after a year. When the aircraft came to an abrupt halt after the short run on the tarmac, he felt his heart lift. Stepping out with his wife and two children, they were greeted by a strong heat wave. Then, as they walked down the stepladder, the distinctive Chennai heat embraced them, akin to the warmth they would soon be engulfed in. It is this warmth of people that they missed most in their adopted hometown of California, in the US. Raghu smiled at Devika, his intense eyes shining. She noticed his handsome face light up. He was home where he truly belonged. As they walked into the arrival hall, stepping out of the coach, the children took Raghu's hand on either side. Devika trailed behind them, as she did in her zeal at the prospect of moving back to Chennai.

Their eight-year-old daughter, clutching Raghu's right hand, wore a baby pink georgette short-dress with halter neck. Her long hair pulled away from her oval face in a ponytail, accentuated her big brown eyes. Her brother, all of five years, wore blue denim trousers and a red T-shirt with Spiderman embossed on it. His brown hair lined the forehead of his chubby face. After they had collected their baggage, tugging at his father's arm manoeuvring the baggage trolley, the boy propelled him to walk faster.

"Papa, where are our grandmas and grandpas?" he enquired, straining his head to look amidst the waiting crowd outside the airport terminal.

Both children had looked forward to this trip. Their grandparents spoilt them, humouring their every whim. Devika, dressed in an elaborate *salwar-kameez* for the benefit of her in-laws, walked uncomfortably, groggy from the sleep she had been awakened from before landing.

The two sets of grandparents eagerly leaned over the metal

railing facing the exit gate, in an attempt to spot the children first. Their aged faces and dull eyes shone from anticipation as much from the bright lights overhead. It was Devika who first spotted her parents alongside Raghu's. It was difficult to miss them even in a crowd, she thought, smiling to herself. Their mothers wore blue and green Kanjeevaram *sarees*. They had draped strings of jasmine flowers, around their buns of grey-black hair. The fathers wore white *veshtis* along with starched white *kurtas*. The elderly couples, friends now, often met to discuss their children and grandchildren, thus drawing refuge from their loneliness. The visits of the children and grandchildren, was as good as a festival now. They looked ahead to all the celebrations they had planned, with time spent between both the homes. Each household had their share of hosting and revelries.

Raghu and Devika had visited Chennai along with the children, only last summer, though they usually visited every two years. These all-family visits meant incurring a huge expenditure and so were spaced out, their parents visiting them in-between. It was difficult to avail long-leave as it is, from their high-profile jobs. Then the children's vacations had to be coincided with. This didn't leave one the option of travelling on low season fares. Gifts had to be taken for everyone in Chennai – distant relatives and the domestic-help included. Added to all the Indian stuff Devika took back for herself and for their home from every trip, they had to take gifts for friends in the US, including *sarees* and dress-material. Though they earned well, and had a good lifestyle, it was with both Raghu and Devika working very hard, juggling the pressures of bringing up the children without the family support they could have had here.

Raghu and Devika had met at a prestigious American University while pursuing their Engineering degrees. Their commonalities were restricted to their being from Chennai. Raghu was soft-spoken, warm and popular for his down to earth congenial personality. Devika was reserved, came across as snobbish due to her cut and dry style of talking. While completing their MBA at the same institute thereafter, it was their common origins contrasting with their diverse personalities that had been catalysts to their friendship. Their recruitment into separate multinational

   Shuvashree Chowdhury

companies, offices located at a distance from the other, did not put an end to their friendship. In fact, the effort in meeting after extended work hours had tested the friendship – culminating into love, marriage and children in a short span. Their expensive college education had ensured their jobs came with meaty roles and matching compensation packages. Raghu, in a few years, led the marketing function of his company while Devika headed the R&D in hers.

They soon bought a large two-storey house with a sprawling lawn in the front; the back of the house accommodated a peanut-shaped swimming pool amidst a well-kept garden. Both of them drove high-end latest model cars. The children went to the best schools. Life was good. All they asked for now was their children have a good upbringing, imbibing Indian culture and values. So what if their speech and accent, the clothes they wore, were American? Raghu and Devika also spoke with heavy American accents now, as it was easier to relate to people than with the Indian accents they spoke in when they came to the US. Devika wore a *saree* or a *salwar-kameez* only on Indian festivals now, celebrated in the US with great aplomb. In spite of the comforts of living in California, the Krishnamurthy's reminisced life in India. They fondly recalled their growing years, narrating stories to the children, who now learnt Indian classical music and dance like they themselves had in India. Their daughter took *Bharat Natyam* classes. Devika procured dance costumes and jewellery for her from Chennai. Their son had started sitar lessons and seemed to have a flair for it. The children were familiarised with Indian art and culture, as much as possible.

Every time Raghu and Devika visited India now, they realised dejectedly how much their parents and relatives had aged. It wrenched their hearts to discover new ailments keeping pace with the ever-increasing wrinkles and grey hair. It was also getting difficult for their parents to visit them in California. The distance seemed more than ever now, and they found the differences in climate, surroundings, culture, widening with every trip. It was after much deliberation, after his visit to India last year that Raghu decided he would move back. Devika was not ready for that yet. She missed home and her parents, but moving back to Chennai, with its male chauvinistic streak and conservatism was a thought she far from cherished. She loved her life, most of all her independence in California.

It was on their visit in the summer of 2009, a year after the trip wherein he decided to move back to India, that I first met Raghu. I was at the time executive search consultant with a reputed firm in Chennai. He had been referred to me by his friend, whom I had placed as CEO of an FMCG company. After a brief telephonic conversation, I had asked Raghu to email me his professional resume, and then going through it had requested him to come and meet me. As decided, he came the next day at 3pm. He was flipping a page of the *Business Line* magazine, when I met him at the reception area of our office, on Radha Krishna Salai, not far from the City Centre mall near the Marina Beach.

"I'm Raghu Krishnamurthy," he said standing, shaking my hand.

I proffered my business card, which he accepted, glancing briskly at it, then appraising me with a hint of a smile – perhaps expecting someone older as senior executive search consultant. I wasn't surprised – I didn't look my thirty-seven years. Moreover, after all the years of being a working woman, I took smirks of men in my stride.

Raghu was of above average height, moderately built, fair complexioned, with piercing brown eyes, sharp facial features, and wavy brown hair. He wore a formal blue shirt with beige trousers. I led him into an adjoining glass-door meeting room, with four blue-cushioned chairs, around a circular glass table set on a steel base. On the table were two glasses of water covered with coasters, a telephone and a few magazines. In one hand I carried a notebook and a copy of Raghu's resume. With the other hand carrying my mobile phone, I gestured to Raghu to sit down.

"Would you prefer a hot or a cold beverage?" I asked.

"I'd like a south-Indian filter coffee, if that's possible," he replied.

I nodded and dialled the pantry for it. Raghu then briskly took me through his experiences and educational qualifications projected on his CV. We talked of his interest in returning to India, stemming from his parents and family living here.

                    Shuvashree Chowdhury

"So what do you think are the job opportunities in India, for someone with my qualification and experience?" he asked, taking a sip of the coffee the bearer had brought us.

"Honestly, Raghu, with the availability of qualified and experienced talent in India now, companies are not keen to hire senior persons from overseas. They prefer those with experience in the Indian market, especially for sales and marketing functions."

Raghu looked crestfallen. Then, after a moment's silence, not willing to give up, he said forcefully, "You have to do something... please."

"Let's see, there is this head of marketing position I'm working on...." I said thoughtfully, convinced of the seriousness of his intention. As Raghu looked up at me hopefully, I continued, "They are in the entertainment business. They own a chain of cineplexes. Perhaps their requirement for a head of marketing could be suited to your experiences and skills."

"That should be interesting," Raghu replied excitedly, "Please check."

"Since the entertainment, cineplex business is still in the early stages in India, they might welcome someone talented with international exposure."

I briefly discussed with Raghu the position dossier of this head of marketing position. Raghu agreed the requirements for the position were in line with his qualifications and experience.

"I will email the formal brief of the position to you. Also, please go through their website," I said, in ending our conversation, as we stood up to leave the meeting room.

After Raghu left our office, thanking me repeatedly at the reception area, I called my client – the CEO of the cineplex company. I got an appointment with him for Raghu. We had already shortlisted two candidates to meet with their MD, but I requested him to meet Raghu, before the final meeting with the MD. On meeting the CEO, after a brief chat, Raghu was taken on a tour of their offices spread on a five-floored building, located in central Chennai. Then he was taken to the cineplex closest to the head-office. Raghu was impressed by what he saw. That things had progressed so much in India, was an eye-opener for him. The CEO named Ian, an expatriate from New Zealand, was impressed with Raghu's keen observation, derived from the feedback and marketing plans he suggested. Also taken in by Raghu's charming disposition and having struck a rapport with him, Ian introduced him to the MD informally.

After his discussion with Ian and the MD, Raghu was convinced this was a professional place to work in. He liked their progressive thoughts and plans for the future. After a couple of more meetings, the MD had with all the shortlisted candidates, Raghu was selected for the position. Raghu's international experience stood him in good stead; it was in sync with their expatriate CEO and the company's developmental plans. They were looking at a complete overhaul of product and services, an upgrade of the overall movie-going experience for the customer in line with international standards. Raghu's inexperience in the Indian market was luckily overruled with his Chennai origins and fluency in Tamil. This would help him learn, adapt to situations here, and relate to local customer psyche soon.

When Raghu had called me after the first meeting with Ian and, much to his surprise, the MD, I had asked him: "So what makes you certain this is the company you would like to work for?"

"A number of things actually," he had replied, "But there is one thing in particular. When their head of human resources was showing me around the offices and the cineplex, I asked to see the washrooms at both."

"Why would you do that?" I asked laughing, "How did you find them?"

"The washrooms at the cineplex were impeccable, luxurious, at par with international standards," he replied, "A sign of excellence. Their vision of world-class product and service is evident. I was impressed."

Raghu returned to California with Devika and the children, his fifteen-day leave running out. His offer letter would be emailed to him shortly he had been assured by his new employers. He kept in touch with them, as well as with me, calling or emailing us. The financial terms of the offer, when he received it, were meagre as compared to his current compensation in dollars. But he had been asked to keep his expectations low anyway. The company had brand equity and would help restart his career in India, is what he

          Shuvashree Chowdhury

had been advised by family and friends. So Raghu was willing to step down on the financial package. What was most important to him was that the posting was in Chennai, his hometown. He could live in the ancestral family house, which fortunately was in top form, as he had recently financially helped rebuild it. The cost of living in Chennai was much lower than in California; luckily the children were still very young and would adjust to life here easily. On weighing the situation overall, Raghu considered he was lucky to have this job offer worked out so soon.

Raghu broke the news to Devika one morning, over coffee. He carried a copy of his offer letter on the tray he brought to their bed. While pouring the coffee into two mugs in the kitchen, he had smiled to himself imagining her radiant face on seeing it. Devika was tall, slightly overweight, though attractive in an unconventional way – with average facial features. She had a luminous fair complexion and bright eyes. With her long, thick, wavy hair cascading to her waist, Raghu thought she looked almost as when he had first met her in college. Even now he could lose himself in her large black mysterious eyes. However, to his dismay, on reading the offer letter, Devika did not smile as she sat up in bed, and neither did she look pleased, only surprised. Though she knew of the meetings he had had, she had not expected an offer to really come through so soon, if at all.

Looking up, noticing Raghu's crestfallen face, Devika realised with dread how much he had wanted this. For her, merely considering a move had been one thing, but actually moving, quite another. At forty-four years, only a year elder to her, Raghu looked much older. A lot of his hair had greyed, the fair, smooth skin of his face roughened, and crow's feet were prominent along with the dark circles under his eyes. This was a result of the less than four hours of sleep a night, a lot of travelling, hotel food and lack of exercise. Looking at the anticipation in Raghu's eyes, still wearing his checked black and white night suit, Devika's face softened, and then broke into a tender smile. She fondly recalled how he had been one of the most sought-after Indian men in college. His intelligence, though, had been his most attractive attribute. Not wanting to disappoint him, she extended her hand, placing it over his on the bed in a placating gesture.

"This is great news, Raghu," she said cheerily, "Though, I'd say, let's take some time to think things over before you accept the offer. Shall we?"

Raghu's face brightened. Devika's support meant a lot to him. In the following days, they discussed every aspect of the move, including children's schooling, her job opportunities in Chennai. He discussed with close friends in India, high on the corporate ladder, on the compensation break-up of his offer letter, the tax incidence, legal implications. Then one day he called me to say the salary package offered to him was not commensurate with his position and requested me to get it revised. Also, that he expected the company to give him a car, instead of incorporating its cost into his salary package along with the responsibility of lease payment for it. In alliance with the CEO, Ian, who was convinced of Raghu's perceived value in concurrence to his current expansion plans, I was able to get Raghu's offer revised.

It was after a second and then a third revised offer was made to Raghu that he and the company reached a consensus. I was relieved. I could now collect the second cheque payment, having received the first as an initial retainer to start work on this position. The third and final amount would be payable once Raghu joined. In the meantime, Raghu updated his knowledge of the Indian market, the changing trends with a view to the worldwide recession now. He read as much as he found on the net and from books, in readiness for the new role. He was excited, looking forward to embarking on his new life in India along with the new job. It was when over a week had passed since the final offer letter was sent, and I did not get a copy of Raghu's acceptance letter, that I fretted. What if he didn't take up the offer? I had worked very hard over this mandate, from making the initial long list of companies along with our research analysts, to assessing a number of candidates and finally negotiating Raghu's offer. If he did not accept the offer, I would have to do it all over again, more importantly, I had a monthly target to meet, from which I was far away.

One morning, I had barely settled into my workstation, switched on my laptop, when the direct phone rang. It was Raghu.

"I just need a little more time to accept the offer," he started abruptly on recognising my voice from the hurried 'hello', and then said, "Please talk to the CEO, Ian, tell him that I need a little time to sort out relocation issues."

"But Raghu," I replied with a touch of impatience, "I thought you had already decided," and then composing myself, in an even tone, I added, "You can take time in joining, but why the delay in accepting the offer?"

"I need a little more time in accepting the offer as well," he insisted. "Devika and I are re-evaluating the pros and cons of our moving right now."

"What really is the matter, Raghu?" I asked, alarmed. "Please tell me now. I think I deserve to know, don't you think so?"

"It is nothing to worry about, really," Raghu replied in his usual charming tone, with the American accent, and then sombrely added: "We're just thinking a little. Devika is having some problems at her workplace."

"But what has that got to do with your accepting the offer?" I persisted. "She is going to quit her job to join you here, isn't she?"

Raghu remained silent.

"Isn't Devika quitting her job in the US, Raghu?" I repeated.

"Devika's company has just laid-off 150 employees, at various levels," Raghu blurted, "Luckily, she was not amongst them this time," he paused, perhaps for me to comment, but I remained silent trying to gauge the point he was trying to make, so he continued: "She fears that if she gives up her job now, with the current global recession, she will not get another, especially not in India without relevant experience there."

Devika was the deterrent to Raghu's acceptance of the offer. I had rightly gauged her reluctance to return to India.

"What is the guarantee Devika will not be in the next list of layoffs?" I said cynically, "Then it will be worse than having quit herself, won't it?"

Raghu remained silent, in the face of my perceptible anger he knew was justified. I had worked hard to get him this offer, taking advantage of my rapport with my clients. I had pushed his candidature over the two shortlisted ones. Then I had negotiated his salary several times for a better package, till the final offer was made to his satisfaction.

"Well … you may be right," he said, after a prolonged silence, "But Devika is shaken with the mass layoffs at her company. She cannot consider giving up her job at this point. With the global downturn, she feels it would be stupid to leave a well-paying secure job for uncertainty in India."

"Raghu, but what about you, what do you really want?" I said evenly, coming to terms with reworking the mandate, yet taking another chance at convincing Raghu. "I thought you really wanted this."

"Yes, I did," he replied, unhappily. "In fact, I still want to return to India, to Chennai, to where I belong. However, leaving Devika and the kids back in the US is not an option. I hope you understand."

"Yes, of course, I do, but I thought you could convince Devika, telling her how lucky you are to get this opportunity."

"I tried. I really tried," he said firmly, sounding exasperated. "But, you see, there is another problem. After my return from India, I put our house up for sale, but there are no buyers yet. Well, not at a price remotely close to what we paid for it. The value of real estate is at an all-time low. "

"Raghu, it's just bad timing, what else can I say?" I said, empathising with his desire to return to India now thwarted by the current global recession. "I'm sorry for pushing you. I understand you need to sort things."

"Thank you! Thanks a lot," Raghu blurted, cheered. Then in a sombre tone, he added: "You know what? I haven't slept well for days, worrying about what to do. All I need is a little more time. Please bear with me and hold the position a while longer, will you?"

"I'll try to hold it as long as is possible, Raghu, but that won't be very long. You know how crucial this position is, in their current expansion mode. I'll still try and convince Ian to wait for your acceptance letter, but you had better firm your mind fast."

At this time, I was under a lot of pressure myself. My personal target of six lakh rupees a month – not revised in spite of the global recession, was daunting. My company, with a strong international presence, was perhaps of the view that India and Asia Pacific countries could generate business to manage costs,

		Shuvashree Chowdhury

Europe and the US being at an all-time low. My email inbox, along with my colleagues', was swamped with fresh CVs daily. People called daylong, anxiously enquiring about suitable openings or for feedback on interviews they had attended. We were juggling between lengthy meetings and writing out detailed candidate assessments – mandatory for the top positions we handled. Our clients were now more stringent in their selection processes, as salaries were dearer. We saw the anxious, at times desperate, faces of senior executives with successful careers so far, now left in a lurch, some without jobs, others serving notice periods. Their families accustomed to high incomes, leading lavish lifestyles thus far, now forced to curtail. In case of single-income households the panic more pronounced.

I had to conversely work with the economic pressures faced by my clients in the consumer, retail and services industry, that I worked with. Organisations faced fund liquidity issues, along with over-staffing. They were laying-off mid-management positions for senior positions. These new positions created to bail ailing companies out of flagging bottom-lines, were crucial. They engaged reputed search firms like ours, but they were not willing to pay our regular high retainer fees or service charges. They insisted on discounted rates and terms, which smaller search firms, reacting to the downturn, were giving. These firms slashed service fees, worked without signing amounts, also agreed to work non-exclusively on position mandates, making competition thick. Above all this, organisations deliberated over selected candidates, and their compensation packages.

As executive search consultants, our monthly revenue targets could be achieved in three parts, from the corresponding positions we worked on. The first part we received as signing fees for a position, the next at the time of the selected candidate's acceptance of the offer, and the final amount at the time of his joining. The closure of any position – from our being signed up till a candidate's joining, could be spread over six to nine months. We planned our targets in advance. But in the current economic situation, in spite of all plans and efforts in their execution, we could not meet monthly targets. My colleagues and I from the consumer, retail and service industry vertical across India were most at risk of losing our jobs.

With Raghu's indecision impacting my performance and my job, I was very upset, for I had gone out of my way to help him.

One morning, more than a week since our last conversation, Raghu called me. It was late night in California. He had waited up for me to come into the office, so as not to inconvenience me before that. He knew of the heavy Chennai traffic at peak hours I drove to work in, of my need to wrap up household chores before leaving the house. Over several telephone calls and a few meetings, in the past month, we had chatted on various issues. Raghu had told me, among other things, how Devika was always rushing to work similarly, after tending to the house and children.

"I've really been in a big dilemma," Raghu said, after we had exchanged the usual pleasantries. "There is no way we can sell our house at this time. I just don't know what to do. Devika and I have discussed this ... and...."

"You've come to a decision ... right?" I interrupted.

"Well ... actually, yes," he replied, in a sombre voice, "And you have to believe me, it was the most difficult decision of my life. Devika and I went out to dinner last night, to talk things over and take a final call."

"And your decision is ...?" I asked, even though I knew what his answer would be, having sensed it in his voice.

"We have decided to stay on in the US for now," he replied crisply, "I think it's best under the circumstances."

I remained silent. The uncertainty so far had been killing. Though disappointed, I slowly began to relax. There is nothing as painful as indecision, in my view. Luckily, I had reinitiated the search process for this head of marketing position in the past few days, anticipating Raghu's decision. It was going to be more difficult to fill this position now, with the global economic condition worse, added to the need to match Raghu's standard. The two previously shortlisted candidates had accepted other offers. Moreover, good candidates were not inclined to switch jobs lately, due to the insecure job market.

"Hello," I said into the phone, a few seconds later, suddenly recalling Raghu must still be on the line.

"Hello," he responded, "I know you must be so upset. I wish there was some way I could make this all up to you."

     Shuvashree Chowdhury

"Okay, then …" I said abruptly, and then after a pause added: "You can start with telling me what the deciding factor in turning down this offer really is, Raghu."

"Devika is not willing to give up her job," he replied squarely. "She is very insecure about not finding another, with the current recession."

"But what makes Devika so certain she will not get a job?" I asked. "She didn't really try in India. Did she?"

"She sent her resume out to people, even to your firm, but nothing worthwhile came up for her," Raghu replied matter-of-factly, then in a soft voice added, "You know we started our careers together. I cannot expect her to just throw up her career that she built till now, only to follow me."

"Raghu, I helped you up to this point, only because of your keenness," I stated firmly, "You stayed connected and did not give up."

"I know. I can never thank you enough for your help." Raghu promptly replied. "I only wish something could have worked out for Devika, too."

"Raghu, you know what, Devika could have called me. We've met over dinner here, remember," I replied crisply, and then, trying in vain to control my irritation, I added cynically, "Rather she called our reception and told them she is an Engineer with an MBA, from the US. So she was connected to the manufacturing vertical, assuming they were the right people to help her. I learnt from my colleague, she did not show any flexibility on career options and compensation. 'This lady will not fit in culturally with any of my clients' is what my colleague categorically told me, when I pressed him on helping her."

Raghu remained silent. He knew his wife well. I had met Devika when I had taken them for dinner to my club. Raghu had wanted to see the Presidency Club, planning on applying for a membership when he returned to Chennai. But it was really from my chats with Raghu, incidents he had narrated, that I had insights into Devika's personality. She was usually high-handed, tending to look down on people if they were not well dressed or didn't speak well in English. On their last trip to India, she had carried a bottle of Evian drinking water, wherever she went. She was class-conscious, never availed public transport, would not consider sitting with workers at a factory or sharing a meal with them. India, to her, was a backward, underdeveloped country, so were the people who lived and worked here. She had no patience and little regard for their intelligence and capabilities, unlike Raghu, who was very respectful and humble. Little wonder few wanted to help her.

"I just happened to go through Devika's CV in detail," I said, interrupting the silence since my giving Raghu feedback on Devika. "She heads R&D in a food processing company, right? We could have looked at her for something in the FMCG space as well, in addition to the manufacturing sector."

"I suppose, but she's not a risk taker," Raghu replied, "Initially we had planned she would come to India along with me, then look for an assignment for herself. One of us would have to find a job here first, we realised. But now she is not sure. Is it possible for you to have a chat with her? Maybe you can convince her."

"Sure. I'll try," I replied.

It was little effort, I thought, if it might lead to Raghu's taking up the position here. Raghu called me the next morning, and put me on to Devika. After initial pleasantries, I tried to convince her that as R&D head in the food and beverage industry, there would be opportunities here. Indian companies could well do with international expertise.

"But it will be very difficult to get Raghu another opportunity," I stated, "Since he has no experience in the Indian market, crucial to a marketing head role. In fact, he was very lucky with this offer as it is."

After we hung up, thinking I had convinced her, I emailed Devika job leads, along with contact details. I asked her to write to them directly.

It was a week later, Raghu called me one morning as he usually did.

"We are still unable to find a buyer for our house," he said morosely, and then very abruptly blurted his decision, "I will have to let this offer pass at this time. I am really ... really ... sorry."

I was astounded. But decided to accept their decision and let go. After all, I had tried my best. My productivity and performance were not always in my hands. In spite of all the hard work, I

 Shuvashree Chowdhury

would still be low on target achievement that month. This is what frustrated me about my job. I firmly decided to go all out finding another candidate soon. Luckily, in a short time, I was able to find a good fit for the position. The CEO, Ian, and their MD were both happy with the new find, so quickly a fresh offer was made to him and, this time, accepted as well.

A few months later, the new candidate had resigned from his current position, serving his notice period, and due to join in a month's time. One afternoon, on returning from a client meeting, as soon as I sat at my desk, the telephone rang. I picked up the receiver to Raghu's familiar voice. "Hi," he said in a cheery voice, "I hope you are not still angry with me?"

"Raghu, is that you? … Ah … I … well … not anymore." I stuttered, and then smiling into the phone, I added: "But I have to admit that I cursed you for quite some time. I think it was until I received your new-year card … that's when I stopped being upset with you."

"I don't blame you. I'm still cursing myself," he replied laughing softly, and then in a low voice continued, "After I put you through so much trouble and awkwardness with your clients, I was embarrassed to call you, so I sent the postal card. I prefer them to e-cards as they are more personal."

"Thanks for the card, Raghu, it was thoughtful of you. Initially, I was upset, but I'm alright now, you don't need to apologise repeatedly."

"It's very kind of you to let me off the hook so easily," Raghu replied humorously. "How's the search going, found anyone yet?"

"Yes, I was lucky. The offer's been made and luckily accepted this time."

"Ah! I'm late," Raghu muttered, almost to himself. Then, after a pause, wherein I wondered what he had meant, he added: "But I'm really happy for you. It all worked out well in the end. "

"Yes, it did, didn't it?" I said cheerily, and then gauging Raghu sounded more dejected than happy, I added. "All will work out well for you, too, Raghu. Things have a way of working themselves out. You just have to have faith. So tell me, how are the kids? How are things with you and Devika?

"Well … not good … not good is an understatement really. It's pretty bad," Raghu said falteringly. "In fact, I was wondering if it was too much to expect you to find me another job opportunity."

I remained silent for a while – angry, hurt, and then said, "No Raghu, not again. You think this is a joke or what? I will not help you, until you and your wife finally decide and commit you really are ready to come home."

"Now it is not only a matter of wanting to come home. I need a job," he replied wryly, "And there's no better place to look for one now but India."

"What does that mean, Raghu?" I asked impatiently.

"My company's given me two months to find another job," Raghu replied crisply "It was kind of them, considering many were laid off without notice."

"I'm sorry, Raghu," I blurted, flabbergasted. But then had I not heard enough stories of layoffs in the past year to be surprised?

"I guess I really deserved this, didn't I?" Raghu stated, dejectedly.

"No, Raghu, don't be disheartened. We will work something out over again," I said cheerily, sounding more confident than I felt.

"Please see what you can do," Raghu said persuasively, and then added softly in his charming tone, "I would be tempted not to, if I were you. But my hope lies in that you don't think only with your head like me. It is usually the case with women. Please be an angel and wave your magic wand again."

"I'll see what I can do, Raghu," I replied, smiling into the phone.

          Shuvashree Chowdhury

20. *It's Still a Man's World*

Priya walked into the hotel lobby with trepidation, handing over her car keys to the valet. She walked across the ornate, fresh-flower-bedecked foyer to the reception area at the far end.

"I am here to meet Mr Kurien," she announced to one of the front office executives in a navy blue business suit.

"Certainly ma'am," the young lady replied, flashing a warm, cheerful smile, bright from the amber lipstick she wore. "He is in the business-centre. Please take the elevator to the first floor. It will be to your right."

Priya noticed the lady's smile reflected in her eyes, enhanced by the thick eyeliner, mascara and the blue eye shadow she wore. Her hair pulled back in a French-roll gave her appearance a professional edge.

As she stepped out of the elevator onto the red-carpeted corridor of the first floor, Priya met an elderly gentleman.

"I'm Venkatraman," he said, spontaneously holding out his hand to her to shake, "And you must be Priya?"

"Yes, yes, of course," she smiled warmly, shaking his hand firmly.

"Come this way," he said, taking a step along the length of the corridor, "It wasn't difficult finding this place, was it?"

"No. Thanks for asking," Priya replied, falling in step with him.

Venkatraman or Venkat as he was better known to everyone was the human resources head of the company Priya had applied for a senior role. It was a month since she had received a letter confirming the interview date for today. Venkat was of medium height and built she noticed, meeting him for the first time. His eyes, warm and friendly, stood out in a gaunt face through the thick glasses of his spectacles. His hair generously touched with grey, both on his head and his thick moustache, were accentuated by the grey suit he wore. With an air of assurance, he walked down the corridor flanked by brass-rimmed paintings and then abruptly he stopped, walked into a room to his left. Priya followed him.

There were four men seated inside, Priya noticed, dressed in business suits, crisp shirts and ties. Candidates for the same position as her, she decided.

"Please wait here, Priya," Venkat said softly. "We will call you into the conference room shortly."

"Thank you," she replied politely, as Venkat walked towards the exit.

Sitting down, Priya appraised the medium-sized room. The four men seated apart, cups in hand, were sipping tea; munching on sandwiches and fruitcake. She noticed a table at the far end. Two waiters were standing behind it.

One of the waiters, on noticing Priya, walked up to her.

"May I get you something, ma'am … tea, coffee … sandwiches?" he asked politely.

"Thank you. Only tea, with no sugar, please," she replied.

After the waiter retreated, Priya took out a small mirror from her handbag. She stole a glance at her face, with the almond shaped brown eyes, shapely nose and a splendid smile. Her hair and make-up were in place; she slid the mirror back. A good amount of time had been spent that morning over deciding on wearing a western suit or a *saree*. Once opting for a *saree*, the confusion had been over which one to wear? She had chosen a peach coloured, crepe-silk *saree*, with soft floral designs that enhanced her fair complexion. She looked beautiful and felt confident about herself. On her ears, she wore diamond and pearl-drop earrings. On a short chain, a pendant rested below her neckline emphasising her high collarbones. Her below-shoulder length hair fell about her slender neck. The only make-up she wore was eyeliner, mascara and a peach-coloured lipstick. The waiter returned, extending to her a tray, from which Priya took the teacup and saucer. The very first sip of the well-brewed Darjeeling tea was refreshing, the rest uplifting her self-assurance. As the waiter left, reclining on the back of her chair, Priya was reminded of the events leading up to her sitting here.

It was at a FICCI (Federation of Indian Chambers of Commerce and Industry) meet that Priya had met her prospective employer,

        Shuvashree Chowdhury

Ravi Kurien. He was tall and lean, with greying hair that made him appear to be in his mid-fifties. With a broad forehead, piercing eyes, a sharp nose and thin lips, he was above average looking. They had been attending a day-long awards function wherein as managing director of his FMCG company, after receiving an award, Ravi had made a speech. This was followed by a presentation on how he had taken his company to its current stature in the last five years. At the tea break, introduced by common associates, she had met and congratulated Ravi Kurien, interacting with other senior officials of his company, knowing some of them. She worked with a rival organisation, as GM-marketing, and was well known in social circles.

"Your company has done very well for the few years you've been around, as compared to ours," she said appreciatively to Ravi, after being introduced.

"Thank you!" he replied beaming. "Coming from you, I'm indeed flattered."

"My intention was not to flatter you," she laughed. "I sincerely meant it."

"Why don't you join us, Priya?" one of Ravi's senior executives blurted, as if out of the blue, looking her in the eye. Then turning towards Ravi, as though seeking his opinion, he asked: "Wouldn't it be great?"

Priya looked shocked, embarrassed, the expressions flitting across her face involuntarily. She had gone overboard with her praise, she realised. She had only intended to be polite, not show undue interest in his company. Everyone in the small group looked from Ravi to her and then back to Ravi.

"I work for your competitor, you know!" Priya grinned awkwardly.

"Of course, we know that Priya," Ravi Kurien replied grinning, "Don't you think we keep track of our competition? I also propose you join us. You won't regret it."

Priya mentally writhed at his intense, mirthful gaze, but decided not to respond. The situation could only get worse she knew. She just smiled back, excusing herself to go and get another cup of tea.

She sat through the meeting that lasted another two hours,

repeatedly going through the events of the tea break. She should have been more formal in her interactions with Ravi Kurien, she reproached herself. People in the industry would be talking about this incident, twisting the story beyond recognition.

That evening, dinner plate in hand, in front of the muted television, Priya had relayed this incident to her husband, Shekhar. He had had his dinner of penne pasta at the dining table, along with their only child, Amit, who was eight years, earlier. Priya often got late returning from work, sometimes after 9pm. The drive home from work in the outskirts of Chennai, took an hour to two, in the heavy traffic. Priya insisted Amit have his dinner by 8.30pm, instructing the cook to serve both father and son by then. After dinner, Amit waited up for his mother's return, spent time with her telling her of his day, before she tucked him into bed, reading to him till he fell asleep. This ritual had been completed that evening before Priya broached the topic of her meeting Ravi Kurien with Shekhar. Listening to her story patiently, Shekhar suggested she think it over, weighing the situation judiciously.

"What is there to think about, Shekhar, I'm quite happy with my current job," she said. "They treat me well, and the job is fulfilling."

"Coming to think of it, Priya," he replied thoughtfully, "You have held your current position of GM-marketing for the last three years. There is no way you are going to move up to being vice president here anytime shortly, and you're already thirty-seven years. If these people offer you a meatier role and a bigger compensation, why not consider it?"

Shekhar's words remained with Priya, hovering in her mind for the next few days. There was truth in them, she thought. Though being a top-ranking alumna of premier institutions and a smart, conscientious worker, she had not been ambitious from the start. Shekhar – chief executive now, at a multi-national company, had guided the course of her career since they had met, with his foresight. Older than her by twelve years, he had been her boss in her first job after business school. She still remembered her crush on him, going about him all starry-eyed. It was his wittiness that she had fallen in love with. Shekhar was tall, athletic and had an intelligent-looking face. His rimless glasses added to the intellectual look. The years had not changed him much, except that his now salt and pepper hair enhanced his distinguished look. Priya, however, had changed a lot since they first met. She now looked more mature than she did then. Her plump oval face with the wide eyes and waist-length hair had been replaced by a lean face with sharp eyes and shoulder length hair. The changes added up to her current sophisticated and corporate look.

Priya, bracing herself for the challenges she envisioned in the new job, after detailed discussions with Shekhar, agreed it was time to move on. She abhorred change, was apprehensive to realign to a new culture and environment, and of striking new equations and relationships. Though comfortable in her current position, she agreed she could not turn down a better role in a prestigious organisation. Moreover, Ravi Kurien's company was growing so fast, hers would certainly be a challenging role. She called Venkat, the HR head I had a good rapport with, who then routed her to me. I was the executive search consultant who had clenched the exclusive mandate on this head of marketing role, and we had already shortlisted a few candidates.

At the formal assessment meeting, I realised Priya was indeed the most suitable candidate so far. I put her onto the particular division's chief executive that this position would report to. They had a preliminary discussion after which I intimated Priya of the meeting with the board of directors at their office shortly. I forwarded an email from Venkat on behalf of the HR department for the formal final meeting a month later at a hotel. In the course of our interactions, Priya and I struck a friendship that lasts even today.

It was shortly after 7.30pm, that Priya arrived at Ravi Kurien's office building, for the meeting with the board of directors scheduled for 8.00pm. There was no one at the reception area on the first floor, except for a security guard. She did not need to give him her antecedents. He had already been briefed of her expected arrival. Having reached early, she sat for a while on one of the grey sofas in the reception area, glad for the time to compose herself. She had rushed straight from the office. Picking up a magazine from the tinted-brown glass table in front, she flipped the pages distractedly. Then, sharp at 7.50pm, she got up from her seat. Escorted by the security staff, she walked past a hall with numerous workstations, each comprising a flat-screen computer and a black telephone, on her way to take the lift to the fifth floor. All the stations were vacant, as the staff had already left for the day. The lift did not stop at any floor but the fifth, offices on the other floors all vacant by now. Opening the lift door, she stepped directly on to a dimly lit lounge.

Priya took a deep breath, which she held to a count of six and then let out. Looking around her, she noticed the hall was furnished with a number of black-leather single or triple-seat sofas, with glass centre-tables. Several men in business suits were seated in clusters. The walls displayed wood-framed photographs of a wide array of company events. At the other end of the hall, was the bar counter, with black-seat stools lining its front. Three uniformed-waiters stood behind. Having just concluded their board meeting, Priya supposed, the directors and senior employees were lounging with drinks. Seeing her walk in, most of them looked up. She felt their glances in spite of looking straight ahead. Wearing an aqua-blue and white printed georgette *saree*, being the only woman there, their curiosity at her entry was natural. She squashed the unease, looking to find a known face, telling herself she was here on business, so how did it matter that there were no other women.

A middle-aged man walked up to her, offering her his hand to shake.

"It's good to see you, Priya!" he said.

"Good to see you too, Mr Mathur!" she replied, shaking his hand firmly.

Priya was relieved at meeting someone she knew. Atul Mathur was the chief executive with whom she had met for preliminary discussions. He was of medium height and built, with a receding crop of greying hair and curious eyes. His warm smile made her relax somewhat.

"Please take a seat," Atul said. "I'll get you a drink. What would you like?"

"Any fresh-juice would be fine," she replied.

"Now come on, you can't have only juice," he grimaced. "We

have some good Scotch, perhaps you'd like some. How would you like it?"

In a room full of strange men, awkward from it, also since she was here for an informal interview of sorts, Priya wondered if she should take alcohol. She did have an occasional drink, but drinking with strangers was not her style. She was about to decline the offer of the Scotch when it struck her that this might just be a test of her socialising and public relations skills. She decided to play along.

"Ok, I'll have it on the rocks then, please," she replied with determination, to show Atul she could just as easily be one of the men, as he walked to the bar.

A waiter came over to where she was seated. He placed on a coaster on the table, a cut-glass tumbler of whisky on ice-cubes. Stirring it slowly, she took a sip. Then she looked around for Atul, but he had disappeared, leaving her again by herself. She closed her eyes briefly, when she opened them, to her surprise, she saw Ravi Kurien, the MD, bending to her level. Embarrassed, she stood up. He looked amused. She recognised his grin, from the FICCI meeting, which in time she would consider his talisman. He looked freshly shaven, wore a black business suit with a red tie. Like him, the others in the room were all formally dressed, for the meeting that had just concluded.

"When you are bored, you can join me on the balcony just outside," Ravi said, with a casual friendly wink.

Still gathering her wits about her, after the embarrassment of his catching her with her eyes shut, she nodded in response. He then walked out into the balcony, which opened up from the bar side of the lounge.

Priya sat down, took a sip of her drink. The sharp sting in her mouth and throat seemed to bolster her sagging confidence. She wondered what the purpose of calling her here was. If this was a test of her networking skills before her final interview, as she assumed, sitting alone was not going to make a good impression. Slowly she made a conscious effort to make eye contact with people seated nearby, smiling. Why did she get the feeling of being watched on a close-circuit-television camera? She wondered.

Priya got up, leaving her drink halfway. Feeling more self-assured than when she had arrived, she walked graciously across the hall. Stepping into the large balcony, she found she was facing Ravi. He was seated on a wrought iron chair, around a table with two other men. He saw her.

"Come, come here," he waived. "I knew you would get bored in there."

Walking over to his table, Priya noticed in the dim lighting, there were three other tables in the balcony, similar to the one Ravi sat at, unoccupied.

"Those men inside are so engrossed in their drinks, that even a beautiful lady like you could not break their concentration," Ravi said, grinning at Priya. Then, as a waiter pulled out a chair for her, he said: "Come sit here, Priya."

"Thank you," she replied, sitting down. "I am your guest, and everyone's figured that by now, so perhaps they are waiting for you to introduce me."

Ravi nodded smiling.

"Gentlemen, let me introduce Priya," he said, as the other two men nodded at her. "We are considering on using her skills and experience, to head the marketing function, for one of our larger divisions. And Priya meet my close friend Satish Chawla. He's an industrialist. And this is Suresh Babu, an IG of Police."

Priya nodded at each man, smiling politely.

"Priya, what will you have to drink?" Ravi asked, turning to her.

"Well … I left my unfinished drink inside on the table," she replied.

"Get madam's drink here, will you?" Ravi said, waiving to one of the waiters hovering nearby, waiting for his instructions.

The waiter returned with Priya's glass, placed it in front of her. In the course of the evening, they were served a series of delectable vegetarian snacks and succulent meats. The conversation ranged from politics, industry, to national and international happenings. Priya was able to hold her own, also when either or all the three men were on different sides of the discussion.

"You are rather slow with your drink, Priya," Ravi said, when just about to ask the waiter for a refill for himself.

 Shuvashree Chowdhury

Priya merely nodded, smiling, choosing not to respond. She realised it was not going to be possible to sit much longer with one drink, definitely not for the rest of the evening. So she drained her glass in one last swig.

The waiter promptly returned with a fresh glass of Scotch on the rocks for her. Priya mentally noted to eat well, punctuating every sip of her drink with a bite or two of food. She was not a habitual drinker, definitely not used to downing Scotch on the rocks. The last thing she needed was to become tipsy and lose control. After all, her drinking now was to impress her prospective employers, not to prove how footloose and fancy-free she could get after a few drinks. This interaction could possibly seal her fate on the prospective position. She knew she was under observation, for whether she could swim through the evening at ease. Priya, in due course, was introduced to other board members. Each one came out to the balcony in turns – to exchange pleasantries with Ravi, or so it seemed to her. She shook hands with them and made polite conversation, ensuring her smiling, easy charm and grace, were in place all through the evening.

Priya got up to use the washroom. On her way, she came across Atul, the chief executive, who, thinking she was leaving, asked her: "Can I drop you home?"

"Thanks Atul, I've got my car here," she replied with a smile. "Though, I'm not leaving yet."

She could not help wondering how a woman was expected to be bold, independent, fit into a man's world, yet have to rely on a man to drop her back home. It was very late already, but Priya was finding it difficult to leave before anyone else, especially Ravi, did. Her visit to the washroom was a run-up to her escape. Luckily, when she returned to the table, Ravi and the others were standing and ready to leave. Priya shook hands with the three men and said good night. She drove back home relieved, having pulled off the perfect socialite act. In fact, she had been a shy, introverted, reserved child. At thirty-seven years, the world saw her as a confident, extroverted woman, with excellent communication skills, which in reality came to her at the cost of much internal unease.

The morning after, Priya awoke to a text-message from one

of the men in Ravi's company she had met the night before. She recalled giving him her business card, since he had asked for it. It was a lengthy message, wishing her good morning, as well as a good day, along with poetic form. She ignored it as a one-off group forwarded message. The next afternoon at work, she got a call. It was Ravi Kurien himself.

"Hi Priya, how about we meet at my club this evening," he said without prelude. "Maybe we could go to the Taj for dinner, if you prefer, or there is this Italian restaurant close to my office, the food is awesome."

Priya was astounded. She had not considered meeting him socially, having met him at his office premises last evening, so how did the venue matter? But she knew there was no way she could turn down his invitation, without turning down the job opportunity completely. She had to play smart, she decided.

"How about we meet at your club?" she replied. "At 7pm."

It would be a safer place to meet than at a hotel, she thought, and socially more apt a place to meet a prospective employer.

"Alright, see you at 7pm at the Gymkhana club then. We'll go to dinner thereafter at the Taj Coromandel," he insisted. "It's pretty close from the club."

"We'll see about that," Priya replied cheerily, mentally on her guard.

That evening, Priya met Ravi Kurien at the Gymkhana club's front lounge. Dressed in a half-sleeved, collared black T-shirt with blue-jeans, he looked different as compared to the two times that she had seen him in business suits. After his regular workout at the gym and a game of squash, he looked fresh and relaxed. His hair was damp, brushed back and slickly set around his face that was aglow after the exercise. Priya was dressed in an olive green boat-neck viscose top, over a pair of dark blue jeans. Ravi appraised her appreciatively before he led the way to the bar, to the left of the lounge.

Inside, they took a window seat to the right, overlooking the lawn. They were lucky, as it got vacated just as they entered. A waiter walked up to their table promptly, on recognising Ravi.

"Should I get your regular drink, Sir?" he asked. After Ravi nodded, he turned to Priya and asked: "And for you, ma'am?"

                    Shuvashree Chowdhury

"I'll just have a fresh fruit juice, please," she replied.

"Now don't be a spoilsport Priya," Ravi interrupted briskly. Then, in an assertive tone, he added: "Perhaps you'd like some vodka with orange juice?"

Priya asked for a gin with lime cordial instead, feeling compelled to have an alcoholic drink, but standing her ground all the same. As the waiter retreated, Priya looked about her. It was a rustic place, with dim-lighting and minimalist décor. A Friday evening, there were a number of couples and families. Most were looking at the large-screen television, high up above the bar counter where a cricket match was in progress. The television set was muted, the buzzing sound of conversation, clinking glasses, cutlery on crockery, was clearly audible.

The bar did not permit smoking, so Ravi, stepping outside for a smoke in the lawn, asked her to join him. She followed, but a non-smoker, she did not accept a cigarette when he offered her one. They sat at a table outside, and the conversation moved to their respective families and interests. A waiter brought over their glasses, of Ravi's Scotch and soda, her gin and lime cordial, and a platter of mixed kebabs from their table inside the bar. Priya's face shone with pride as she told Ravi about her son, Amit, and husband, Shekhar. Ravi perfunctorily told her of his wife, Anu, who had been his classmate at engineering college and the mother of their now college-going son. Ravi finished his cigarette, then briskly auto-dialled a number from his phone. To Priya's surprise, it was the Taj Coromandel, as she figured from his conversation with the manager of a restaurant there, checking if he would reserve a table for them. It was clear the manager knew Ravi well as a regular guest, making her discomfort in accompanying him sturdier.

Priya was piqued that Ravi did not find the need to seek her consent on the dinner reservation, assuming she would just go along. She remained silent but determined that she wasn't going. Ravi hung-up, a table reservation made for half an hour from now, at 9pm. After finishing their drinks, Ravi's two pegs of Scotch and her single gin, and part of the plate of chicken kebabs, they rose to leave. Ravi briskly signed the check the waiter brought, and then waving to a group of people at an adjacent table, he walked to the lounge through which they would exit. Priya followed him. On seeing Ravi, the valet dashed off and returned with his white Mercedes car, parking it on the porch right in front of the gate. The valet got off and handed Ravi the key who lithely slid in behind the wheel.

"Come on, let's go, Priya," Ravi said, in an urgent tone.

Priya was on the phone then, talking to her husband, Shekhar. She signalled to Ravi with her hand to wait a minute. After a few more brief sentences into the phone, as Ravi watched her, with the ignition and AC on, she hung up.

"Ravi, I'm so sorry to tell you ..." she said haltingly, "I'm unable to come with you now. Something really urgent has come up."

"Now c'mon, Priya, what is so urgent that you cannot have dinner and go," Ravi replied impatiently.

After a dramatic pause, conjuring up an apologetic face, Priya replied in a single breath. "It's my son, Ravi. He is suddenly very unwell. An asthmatic attack presumably. My husband says he is crying ... wants his mommy ... he is only eight you see ... I need to rush home immediately."

Ravi looked at her suspiciously, trying to hide his disappointment.

"I'm so sorry Ravi, I'm sure you understand. I'll catch up with you shortly, I promise, I will," she added, hurriedly.

Ravi did not reply, but involuntarily the muscles of his face tautened, his jaw line clenched at the rejection. Briskly composing himself, he tauntingly gave her a menacing look. Then revving the accelerator of his car, he dashed off abruptly.

Still standing on the porch, in relief, Priya called her husband, Shekhar.

"Thank God, he's gone," she blurted into the phone, still gasping from the breathless explanations to Ravi.

Shekhar had been watching a movie with their son, who was hale and hearty, munching out of a bowl of popcorn, when she had last called him.

"Come home now, Priya, we'll talk," he said distractedly from watching the movie, "I'll get Amit into bed by then. You can kiss him goodnight later."

            Shuvashree Chowdhury

"Okay, you do that," she muttered, walking to her car. "I'm just leaving."

She had consciously self-parked her car, rather than give it to the valet, so as to have full control of her departure, not knowing how the evening would go. As she walked amidst the line of cars towards hers, a shiver ran down her spine. It was obviously not from the October Chennai weather, so it had to be the indignation of the evening.

As she slid behind the wheel, opening the door of her grey Maruti Swift to the lavender scent of the car freshener, she felt a sense of refuge. As she reversed the car, drove to the exit, the stereo playing her favourite fusion music, Priya could not help comparing the car's manoeuvring to that required in handling male attitudes and their brittle egos. The business world, at times, seemed to her like a jungle abounding in dangerous wolf-men, the way out of which was to duck and dodge, till the wolves disappeared, rather than go underground. It was pointless getting into a confrontation with them, perking their defences, aggression even, to finally be devoured by way of being forced to quit the career race or relegated to the last rungs of the corporate ladder. She was still going to contend for the position in Ravi Kurien's company, Priya firmly decided, as she drove in through the iron gate of her apartment complex.

In fact, now she was going to take on this position as a challenge. Having come so far in her career after much struggle, she owed it to herself to prove she could do better than merely survive in a man's world. Priya decided, on her way up in the elevator to her apartment, she would not allow the likes of Ravi to intimidate her, like when she was younger. She had the experience and the relevant skills for this position, she was confident. She would have to make it clear that though she wanted this position, she would not be in a compromising position in lieu of it. After narrating about her evening to Shekhar, starting with the telephone call from Ravi in the afternoon, Priya felt ready to take on any number of Ravi Kuriens who stood in the way of her and this position she sought. In the coming days, Priya had to turn down invitations and overtures from other directors of Ravi's company. They had clearly misread her charming disposition and company, amidst them, that evening over drinks at their office lounge.

One called seeking to meet her for coffee or a drink, and another asked her out to dinner. One of them called her merely to have a chat. Though irritating, Priya found the situation hilarious, flattering even. 'Boys will be boys,' she thought, whatever their age. These men, mostly over fifty, were enthused as of a new toy, by the thought of a chase. The fact that she was strikingly beautiful, in addition to the candour with which she interacted with them, had been the bait. Priya played along politely, turning down their advances tactfully, so as not to antagonize them. Why would they not look beyond a woman's beauty and respect her for her capabilities, she thought? Ironically, this was the case with other women too who felt a good-looking woman had all the advantages, little understanding what she has to bear to survive with dignity in a man's world. With premier institute engineering and MBA degrees, an impressive past work-record, Priya was very good at her job.

Just because she fit into a man's world with ease when required, would have a drink or two, as well as participate effectively in their conversations, didn't mean she would go to any lengths to get a job. In fact, her socialising and networking skills gave her an edge at her job. Priya knew by now that being attractive could be more of a nuisance at work than help. It came in the way of being assessed on merit and capability. In the past, male bosses had taken offence to being turned down as personal rejection, giving her a harrowing time thereafter. Worse still was the attitude of women who attributed her successes to being easily 'available' to men. In fact, ironically, all her life since her first job, she had to work much harder than most to be taken seriously. Priya had met Shekhar, her husband, at her first job. As her boss, he had valued her work, sincerity and efforts. This, in turn, brought on her unwavering respect, love and faith in him till date. He had aided her struggle up the career ladder through his mentoring and support. He knew how in her bid to be taken seriously, Priya, at times, came across as aggressive to her peers as well as seniors. But under that tough, businesslike exterior, the woman he knew well and loved was a warm and kind soul.

     Shuvashree Chowdhury

After Priya declined Ravi's dinner invite the evening at the Gymkhana club, he did not call her again. She realised this might be the end to her prospects of working in his company. Should she let it slip, or should she try and salvage the situation? After much deliberation along with Shekhar, Priya called him.

"Hi Ravi, this is Priya," she said cheerily, and then in an even tone added, "I'm calling to apologise for that night, I had to turn down dinner with you."

"Hmmm … that's all right," he grunted in response, sulkily.

"By the way, I've been in touch with Venkat, as you suggested," she said, ignoring his sullen response, "about the marketing role."

"Ah! That's great," he replied, his tone still sullen.

How like children men can act in dealing with rejection, she thought, smiling. She had to fix her equation with him, put in on the right track from the start or it would be difficult in handling, going ahead.

"I want to learn how to play squash, Ravi," she blurted. "It keeps you so fit, I've noticed. Would you mind teaching me?"

"Sure, why not," he replied, a lilt in his voice, just as she had expected. "You could come over to the club in the evening sometime, how about tomorrow?"

Priya met Ravi in the squash room at the club the next evening, dressed in a sweatshirt, track pants and sneakers. Ravi had already signed her in the visitors register at the entrance. There were a few young boys around, drenched in sweat from their practice. Ravi had an extra racquet and balls ready for her. Priya attempted initial shots the way he showed her, feeling a little self-conscious, at the tiny balls bouncing around wildly beyond her control. Luckily, she was agile, since she worked out at a gym and swam sometimes, so got the hang of it soon.

"It's enough for the first day," Ravi said abruptly after a while, by which time Priya was panting and perspiring profusely. "Let's not overdo it."

Priya stopped the ball that bounced back towards her with her racquet, after she struck it, and nodded, picking up a bottle of water and taking a swig.

"Come, let's have a drink now," Ravi smiled, "I'll see you at the bar after a quick shower."

Priya nodded. Ravi had already played his share for the day, in the way of exercise, before her arrival. They proceeded to the respective changing rooms.

Priya walked into the bar in a light pink T-shirt, accentuating her flushed face, teamed with a pair of light blue jeans. Her hair was damp from the shower, needing a few more blows from the hairdryer that she had curtailed since she would be late. Ravi was already at a table, a glass in hand. He waved to her, noticing her step in. He ordered club sandwiches to a waiter standing alongside, after looking at her questioningly, and she nodded in assent before sitting.

"Priya, I was just thinking," Ravi said in an urgent tone, after the waiter left, without meeting her eye. "Maybe you could come to my farmhouse on the East Coast road for a weekend. I have a good squash court there. You could master the game in two days. When you are back, you will be able to play by yourself." Then, smiling conspiratorially, he added, "Perhaps we'll have a corporate membership worked out for you by then, once you've joined us as head of marketing."

Priya looked shocked, then composing herself since he was studying her expression, she said smiling: "That would be really nice, Ravi, but that's quite an improbable idea, don't you think?"

"But why, what's the improbability?" he replied with a quizzical look.

"We are both married, Ravi ..." Priya said, grinning mischievously in an attempt to make light the situation, "And unluckily to other people."

Ravi burst out laughing, and then composing himself, still smiling said: "Ah! That indeed is a problem, isn't it? When did that ever stop anybody from taking a holiday? Marriages are meant to come back home to, aren't they?"

He was laughing, Priya thought relieved. She had to somehow maintain this humorous-thread in their conversation for the rest of the evening and thereafter.

"I'm as yet to look outside of my marriage for a vacation partner, Ravi," she said, grinning at him. "If someday I do, you will be topmost on my list, I promise."

Ravi roared with laughter, and through it, he blurted,

     Shuvashree Chowdhury

"Sure … my friend, sure. I quite like your sense of humour."

Priya, watching him intently, knew she had got her message across, luckily keeping his ego intact this time. After that evening, Ravi was no more a problem. With him taken care of, Priya was able to deal with the rest of the directors.

"You are like an elder brother to me," she told one of the directors, after his second invitation to coffee. "I'm so lucky to have found one in you."

She followed this by asking him for professional advice. In this way, tactfully, Priya soon befriended the other directors, too. With her easy-going manner and sincere compliments, it was not difficult. As for the men, having tried their luck in wooing her, they gave up, accepting her as a friend, as one of them.

* * *

"Priya, it's your turn now for the meeting," Venkat announced, breaking her reverie, "Please come with me."

"Yes, yes," she replied, standing, then following him to the door.

She briskly ran her fingers through her hair, ensuring it was in place. As she walked with Venkat, she ran her hand over her *saree's* front pleats to ensure they were in place. On entering the conference room, she viewed the semi-circular seating. The eight directors, all of whom she had previously met, were seated behind the horseshoe shaped table. In front of each one was a glass and a bottle of mineral water. To the open end of the horseshoe was a vacant chair.

"Good evening, Priya," Ravi said cheerily, on seeing her.

"Thank you, Ravi," she replied in a formal tone, and then with a quick glance around, she added, "Good evening, everybody."

"Perhaps you would like to individually meet everyone, first," Ravi said authoritatively, leaving no doubt as to who was the boss here.

Priya nodded, walked over to the first man seated at the end of the table.

"Hello! I'm Priya Sen," she said smiling, offering him her hand to shake.

"Nice to meet you again, Priya," the man who she had made her elder brother replied, shaking her hand warmly. "I'm Gautam Sinha."

She nodded, moved to the next person repeating "Hello! I'm Priya Sen."

Again the man introduced himself, shook her hand. Then she moved to the next, and thus, in similar fashion, Priya met everyone in the room individually.

"Please take your seat, Priya," Ravi said, on completion of the introduction round. Then, after she was seated, he continued: "Could you tell us more about yourself, Priya, briefly take us through your work experiences so far."

She nodded. Then, after a few seconds to compose her thoughts, she spoke:

"I am a marketing professional with an engineering degree followed by an MBA – specialisation in Marketing," she started, and then recounted her work experiences starting with the last, up to her first job after campus recruitment.

"Perhaps you'd like to tell us a little about your family background," Ravi prodded, just as she finished talking of her work.

"I'm a Bengali, who moved to Chennai after my marriage to a Tamilian man," Priya said promptly, as if on cue, "It's been over ten years that I'm in Chennai now. My husband is the chief executive of a manufacturing company and we have a son. My parents are retired professors and live in Calcutta. I have a brother who lives in the US."

"Alright Priya, now that we've been formally introduced to you, our new head of marketing ... Congratulations! Welcome to the team," Ravi announced theatrically, even as Priya stared at him, trying to comprehend his words.

This was hardly the kind of interview she had in mind, while she waited. She had imagined a panel discussion or something more technical, formal perhaps. Moreover, what were the other men in the adjacent room waiting for?

"Priya, I'm certain you will add value to your role in our organisation, as well as to your own career and life," Ravi continued, in the face of her silence. "This was only a formal

     Shuvashree Chowdhury

meeting with the board of directors. We had already decided on taking you. Moreover, we want you to select your second-in-line. The men waiting in the adjacent room are shortlisted for the position of the General Manager—Marketing. We would like you to join us in selecting a suitable candidate."

The situation having sunk in by now, Priya was thrilled, she had climbed another rung. She knew the compensation would be negotiable, and she had me to handle that, so she need not worry. Each of the directors came up to her and congratulated her warmly. It is still a man's world, Priya thought wryly, going by the events leading up to now. A woman has to fit into their world, assert to make her presence felt. However, if a woman stands strong, while maintaining her femininity, the world truly is her stage. She can take the bows, with men and women respecting her for her skills and intelligence, in addition to her beauty.

What Priya wanted to do foremost was call her husband, Shekhar, to give him the good news. After all, it was his initiation and unending support that had got her to this stage.

21. *The Price of Success*

I rushed outside to the waiting taxi. It was 8am. It had been assigned by my office, to drive me to a place two hours from Chennai on the Trichy highway. I was to attend the launch-ceremony of an ultramodern textile factory there at 10am. It belonged to a client company. They wanted me, as their executive search consultant, along with other patrons, to witness this progressive stride. As I slid into the back seat of the white Indica car, I notified the driver I did not know the exact location. That once we got to the Trichy highway, we would have to ask for directions elaborated on the invitation card. As the taxi pulled out of my street, I looked back up at the balcony. My husband was standing there as I had expected. He came out to wave me goodbye the days I left early or was going out of town on work, which was often. I waived to him, a hand outside the window, swathed in a smug sense of emotional security.

Once the taxi hit the main road, I settled back on the seat, and asked the driver to turn up the stereo. Through the maze of mounting office hour traffic, once we left the city, the view that flanked the broad highway was picturesque. The expanse of greenery ended at the foot of low hills in the distance. At places, I caught glimpses of the shimmering sea, at others narrow streams going out to meet the Bay of Bengal. My eyes glued to the scenery, listening to old Hindi film songs of the 1970s, it was a very enchanting drive that made me very nostalgic. I handed over the invitation card to the driver for the address to our destination. He stopped the car, locked it from the outside out of concern for my safety, and got out to take directions. My office used his company's fleet of cars for all employee travel and they, in turn, reciprocated, by duly valuing the patronage, by taking care of us.

After a few stops, wherein the driver asked for directions from local shopkeepers, as I had suggested, we finally drove up to the imposing iron-gate of the factory premises. It was well

Shuvashree Chowdhury

past 10.30am, and I had spent the past half hour despairing on the delay. It was caused in addition to the heavy traffic, by our inability to find the place. After registering at the security post, we drove in through the gate, over the cobbled road, amidst lush green fields. There was a colossal tarpaulin cast in front of the lawn overlooking the huge main factory building, separated by a metal road. Approaching there, briskly retrieving my compact-case, I brushed the puff over my face, tidied my hair, and then touched-up my lipstick. The driver pulled up on the road between the factory and the tarpaulin-covered area. I got off the car amidst a sea of business-suit clad men and women, of varied nationalities – going by the skin colours.

Stepping under the festive-looking tarpaulin, I looked around and noticed that refreshments were served on self-service tables to one side. A number of people had a cup and saucer in either hand. Whether or not they had a cup to their lips, they had a formal smile. Initially planning on wearing a business suit, I had draped an off-white chiffon *saree*, with printed tender green and yellow twines, with a yellow blouse. To my surprise, I was one of only three or four women clad in a *saree* among a few hundred people. I helped myself to a cup of coffee, smiling and nodding politely at those who looked my way, in the hope of opening a conversation, preferably with someone from the host company. In the crowd, I had not yet found anyone I had interacted with earlier, in my short stint as their executive search consultant.

"You look lost in spite of that dazzling smile you're wearing," a baritone voice said in my ear from behind, its familiarity freezing my smile.

I involuntarily took a step forward, before turning around. My gaze first rested on the broad chest and then the shoulders, in a white shirt and a matte-red tie, under the lapels of an azure-grey suit. I then let my gaze move up to notice the familiar childlike grin, way above my head – due to his imposing height. Then, as I saw the brown eyes twinkling in amusement, recognition dawned. I almost dropped my coffee cup in shock. It was the same boyishly handsome face, with the small nose, wide mouth and broad forehead under a short, smart crop of thick black hair. I stared at him in disbelief. What was he, Tushar Bhatia, doing here? It must be more than a decade ago that I had last seen him. The memory of that was fudged now, but conversely, our first meeting and many a subsequent one, were as vivid as though of the day before.

* * *

The clock said 7pm. Another working day as airport reservations and ticketing in-charge of a reputed airline was over. My office was adjacent to the Calcutta airport arrival terminal. I checked on the status of the flights for the evening, ensuring all my night-shift staff was logged on to their headsets, the telephone calls flowing smoothly on the computerised Alcatel monitor system.

As I was about to step outside into the cool November evening, one of the staff called aloud: "Ma'am, there's a call for you."

"Please take the message, Vishal," I replied, briskly turning around. "It must be for seat confirmation. I'm going crazy with this Diwali rush."

"It's a frequent flyer, Mr Bhatia. He insists on talking only to you." Vishal replied urgently, a finger on the silent button of his phone-box. "He says it's very urgent and he must talk to you right now."

I returned to my workstation and slipped on my headphone, quickly logging in to enable me to take the call.

"How may I help you, Sir?" I said into the phone.

"Am I talking to the reservations manager?" the authoritative voice at the other end enquired in a hurried tone, but before I could reply, he continued breathlessly. "You've got to help me. I'm a frequent flyer, my name is Tushar Bhatia. I had a time-limit booking for the Mumbai flight, departing at 8.10pm. It must have got cancelled by now. But I have to get to Mumbai this evening, somehow. I am on my way to the airport, stuck in traffic. Please keep my ticket ready, I will come and pay for it."

"That will not be possible, Mr Bhatia, I'm really sorry." I replied politely, but firmly. "That flight will be boarding very shortly."

"But you have to help me," he pleaded "You could keep the boarding card ready so as not to waste time, I will come and pay. I'm a very frequent flyer. You can do this much."

     Shuvashree Chowdhury

"I wish I could have helped you. But that won't be possible, Mr Bhatia. I'm sorry," I reiterated. "I cannot risk delaying the flight, in case you don't make it on time."

"I know that you will," he blurted arrogantly, then hung up. "See you."

I took a few seconds to act. He was right, as a customer services manager I would at least give helping him my best shot. I asked a staff to print his ticket, with payment mode as cash, then called the backup office to request them to check him in, print his boarding card.

"I'm not going to take a delay," the duty manager cribbed, when I requested him, telling him the circumstance, "It's all at your risk."

"Don't worry," I said in a placating tone. "I won't delay the flight. I will inform you in time to off-load Mr Bhatia if required, or send his ticket coupon on time."

I called my mother to inform her I would be late in reaching home. As I would have to wait till this particular passenger was onboard the flight or ensure he was offloaded since he had been checked in.

I had just hung up, when someone rushed into the office. In an authoritarian tone, he hurriedly announced: "Hi, I'm Tushar Bhatia."

I looked up in the direction of the rich baritone, to find a youthful face, incongruous to the voice and tone of its owner. Over the phone, I had assumed the owner of the commanding voice to be a man in his fifties, but in person, he looked below thirty. Then, as he looked at me with an expression, as if almost about to break into a grin, I recognised him as the man I had encountered a few times. I comprehended with much amusement, that his almost missing his flight, calling me so urgently, might all be a ploy to get my attention, as he had tried to a few times before. This was since he had seen me one morning, very early, when I was waiting at Mumbai Airport to take a return flight to Calcutta.

Tushar, his name that I just learnt, had been strolling where I was seated in the departure terminal, after security check. It was 5am, very early after a late night out with friends at Colaba, subsequent to a daylong training session. But I did not miss his imposing height, at over six feet two inches, broad athletic frame in a royal blue shirt, beige trousers with a yellow tie. Soon my flight had been announced. I moved in queue towards the departure gate on the ground floor, noticing him a few heads ahead, from his blue shirt and beige trousers, his thick black well-styled hair. I had dressed well in spite of the early hour, in a light pink Lycra top and fitting blue jeans, my long hair lose to my waist. On my face, I wore eyeliner and lipstick, from sheer habit borne out of grooming regulations since joining the airline three years back. On the flight, Tushar passed my seat at a rear side window, on his way to the washroom, twice. I noticed him looking at me, so I looked back up at him. Then, at the arrival lounge, picking up his suit-hanger bag from the conveyor belt, he walked past me very close, ensuring I noticed him yet again.

After that, it was a month ago, when our paths had crossed again. It was at the boarding gate, for the same flight to Mumbai he wished to take this evening. In order to fill in for staff shortage, I had been collecting boarding card stubs at the commencement of the aerobridge. When a boarding card was suddenly shoved right under my face, instead of handed at waist level, as is usual. I looked up to see who the perpetrator of this defiant act was. To my bewilderment, it was the tall man who I had taken notice of, when he travelled with me to Calcutta from Mumbai. I took his boarding card, pretending not to notice him, perfunctorily returning his portion. But not before I caught him glance at the nametag I was wearing below my left shoulder and register my name to mind. This encounter had been at such proximity that I had also recorded his boyish face with the intense brown eyes to memory.

Vishal, the staff who had taken his call first, looked at me on Tushar's announcing his arrival. I nodded, signalling him to proffer the ready ticket to Tushar, who promptly opened it, read the fare, and then paid for it in cash.

"Thank you so much!" Tushar said, looking at me over Vishal's head.

"You're welcome," I smiled. "But you will have to rush to collect your boarding card, or the flight may still go without you, in spite of the ticket."

                    Shuvashree Chowdhury

"That's why you're coming with me," he grinned, "Till I get on that flight."

I looked at him in surprise; the amused look was more pronounced than ever. He was right, if I accompanied him, he would see through the check-in and security check faster, since the counters had already closed. Moreover, I would be safe in ensuring there was no delay to the flight, due to my request, if he boarded on time. We strode across the long length of the airport terminal in silence, to the check-in counters at the extreme end.

"I owe you a treat, for all your help," Tushar said, turning to me gratefully, after he was handed his boarding card.

"Thank you! I was just doing my job," I replied.

"Your job doesn't keep you so late, does it?" he said, and then added persuasively, "May I buy you coffee, at least."

"Perhaps some time," I smiled. "Now let's get you through security check and we can have coffee at the lounge after that, upstairs, while you wait to board."

He nodded thankfully, smiling. We briskly strode across the hall. After security check, we took the escalator to the Oberoi lounge. The staff there knew me well, so quickly served us coffee and a plate of cookies, I would sign for later.

"So, what brings you to Calcutta?" I asked after a few sips of our coffee silently. "You're not from here I presume."

"I look after east India, and neighbouring country sales for a Pune based MNC," he replied. "I come almost every week."

"So do you do this a lot? I mean, imagine the airline is yours?" I smiled. "I risked my job, my reputation at the least, to get you on this flight out of here."

"Well, I do tend to get late for flights a lot," he admitted, laughing, and then taking another brisk sip of his coffee, he said, "Something always comes up, or meetings get extended. Though I can stay the night where I am, travel the next morning, like I could have this time too."

I looked him curiously in the eye. There was a mischievous twinkle in them. I was sure he had orchestrated this evening's circumstances to meet me. Learning my name from my nametag at our previous encounter, in addition to knowing the airline I worked for, it was easy. A frequent flyer, he knew its functioning well, to design this meeting so artfully. I fought to control a smile.

A staff rushed into the lounge, and looking at Tushar, announced: "Sir, you will have to board right away. You're the last passenger." Then turning to me, he added: "Luckily someone saw you accompany him here, so I could find Mr Bhatia. The last and final call was made repeatedly. We were about to offload him."

We hurriedly rose, rushed down the corridor to the aerobridge gate in silence. Tushar abruptly thrust his boarding card into my hand, "Scribble your mobile number on the stub, please," he pleaded.

After I unquestioningly obliged, he briskly hugged me, then handing over the other half of his boarding card to the staff at the gate, rushed to the aircraft.

Tushar called me a few times from Pune. On his next arrival in Calcutta late one morning, coming from Dacca, I met him at the arrival hall. He shoved something small into the palm of my hand. It was a blue Christian Dior lipstick case, bearing a magenta shade. He had mentioned over a telephonic conversation the colour would suit me, especially if worn with a black outfit. I was touched by the gesture, the simplicity of the gift, the way he just thrust it into my palm. I don't know; perhaps it was at this point that the mutual attraction between us turned to love, or so the realisation dawned on me then. I took the rest of the day off, and we went out to a long drawn lunch at Park Street. He dropped me back home later. This was the beginning of our whirlwind romance.

In a few months, Tushar shifted base to Calcutta. Now we were able to spend quality time. We went out to dinners, at times to restaurants with live music, and to plays, rock concerts, or to the discotheques. What we enjoyed most was watching films in theatres. We also shopped for things to set up Tushar's apartment, visiting auction houses on Park Street on Sunday mornings. Very soon, he was all settled in Calcutta, and also bought himself a car. But shortly, he became increasingly busy, as, in addition to visiting north-eastern states or neighbouring countries, he also had to visit his office in Pune. It came to us meeting more often at the airport, on his way in or out of town. He was the one who called me when out of town, as this was before the advent of the mobile-roaming facility. It was not possible to remember his mobile numbers, a different one for every city. Our conversations, as always, were still enthused, about a wide array of topics. We still talked for hours, even long distance.

It was over a year since we had first met. Tushar and I had quarrelled over a lady friend of his who kept dropping in on him at home very often. Then while we were still not talking, he had travelled to Pune. I learnt this on checking his flight reservation when I did not hear from him for over a fortnight. When, after a month, I had still not heard from him, worried, I decided to call him, setting aside my pride. I accessed his Pune office's number, from our frequent flyer database. They would surely put me through or convey my message to him.

A young female voice answered my call, with a cheery, "Hello!"

"May I speak to Tushar Bhatia, please?" I asked, assuming it to be the receptionist, not wanting to raise her curiosity yet as to who the caller was.

"He is in the shower," she promptly replied, to my bewilderment. "May I take a message? He's leaving for Zurich right away."

"May I know who I'm talking to?" I asked, still flabbergasted, wondering what he was taking a shower in office for. "I would like to talk to the Tushar Bhatia who heads northeast India sales.

"Yes, yes this is his residence," she replied, emphatically adding, "I'm his wife. Who should I say called?"

After a long pause, identifying the voice of the woman we had fought over, realising how right my instincts were, in a proficient tone, I replied: "I'm calling to reconfirm Mr Bhatia's flight to Zurich. Please inform him it's on schedule." Then fighting to hold the tears that had sprung to my eyes and control my quivering voice, before hanging up, I added: "Have a pleasant day, Ma'am."

* * *

At the launch of my client's factory, near Chennai, I looked squarely at Tushar Bhatia, towering over me. To my surprise, I did not find the animosity I expected to feel. He looked at me unruffled, smiling warmly, rather seemingly delighted to see me. I was amazed that someone who backstabbed me so craftily could be so poised in my presence, even if such a long time after. Then, I recalled he didn't know the extent of my awareness of his betrayal, of my talk with his wife, who I figured to be the same woman we had argued about.

"It's really good to see you too, Tushar," I said in a friendly tone, as though happy to see an old friend. "What are you doing here by the way?

As I appraised him, I noticed he was not as handsome as when I had last seen him. But perhaps my opinion stemmed from the fact that I was not in love with him as I was then. On noticing him closer, I decided there was some truth in my view. Even though still good-looking, Tushar had gained weight, the skin of his face had aged, and there were dark circles under his eyes.

"Well, I should be asking you that," he grinned. "This factory belongs to the company that employs me now."

"Ah! I see," I replied, surprised at the sheer coincidence.

The HR director who I know well walked up to us then and shook my hand.

"It's good you both have already met," he said. "I meant to introduce you." Turning to me, he added: "Mr Tushar Bhatia is our managing director."

I looked at Tushar in surprise. Then just as the HR director turned to him in order to introduce me, I interrupted saying, "I've already introduced myself to Mr Bhatia. But his name isn't on your website yet. I just happened to look it up."

"Yes, we will change the MD's name on it," the HR director replied. "Mr Bhatia joined us very recently. We planned on revamping our website after the launch of this factory and the official announcement here of his joining."

The HR director, excusing himself, proceeded to attend to other guests, leaving Tushar and me to the oddity of being brought together, after our abrupt past.

"It's really good to see you," Tushar said, looking at me, a nostalgic glow in his eyes, in a warm and caressing tone. "You're as beautiful as always."

I was taken aback. He was genuinely pleased to see me, I realised. There was an aura of remorse too. But what I had expected all along was he would avoid me if ever our paths

          Shuvashree Chowdhury

crossed, out of fear of an explanation for his sudden disappearance from my life. I looked at him, trying to comprehend my own feelings – was there anger, hurt, hate or was it all replaced by numbness, a void. All that the cinders of our whirlwind dating retained for me, I concluded, was curiosity – on the genuine cause of its end. Also, there was a dull ache of the betrayal that seemed to have accentuated at seeing him. The intensity of the scalding burn had taken a long time to reduce, then heal, still leaving a scar.

"Thanks Tushar!" I replied casually, looking away so he could not read my eyes.

Tushar signalled to a waiter, who took my empty coffee cup away.

Suddenly, looking intensely into my eyes, he said: "I'm so sorry…" Then, holding my gaze firmly, he added: "I never intended to hurt you, you know. I was sincere about my feelings; you must have felt that too. It's just that at the time, I got so carried away with my career, that I chose ambition over love."

"It's alright, Tushar. You don't have to explain." I said, averting his gaze. "It's a long time since and I'm happily married now."

"Please, please hear me out," Tushar said, in an insistent tone. "I would like you to know what really happened, it is important to me. In fact, I hoped to come across you several times over the years, but this was so sudden. I could not have asked for a better timing and situation than this, though."

I remained silent, in anticipation. After all, this is what I had wanted.

"Everything happened so soon, at the time," Tushar continued, with a distant look. "Suddenly I got a transfer to Europe at our head office, in a better position that I could not turn down. It was so crucial to my career. I was called away to Pune. I didn't know how to tell you that in a few months of moving to Calcutta, I was moving out again. I knew you could not leave Calcutta right away, leaving your own career, your family. I knew also, that the long-distance relationship would not work. So I got married to a girl of my parent's choice.

"To the girl, who kept dropping into your apartment?" I interrupted sourly. "The one who adroitly took charge of your kitchen and then your life, before I had the chance to realise what was happening?"

"So you know?" he said softly, and then looking down, he added: "Yes, it is her. Our families have been very close friends since we were children. Her elder sister spoke to my parents, and they promptly agreed, giving her family their word. I knew the girl I was marrying since we were kids, so thought this was by divine design."

"You make it all sound like a clerical procedure," I said, smiling wryly, "A sales deal you clinched, promoting your position in the world."

"I know it sounds awful, so commercial, so selfish," he replied sheepishly. "It was only about what was convenient for me on my career path. My parents wanted me to get married before I left for Europe, insisting it would help to have a wife. I didn't know how to explain things to you; I was a coward. Also, since you were already upset about her, how could I tell you I was marrying the very same woman? So I quietly packed and moved out."

"I'm glad life has treated you rather well, Tushar," I said wryly, after a long pause, composing myself from the impact of his clarification. "You are successful, aren't you? You're an MD, by what, thirty-six years? Your ambitions and determination have paid off well."

Tushar, not responding to my jibe, enquired: "I hope you're happy with your life? How did you land up in Chennai? Over the years I worried about what happened to you. I even called your old office at Calcutta airport, from Europe, a year after leaving. Your colleague Manisha said you had got married. Do you have kids?"

"I'm married now," I replied, "But I married only two years back, and then moved to Chennai. We don't have kids yet."

"That's very strange … Manisha told me … however," he replied ponderingly, then looking searchingly into my eyes, asked, "I hope you are happy?"

"Yes, I am," I replied emphatically, sincerely meaning it. In a flash I recalled my husband waiving to me from the balcony that morning and smiled to myself. Then I asked him, "What about you, got kids, Tushar?"

    Shuvashree Chowdhury

"Yes, a daughter. She is about seven years now," he replied. After a pause, he added: "Life is ironic. At a time in your life, you chase what you feel is the key to your happiness – success. After you've got it, you look back, wondering about all that you lost in the dash to get what you so badly wanted. By then, what you lost is no longer available for the asking."

"What are you implying, Tushar?" I asked, perhaps hoping there was regret in him, about us. "You were rather ambitious and have got what you wanted at an early age, much before the majority of people do."

"It's true. My success is tangible, glaring perhaps. But no one knows, and of course, no one cares, of the sacrifices I've made to get it." Then he looked sadly into my eyes, adding: "I gave up on love, I was truly in love with you, whether you care to believe that now or not, perhaps still am … in order to marry a girl who I thought would have little expectations of me, and with no ambitions of her own would be happy to make mine hers. You were too smart and capable to be content with a trophy husband who would not have the time for you."

"I never looked at it that way," I replied softly, "But perhaps you're right."

"I've chased success all over the world," he said. "How could I expect you to leave your own career, move with me every time? I don't believe long distance marriages work. My wife accompanies me to all my postings, takes care of home and our child. In fact, I was never around to see my daughter's first steps, hear her first words or realise when her first tooth appeared. Now that I have what I wanted careerwise, can I get back my love or my daughter's childhood? Life has passed me by. Everything comes for a price, and I've paid dearly for success."

"Sir, everything is set for the ribbon cutting," a woman interrupted us.

Tushar nodded. As the woman dashed off, he turned to look at me again.

"I am so happy you're here today, to share a moment of another rung of my success," he said softly, his face sad. "Things have a way of coming full-circle, don't they? Most of the guests here are our international clients, prospective buyers for the new textile mill. As I make my inaugural speech, introduce myself as the new MD, it will give me such a warm feeling to know you're in the crowd."

"I think you'd better rush now, Tushar," I said. Then, looking into his eyes, I added softly: "I'm very happy for you, I sincerely am. Always remember that without the sacrifices, you might never have made it so far. In life, you win some, and you lose some. You have won a lot, that's what you need to focus on."

He nodded, gave me a brisk hug like old times and walked over to the gateway of the factory, barred by the bunch of ribbons that was to be cut in the inauguration.

At the gate, Tushar turned around, smiled at me. I smiled back. In spite of everything, I never hated him. I was happy for his success. The chief guest cut the ribbon, after which we all walked inside, to the auditorium. Shortly Tushar came on stage. I could not help going over our conversation. Had we been married now, our marriage might not have worked out, I concluded. Living in his shadow, more often than not in his absence, would I have been content with the money and perks as compensation?

After the speeches, we were taken on a tour of the factory, which was followed by a business lunch. It was arranged in the auditorium, rather than the smaller canteen, while we went around the factory. Over lunch, I met other key personnel of the company, introduced by the HR director. At the door, leaving the auditorium, Tushar shook my hand firmly, just as he did of all other departing guests.

"It was nice to meet you, Mr Bhatia," I said formally, due to the presence of people around us.

"Very nice to meet you too," he replied. "Thank you for coming!"

     Shuvashree Chowdhury

22. First They Laugh, Then They Copy

> "*First they ignore you, then they laugh at you, then they fight you, then you win.*"
>
> *- Mahatma Gandhi*

I started playing lawn tennis at thirty-seven years, at my club in Chennai. This was during my stint as a senior executive search consultant. Over and above taking a keen interest in the game, I also thought it would give me a scope to socialise with prospective clients and candidates, who tend to play either golf or tennis, to socialise. The three markers at the two high-class cemented courts, who in turns taught me the basics, were polite, but evidently not much intent on my progress. They assumed my own interest would be short-lived, as is often the case with women in India starting to play tennis late. I went to the court at about 6.30 – 7am, so I would have time to rush back home after a session and get ready in time for work. As I was usually the first one on the courts, the other men would await my retreat, even as the marker on seeing them accelerated his speed, so I would tire and leave soon.

However, as they waited, none of the men, except at times the much older ones, volunteered to play with me. They preferred instead to wait and look at the marker exasperatedly, thus urging him to expedite my session. I felt like a child, running playfully on the court, before a big match is to commence. But I held for at least half an hour, playing four-five days a week. It was my intense participation, in basketball, hockey, baseball and volleyball, in school and college that stood my stamina in good stead. However, it was my self-esteem that would not hold the chauvinistic snobbery longer, and I soon left to join a professional tennis academy. A one-time national level player and her coach husband ran it. Though I continued to swim at the club every other day, to ease my overworked muscles and also build stamina.

At the tennis academy, the coaches and markers were very

proficient. Also, as I was to soon discover, much to my relief, in professional training clubs – they don't treat women preferentially. The first half-hour was spent in compulsory rigorous enhancement, one at a time of our legwork and strokes – forehand, backhand, volleys, and serves. In the second half-hour we played either singles or doubles under vigilance of the coach, on the numerous courts. I was the only woman playing with a dozen or so men, as the one or two women who appeared every other day would drop out after a week at most, unable to take the rigour. The children were coached separately, with much more personal attention, so they would turn into competitive or professional players. Thus, my strength, agility and prowess in the game improved substantially.

On visits to my club now, usually with my husband – either for a swim or a meal, I would at times display my improved tennis skills, to the three shocked markers. This was in the way of driving the point that they lacked ability as trainers, and it was not that I was in want for the acumen to learn to play, irrespective my age. The markers would then sincerely keep asking me to return to playing with them as before. I could not help assuming their motivation in pleading me might be so that people, especially the twelve or so committee members, might attribute my enhanced skills to their coaching. But I was rather enjoying the discipline and rigour, more so the respect and equality at the academy, to wish to return to playing here. Also I was to quit my job shortly to leave Chennai for a few years to move to Calcutta, though I thought it was permanent at the time.

In Calcutta, within a week of my moving, I joined the veteran tennis player Jaydeep Mukherjee's reputed academy in Salt Lake. There I engaged a senior personal trainer, under whose guidance, every morning, I improved my tennis strokes diligently. I played for an hour, till I was so exhausted I could drop dead, and yet the coach pushed me some more. The veterans playing on the other courts at that early hour, also sitting around between their games, who watched me curiously, shortly started applauding aloud my strokes and my perseverance. This gave me immense confidence. Also my coach was pleased with my improvement and proud of his efforts.

I now decided to take on a bigger challenge. I went over to the Sports Authority of India (SAI) office, also in Salt Lake where I live

                          Shuvashree Chowdhury

in Calcutta. There I was categorically told I could enrol only if the coach approved on meeting me. So I marched to the tennis courts right away, this was in the blazing sun, passing all the other varied courts – basketball, football, hockey and the sprint tracks. The coach, after quizzing me for about fifteen minutes, very luckily, took me on, and I signed my application form and submitted it to him. As I was to realise only much later, his sharp and abrupt questions, even as he looked me straight in the eye while I answered, were to gauge my intent in joining here.

The next morning, by 6am, I was at the SAI tennis court, after a brief, refreshing walk past the large green expanse of the football, hockey and other courts. I quickly joined the few others on the court and finished my warm-up exercises. Then, as I waited, looking around, I realised the mostly young male players, aged between fifteen to forty-five years, perhaps, were not interested in playing with me, a woman – a novice at that in their estimation. The intense coaching for the younger, wannabe professional and competitive players took place in the evenings. As I was still awkwardly waiting, a young boy – a teenager, was sharply instructed by the coach, even as the boy looked back at him dejectedly, to play with me.

The coach, Ashok Deo, a middle aged, very fit and agile man from Delhi, with a moustache and a short crop of hair, spoke in a crisp and commanding voice, in Hindi. After observing the boy and me playing for a while, he signalled to the boy to move out, and he took the boy's racquet and his position across me. At first he played very gently and then gradually he built momentum and along with it the power of his strokes, gauging mine in turn, along with my agility and stamina. Only after I was bent over, red in the face and panting like it were my last breaths, also pleading with my eyes for him to stop, did he let me off. I could not help notice he was grinning at me coolly, depicting the least exertion, as if back only from an evening stroll.

I must surely have passed his test, for from the next day onwards, the coach allotted me to playing with a young man of his choice for a while, and this was followed by playing with two teenaged boys. I would play singles, to two boys as doubles partners. The first day, these school boys, who I learnt were in between classes eighth and twelfth, looked at me bored, but were compelled to bear me due to the coach's sharp command. He watched us from afar, instructing us on our strokes or our feet movements, time to time.

It was as he had expected, the boys – different ones daily, would be agile and raving to go, but their strokes were not controlled and practised, nor did they have control of the court or the three balls each we played with. The two boys would run around wildly on the court, even as I stepped around in anticipation of their moves and of the ball. I knew the court well through practice, more so with my maturity. Any sport, I realised, especially tennis – is brainwork, much over and above legwork or handwork, and I had in time attuned to a mental agility. So, it became routine for me to play singles with two teenaged boys every other day. The purpose, the coach told us all stiffly, was so they would improve their strokes, the control of the ball and their steps on court, while me, my stamina and agility.

In a few weeks, everyone including the older men and the few teenaged girls started playing with me. They asked me from where I had learnt tennis and how long I had been playing. The coach would smile smugly, even as I looked back at him gratefully for his faith since taking me on. The others were, after all, aspiring professional players with potential. I respected his ignoring the remarks they randomly made of his intent, since he often played with me while not with most of them. Then, in a couple of months, the coach would ask me to shake hands with the kids standing in a queue after tournaments, simultaneous to giving away their prizes and also to make a speech. The first time he asked me to do that, I was rather reluctant. But when he insisted it was to inspire the children, I did so with moist eyes. I truly felt like a hero now.

"If *Didi* can learn to play so well, even at such a late age for playing professionally, you all can be champions, someday," the coach would say to them loudly in Hindi, as they stood in straight files on the court after the prize distribution. "Do you know what the essential attributes to becoming a champion are? They are optimism, perseverance and commitment towards excellence. I saw the motivation and determination in *Didi's* eyes, the day she came to enrol here."

 Shuvashree Chowdhury

23. *The Night Train to Kanpur*

It was a frantic rush to Howrah station on the eve of that Diwali. Husband and I were to board the Rajdhani Express, for Kanpur, his hometown. Mother was accompanying us to the station. We had arrived by a morning flight from Chennai the previous day, on a two-week leave from our respective jobs. The plan was to spend a night with my mother in Calcutta, then proceed to Kanpur for Diwali with his family. Our annual leave alternated between Calcutta and Kanpur, leaving us little opportunity to travel elsewhere.

Now on the drive to the station, in spite of mother's self-proclaimed expertise on Calcutta traffic guiding the driver, we were stuck in a whirlpool of traffic that even she was overwhelmed by. I was jittery, at the possibility of missing the train, having to spend Diwali at my home, rather than with my in-laws who were expecting us. Perhaps more sad at leaving mother, who lived by herself after father's passing, alone at home for Diwali.

I recalled how mother's arguing with father, on the best route to a place, confusing the driver in the bargain, used to once be a common occurrence. So I took away the baton of charge from her, handing it to the driver by asking him to take the quickest way he knew to the station. He would be more proficient in navigating us through this maze of traffic, emanating from the final Diwali shopping, on his own instincts. We made it to Howrah Station just five minutes before the scheduled departure at 5pm. The car park runs alongside the Rajdhani Express platform, so it was a short, brisk walk to our first-class compartment. At its entrance, we hurriedly located our names on the reservation chart pasted on the sidewalls. Then I warmly hugged mother, still sulking from my high-handedness in the car. She had not interpreted my real intention, of averting my husband's assuming she was delaying us intentionally, in case we missed the train this evening.

As I pulled away from her embrace, I noticed the sadness

in mother's eyes, the loneliness she tried to hide, smiling at us, nudging us to board quickly. My husband rushed inside with the larger of our baggage. I stepped onto the train and then turned back to wave at mother, before disappearing inside. She would wait till the train rolled out of the platform, I thought. After identifying our four-berth coupe, my husband stood at its sliding door, waiting for me. Our berths were along with an elderly couple, who were comfortably seated facing each other, adjacent to the window. The gentleman with all-grey hair, framing the bald patch of his head, had a round, friendly, jovial face. His eyes were big, kind, peering through the thick glasses of a rimless frame. Bulky, he wore a blue-black checked shirt, over light blue jeans, with white sneakers. He nodded at us with a warm smile, as we stepped inside on the red-carpeted floor. We smiled back.

We nodded politely at the lady in a white and pink georgette *saree*, who looked back at us stiffly. She seemed over sixty, matronly, with a plump face, her jet-black – obviously coloured hair, was parted in the centre with vermillion and tied in a bun behind her head. In presuming she and her husband were the sole occupants of this coupe, no one having claimed the other two berths so far, our walking in had clearly disappointed her. Husband and I settled our baggage under a lower berth and a rack above. We then sat facing each other, he beside the gentleman, and me the woman. I looked through the dark-glass window at my mother who was still waiting, looking in the direction of the train, though unable to see anything inside, obviously not us. It saddened me to see her looking so forlorn, especially on the eve of a festival such as Diwali.

Suddenly, I felt like a nudge at the back of my waist, and the train started rolling out very slowly. I looked at my watch, it was sharp 5pm. Impulsively, I got up, briskly rolling open our coupe's door, walked out to the entrance, to wave goodbye to mother one last time. Leaning outward, I waved and caught her attention from the slowly receding train, as she waved back earnestly, least expecting to catch another glimpse of me before the train pulled out. Her all-grey hair made mother look older than her seventy years, or was it the loneliness, that was rushing her ageing lately. I could not help notice, as I looked on, how she had shrunk in height and weight, over the years, though, luckily, still mentally and physically agile.

 Shuvashree Chowdhury

In the five years since father's passing, my marrying a year after his demise and moving to Chennai, mother seemed to have aged in leaps and bounds. With a heavy heart at leaving her alone for Diwali (Kali Puja in Bengal), as she had declined to come along this year to my in-laws, I returned to our coupe.

Just as I sat down, a uniformed waiter came inside, carrying a tray with single rosebuds attached to single fern leaves. He gave each of us one, bowing courteously with a smile. Before leaving, he announced tea would be served shortly. On cue, a waiter came in, handing each of us a tray. The trays carried a tea bag, coffee, sugar, and creamer sachets, along with a stirrer and a cup-flask of hot water. On each was also neatly arranged, a paper-wrapped cheese sandwich, a small packet of Haldiram's *bhujia*, a specially packed box of sweets for Diwali and a Five-Star chocolate. I poured the hot water into my cup, over a tea bag, waiting for the infusion to strengthen. The elderly man did likewise, and then as I did, picked up the thick plastic powder-milk sachet from his tray, struggling without success to open it.

My husband extended his hand, to offer to help him open it. After a moment's hesitation, the man handed the sachet over quietly. The elderly couple smiled at him simultaneously, thus breaking the ice that had ensued between us, since we entered the coupe. My husband on opening the creamer sachet handed it back to the man. After adding its contents, along with sugar from the thin paper sachet, the man stirred his tea silently. On taking a sip, content it was to his satisfaction, he turned towards us.

"So where are you going?" he asked. "The train, I believe, halts at a number of places before Delhi."

"Kanpur," I replied spontaneously. "We are going to Kanpur."

"Are you students of IIT Kanpur?" asked the lady, in a friendly tone.

"No, no," I replied, exchanging an amused smile with my husband – at being considered students, though we were both near thirty-eight years.

It was probably that we were dressed in t-shirts, jeans, with sneakers, that made her assume we were students, I thought.

"Then you must be IT professionals," the lady blurted affably.

"No, he's a journalist, an author too," I smiled, indicating to my husband. "His family is in Kanpur. And we're spending Diwali with them. I'm an executive search consultant, referred to as a head-hunter."

"How wonderful," the lady exclaimed, enthusiastically. "We're going to Delhi for Diwali with extended family. It's been long since we last visited."

"Where do you live in Calcutta?" the lady enquired.

"No, we live in Chennai," I replied.

"What about Calcutta?" asked the lady, "You have any connections there?"

"Yes, of course, my mother lives in Calcutta," I replied, reminded again she was by herself on Diwali. "That is why we took the train from Howrah, so we could spend a little time with her, before proceeding to Kanpur."

"So where do you live?" I asked of the couple, "Calcutta or Delhi?"

"Well, mostly in the US now," the lady replied with a sigh, "That is, we live most part of the year in New Jersey – our daughter's home, the rest at Jodhpur Park in Calcutta, our ancestral home."

"So are you going only to Delhi this time?" I enquired.

"We will actually be visiting a few relatives in Chandigarh. After Diwali and Bhai-Phota in Delhi, we will drive down from there."

The two men, though silent so far, had been listening to our conversation, making their acquaintance through our exchanges. The waiter interrupted our build-up of companionship, bringing in the dinner menu. It was short and crisp, of Indian, Chinese and continental options, with a limited choice of dishes in each category. All of us ordered continental.

After the waiter exited, taking our orders along with the menu cards, the ticket checker walked in. On noticing him, I briskly retrieved our ticket from my handbag, proffering it to him. The lady handed over hers.

"Yours is the next coupe," he said, scrutinising my ticket. "This coupe is for them, Mr and Mrs Sen Verma. The other two berths here are unreserved."

"How did this happen?" I asked, giving my husband a quizzical look, since he was the one who had identified this coupe as ours.

He shrugged sheepishly at me and then to the ticket checker he

                    Shuvashree Chowdhury

said: "We'll move into our coupe now, I overlooked it somehow."

The ticket checker, after handing back the lady's ticket, then mine, retreated with a brisk nod.

"Let's move our baggage," I said to my husband, then turning to the elderly couple, having just learnt their names I said: "We are really sorry for the inconvenience Mr and Mrs Sen Verma. But it was really nice meeting you, however short the time together."

Mrs Sen Verma had the mixed look of someone who on one hand was relieved to have the privacy of her coupe back, but was also disappointed at losing our companionship and the probable chance to a hearty conversation ahead.

"Why don't you leave your baggage in your coupe, then join us for a drink here before dinner," Mr Sen Verma said abruptly, as if on cue, reading his wife's expression. "Moreover, since we ordered dinner here, we might as well have it all together. That is if you don't mind our company."

"Sure, that would be nice," I replied, smiling simultaneously at the couple, and then looking at my husband, I asked "I hope it's alright."

After he nodded in assent, I said to the couple, "We'll be back then."

We retrieved our suitcases from under the berths, our hand baggage from the rack. A waiter helped us shift our belongings to our coupe.

Once there, we realised it being at the end of a compartment, it was a two-berth coupe, unlike the four-occupant rest We settled our baggage under the lower berth and on the upper rack. On our return, Mr and Mrs Sen Verma smiled warmly, happy to have us back. After we slipped into our earlier positions, Mr Sen Verma fetched a large bottle of Blue Label Scotch from his suitcase kept under the berth. He poured its contents, with a friendly wink at my husband, into two glasses from the sideboard, marked with the logo of a train. Then, he brought out a bottle of soda, added some to the two glasses of Scotch. He grimaced all the while looking at the thick-set, crudely made tumblers, as he poured the Scotch and then soda.

"How does the quality of glass matter in this circumstance?" he said cheerily to himself, then handing over a glass to my husband said, "What matters is the good company, isn't it. In any case, we're better off with these obscure glasses, as alcohol consumption is prohibited on trains, I think."

"Ah yes!" my husband replied, as he took the glass from the man.

"I have some red wine for you ladies, if you'd like," Mr Sen Verma announced, looking at me. "I always carry some on trips like this by train."

Mrs Sen Verma and I hesitantly nodded our consent. Her husband poured us red wine, into two more of the crude glasses from the sideboard. Then following Mr Sen Verma, who raised his glass, we toasted to new friendship.

"Our daughter and son-in-law are both doctors in New Jersey. They have a daughter," Mrs Sen Verma said to me softly, nostalgically, bringing us back to where our conversation had been interrupted by the ticket checker.

"Ah, I see." I smiled. "So you have a granddaughter, and only one daughter?"

"Yes, in fact, she's like you," Mr and Mrs Sen Verma said spontaneously, in unison, as I looked from one to the other surprised.

The way they looked at me, their eyes aglow, it was like I was really their daughter. I suddenly felt inexplicably drawn to them as well.

"You know, our daughter, Swagata, is the warmest, liveliest person, so full of life and love," Mr Sen Verma continued, and then looking into my eyes tenderly, he added, "She is a lot like you, even looks the same."

I do not know what it was — the wine, the lulling motion of the train, the cosiness of the coupe, or my just leaving home in Calcutta, tears welled up in my eyes. With a large swig of wine, its warmth permeating my throat and gut, I smiled warmly at him. Mr and Mrs Sen Verma then consecutively described their life in New Jersey very enthusiastically. My husband and I listened as they told us about their daughter, son-in-law and granddaughter. Their descriptions were vivid, and so was their love. They showed us pictures of the family, bringing their descriptions to life for us.

On viewing their daughter's picture, I realised the connection

     Shuvashree Chowdhury

with her. Something about her eyes, facial expressions, smile, were like my own. Like me, she had a long oval face, large black eyes, a wide mouth and long straight hair. We seemed about similar height, same built, perhaps age, too. Having warmed up to the elderly couple, I told them about my parents; of my life in Calcutta before marriage and moving to Chennai four years back. As always, it was such a pleasure talking about my father, our time together. Mrs Sen Verma, whom I was seated beside and turned to, abruptly took my face in her hands, looking into my eyes, as though looking into my soul searchingly. Could it be she was comparing it with her daughter's, I thought. I smiled warmly, letting her find her answers in my eyes. Their stories, illustrating their love for their daughter, her family, had stirred emotions I had squashed since my father's sudden demise, my marriage the next year without him to give me away, then leaving mother to move to Chennai. It is so much easier to talk to strangers, share one's innermost feelings, like we were exchanging intimate stories now.

At 9pm, a waiter knocked, announcing dinner. The men had finished two drinks each by now. We ladies had finished our respective glasses of wine. The waiter brought in individual trays of soup, bread-sticks, along with toast and cubes of butter. After about fifteen minutes, wherein we finished our soup, a cream of tomato, the waiter cleared the trays. He then brought in the first course of our dinner – fried fish fillets with baked potato and sautéed vegetables, for three of us non-vegetarians; stuffed-capsicum with baked-beans and sautéed vegetables for my husband, who prefers to eat vegetarian. The main course of roast chicken or cottage cheese rissole, pasta and boiled vegetables, followed. During the meal, Mr and Mrs Sen Verma's attention was on my husband, in learning about his work, his writing, life and upbringing in Kanpur, followed by his moving to Delhi, and then Chennai.

By the time the dessert course of *kesar-pista* ice cream was served, we were like a family, sharing a cosy meal together at home. It was after long that I had this familiar warm feeling, since my father's demise. Somehow, at meals with my in-laws, it was not the same yet. Perhaps my newness in the family, the feeling of being the daughter-in-law, not the daughter, restricted my letting my guard down, to be able to relax like now. After the waiters cleared the trays, husband and I stood up to leave, to retire for the night.

"Thank you!" my husband said. "We had such a wonderful time."

"Thank you, so much," I added. "Someday I would really love to meet your daughter. I'm certain we will hit it off instantly. Don't you think?"

The Sen Verma's looked at me in silence, for what seemed like an eternity. I was unable to withdraw from their tender gazes, through my own forlorn misty eyes.

"Our daughter and her family are no more," Mr Sen Verma said very softly, breaking away from my gaze, looking away. "All are gone. They died in a car crash five years back. But to us, she is as alive as she ever was."

Slowly, as his words registered in my mind's eye, I stared at him in shock, tears spurt from my eyes. I hugged Mr Sen Verma silently, affectionately, like I once did my father. The look he gave me as I slowly withdrew from his embrace could only be that of a father's. I embraced Mrs Sen Verma, feeling her warmth in my soul. Brushing the tears from my cheeks, I strolled back to our coupe, along with my husband. I lay on my berth, feeling the rhythmic movement of the train's accelerated chugging, reliving the events of the evening in my head, but more the events from a lifetime with my father. After long, I dozed off. We were woken at 5am, by a knock on our door by the attendant, just as the train pulled into Kanpur Central station.

            Shuvashree Chowdhury

24. *Homeless by Choice*

The entrance to my family-owned printing press was in a pathway off a narrow lane, in Amherst Street, the printing hub of Calcutta. In this locality, almost every other door opened into printing presses of varying sizes. There were a number of publishing houses here as well. The massive grilled iron-gate, the pathway that led past our gate ended at, was the entrance to a reputed one. It is to this day home to the works of several Bengali literary titans. The owners of this printing cum publishing house lived on the upper floors of their workplace. They, along with staff and visitors to both our premises, including me, frequented this pathway. It had been a year now that I got off from my car at the start of this short pathway, then walked to our gate. I gingerly avoided an old lady sleeping across the width of the path. At times, I had to wake her in order to step into our gate, at other times, I hopped over all her possessions strewn over the length of the pathway.

This lady's presence was a nuisance to us who used this path, but none of us asked her to go away. It was due to this mental security and also perhaps the comfort, that she had made this path her home, since it was cooler from a four-way play of breeze. Our press's gate was, at all times now, in addition to her presence, flanked by five to six suitcases of varying sizes and colours, from brown to red and black, all belonging to her. Across our gate was the imposing wall of the publishing house, from which, through a series of windows, there was a constant whirring of offset machines and the smell of paper. The old lady, leaning alongside this wall on the ground, had lined a Kerosene cooking-stove and several utensils including an aluminium *handi* and a *karhai*, also ladles, steel bowls and plates. This was her makeshift kitchen area. She also had a thin mattress rolled up with a pillow inside, leaning perpendicular to this wall. A mauve and white coloured straw mat lay horizontally. However, I never saw her use these bed gear, preferring as she did to lie on the bare cemented ground during the times I crossed her.

After three years as an executive search consultant, at the end of almost two decades of employment, I had moved to Calcutta in time for Diwali of the year 2011. It was a unanimous decision husband and I had taken along with that of his following me soon, in seeking a transfer of his job as a journalist. Over several visits to Calcutta in the years since we married, he had developed a fondness for the city, even feeling rooted here. As for me, Calcutta is really the only place I call home. If home is where the heart is, then my home is truly my parent's house in Calcutta. But over and above, that my mother at seventy-two years, was living alone with only a maid, weighed heavily on me. She would not consider leaving her home where she had lived with her husband, or let go of the printing press he had nurtured like a baby. This impelled my moving to Calcutta to live with her, even though planning on shifting to a different floor of the house that was now rented out, once husband joined me.

I thus took over the reins of our family printing press so that mother could be connected to it, yet be hassle-free. Life seemed to have come full circle for me, as working for my father was an option I could have exercised even at twenty-one years or any time since. Husband and I made plans on extension and diversification of the press once he moved here. The staffs at our press told me that over the years that I wasn't around, living in Chennai, they had cajoled, even threatened the old lady at our gate to go away. But she refused to budge, just as long-term tenants do in Calcutta. She was over seventy years, I had presumed from her appearance. The all-grey hair, now orange from the application of Henna – she plaited and rolled up close to her head with multi-coloured ribbons. Her fair face, now heavily wrinkled, would at one time, with its shapely nose on which she still wore a flower designed nose-stud in gold, along with big beguiling eyes and high cheekbones, have been the envy of most women. She wore bright coloured *sarees*, in yellow, orange, and blue. These she draped in the typical way of rural women from UP and Bihar, but way above her rough ankles adorned in silver anklets over bare feet.

I viewed the old lady's collection of *sarees*, of which she must have possessed at least fifty or more. They were strewn over the pathway on a whim, as I got off the car one afternoon, on return from a meeting. At times I passed her while she had her lunch out of a high-rimmed steel plate. She sat on the bare ground, her legs stretched out in front, balancing her plate in one hand. Out of curiosity, from the vantage point of walking across over her head, at times I glanced at the food on her plate. There was always a good-sized portion of fried as well as curried fish, and a single or mixed vegetable along with rice and *dal*. But I had never seen or been enveloped in the odour of her cooking. Perhaps she cooked before working hours, I concluded, so as not to cause more inconvenience around her makeshift home.

She smiled at me as I passed her, at times looking up from her plate, and asked me where I'd been, if I had been away for a while when I travelled to Chennai. I responded to her queries politely in Hindi, and then walked through our gate, thinking of her on my climb up the stairs to my office on the first floor. She also exchanged pleasantries with my mother who came to work for a few hours every afternoon – asked her about my sister and me, and our husbands. From her conversation, the lady appeared mentally stable. Mother, a stickler for cleanliness, was often irritated at the mess in front of our gate and reprimanded her, urging her to tidy her belongings. The old lady nodded silently, and smiled at mother, who then exasperatedly walked into our gate. I'm a stickler for cleanliness myself, but what infuriated me about the lady's presence more was the unprofessional façade of our press due to her makeshift residence there. This was after all the effort and expenses I had incurred to renovate, paint, and spruce the premises, since taking charge recently.

This lady had descended upon our gateway only after my father's passing, and since I had never faced anything quite like this at places I'd worked in before, I had no precedent to handle this inconvenience. Thus, I bore her presence out of sympathy, and our mutual helplessness over where would she go if she was turned away from here. At times, when leaving for home in the evening, I found her squatting in front of the tube-well in the lane at the end of the pathway. She poured steel-pots of water over her head in the process of bathing. I supposed she used the public toilet that was down the lane for bodily functions she considered more private than bathing.

One evening, as I briskly walked past her bathing on the road, and was about to get into my car, I heard her sharp, piercing scream. I turned around worriedly, to find her standing upright, with her drenched *saree* clinging to her, and her waist length hair that was dripping wet plastered on her scalp. She was flinging her arms and legs wildly, yelling at a young woman who looked at her aggressively.

As I stood watching in bewilderment, another young woman, and two young men, joined the two women. The old lady abused all of them in turns as they yelled back at her. It was soon a huge ruckus. But people in the adjacent offices, presses, and houses, perhaps used to this commotion, did not step out. A few passing by, stopped on their tracks to view the drama. I walked closer to the confrontational group, as I was overcome by a protective feeling for this old woman. In spite of my annoyance, she had found a shelter in my heart by now. One young woman, whom I recognised from the neighbouring houses at the far end of the lane, started to rebuke the old lady loudly on seeing me.

"*Mataji*, you are embarrassing all of us, more so – your grandsons ..." she said sharply to her, pointing to the two young men alongside her, "by bathing on the road like this. Why are you living on the road like a beggar? Is it to prove that your two sons and daughters-in-law are ill-treating you? Why can't you move back into the house? After all, we cook for you, don't we?"

Even as she shrieked, the young woman looked towards me simultaneous to looking at the old lady, to ensure I was listening. I stood rooted to the ground with shock at her revelation. A whole family living in an adjacent house nearby, then why was this woman at this advanced age of her life on the street? She was shivering from her drenched state, with her steel pot placed on the ground, flinging her arms as she yelled back.

As if in response to my mental query, she spurted "That is not my home, woman, do you understand! After my husband's death, you all have usurped it. I am an outsider now, in my own home.

     Shuvashree Chowdhury

But I'm happy with my dignity intact under the open sky along with my husband."

I looked at each member of the group, allowing the full impact of the old lady's revelation sink in. Then I slowly walked to my car, the driver following me silently, from also viewing the spectacle he was quite used to. As he manoeuvred the car out of the narrow lane, I tried to effectively navigate out of the maze of my thoughts. Even though I understood the old lady's need for dignity, personal space and independence, I was at a loss in comprehending her choice of homelessness – in opting for a street dwelling over a real home. But then isn't the capriciousness of human existences its uniqueness, I concluded.

I could not help pondering if my husband and I should retract our plans on moving in with mother. What if, with all our good intentions, even if we paid her rent, she felt restricted in her own home someday? But then, this old lady, would by her continued presence at our gate, now I was certain of that, be a constant reminder to me, to be sensitive to mother's dignity in our living with her, even if and in looking out for her requirements.

We tend to overlook in our dominance of the aged, their need for dignity and individuality, even in the face of their physical or financial dependence. Isn't a real home then, where the mind has a free existence, in addition to where the heart longs to be, and not merely the confines of a physical dwelling!

25. *An Emotional Closure*

An hour ago, I had signed a document, in receipt of a token sum of a lakh of rupees, as an advance towards the sale of our family's business – the printing press in Calcutta. It had taken just a few seconds, to bring to a definitive closure a lifetime's emotional journey. This press was the identity I was born with. It defined my father half his life, and all of mine, till signing this document. The other part of my identity is as a retired professor's daughter. The part of my identity I just relinquished, the press, was bought in the year 1956 by my father, as a small unit. He registered it as a sole proprietorship company in the name of 'Allied Printers' that he slowly and meticulously scaled up singlehandedly. As a child, I visited the press randomly with my mother and sister, to pick up father on the way somewhere – perhaps to a movie or to dinner, during our school vacations.

While at the press, my sister and I, we romped around, gave steady instructions as the owner's daughters to staff who humoured us, on what colours and material we wanted all our textbooks bound, which fine letter paper we wished our names printed in, the brand of stationery to be selected for school, or the font we wanted them named in for that matter.

At times, we also went over with father to the press, and waited for him to wrap up work at hand, to then take us shopping – which he did with great aplomb. He would allow us to take our pick of what we liked, usually at the then premium AC market on Theatre Road. We went around choosing, setting aside clothes, shoes, stationery, while he hobnobbed with corporate clients in offices located above, in the same building. Then once he was done with the public relations for that day, he would come down to join us, at times with his friends from the offices above. He would pay up and collect all the stuff we had set aside at the market, many of the shopkeepers knowing us well.

There were those visits to New Market too, where father would accompany us to shops, leaving us to choose clothes and

Shuvashree Chowdhury

shoes, as he disappeared to wrap up meetings with vendors in other parts of the large market. Then he would come back and pay up, cursing our bad choices as he referred to them, even as he sometimes swapped our picks with expensive ones – believing always in quality over quantity. We would then drive back home, munching rolls from Badshah or confectionery from Nahoums he would have already picked up while we were in confusion over what we wanted to buy.

During Vishwakarma Puja, when all equipment is worshipped, our entire family would spend the day at the press. There was an elaborate *puja* followed by a grand lunch, this was also the time when neighbours, clients, vendors and ex-employees visited the press, each treated to a meal or the *prasad* at least. All in all, as a child, the press in my mind stood for a place for a rendezvous during our school vacations. It was when I was in my ninth standard, as part of my economics project, that I pinned father down to take me through the basic working processes of the press. It was only then I cared to understand the press stood for business and our family's earning – at least a major portion of it.

After I completed my Bachelor of Commerce degree, while pursuing a course in public relations, simultaneous to learning German, mother insisted I learn the ropes of the family business. She compelled father to take me to the press with him. He was reluctant, as father did not see it as a place fit for a lady to visit, far from envisioning me running it. He was protective of his two daughters, especially me, his first born, much rather preferring I marry and settle down, or study more and add to my qualifications. In his view, he had struggled all his life only so his daughters could lead a comfortable life.

At the time of my father's passing, my mother, by then retired from service, was running the business. She had been doing so ever since father had taken ill after a stroke. Though mother was far from proficient at this new passion she had acquired, what with her teacher's attitude and lack of diplomacy, having little business acumen. It was only in the last couple of years that I tried to wean out of her aged hands, the control of the press she now clung to as the last vestige of her life with her husband. This was like a favourite doll an older child might cling to, much beyond her years of playing with it.

In taking over the reins, as I was deeply attached to this press, as one is to one's ancestral home, I put all my mental, physical and financial resources into reviving it, but now with my personal stamp on it. I looked upon it as a home away from home, a place that would define me. Perhaps I could even stay over the night here, if I did not wish to go home at night. Now, in addition to new machinery, furniture, a freshly painted façade, new signage and stationery, there was also a grilled balcony with plants in colourfully painted pots. There were elegantly framed paintings and photos lining the staircase and offices. Also, sofas overlooking the balcony, beside a pantry well stocked with snacks, a coffee and tea maker and pretty crockery. In effect, you knew on a visit, a woman owned the place, but more so a daughter from the portraits of my parents that hung about you.

In addition to my emotional investment, I put all of my financial and physical resources into my dream project, including hiring more people, making several corporate client presentations to revive old customers, and to get new signups. It was now that my husband declared his inability to move to Calcutta as we had planned – that had brought me back from Chennai in the first place. It was impractical to move out of Chennai, as he had just been promoted to a much coveted position at the newspaper he worked for. So, here I was back to sacrificing my dream all over again, after several rounds of doing so lifelong. As in no indefinite terms, a career comes before family for me. The only solace I had was to look forward to returning to the comfort of pursuing my literary dream, now that I already had a published novel.

Letting go of a cherished dream mid-flight, as I was in giving up my printing press, after all the effort in taking off – I might have crash-landed emotionally, if not for the literary dream I revived, to cushion the fall. Foregoing a ripe dream is as painful as the amputation of your limbs; let's say, in this case, it being your wings you are brutally eliminating to bring you quickly to hard ground reality. My dream balloon was also wrapped in my childhood memories, fuelled by the longing for the essence of my father's hands. This was in upholding his aspirations for the tree-

    Shuvashree Chowdhury

house he had literally built himself – that he had lived in the attic of the press till he married – in the lonely woods he walked into in Calcutta coming alone from Dacca, in erstwhile East Pakistan.

26. What Emotional Strength Means to Me

"It is not true that suffering ennobles the character; happiness does that sometimes, but suffering for the most part, makes men petty and vindictive." – W. Somerset Maugham in 'The Moon and Sixpence'

I had just joined a new school in standard two, my heart sore in moving from one boarding school to another, so soon. It was a week since the new session had started in January. In the math class that day, I was unable to answer a question the class teacher asked me after asking me to stand up. In spite of repeated aggressive threats, taunts, and assertions – as to how and why I was unable to answer this simple question that surely anyone could from this school, I still would not respond. I could not bring myself to tell her I hadn't learnt the topic yet. I was asked to step in front of the class and a number of questions were flung at me. Each span of my acute silence, with my head bent down low, eyes fixed to the ground to hide the stinging tears of humiliation, was followed by a stinging lash on my hands and back. This was with the thick wooden rulers used back then, over their actual purpose.

After the initial question that I was unable to answer, I didn't hear any question, as I was swamped by the immense pain of the stinging lashes to my tender skin and bones. So I continued to look down, the tears drying before a single drop had spilled out, a fierce pride and stubbornness taking their place, even as I no longer felt the stinging pain that kept showering all over me with acute velocity. I had shut my mind from the pain I was so ferociously inflicted, my heart already numb from the change in school and then admitted to another lonely life away from home. The teacher kept beating me, in view of the whole class, as I stood like a log, not flinching, no drop of tears on my face now set firm. She kept flinging the questions at me repeatedly, thinking she would break me and get me to answer. But I had shut myself emotionally and physically, too far gone for her to reach me. In exasperation, she

 Shuvashree Chowdhury

asked one of the girls – all looking at me in shock, no emotion on my face, to take me and leave me in standard one, where I was to complete that day of my five-year-old life.

That evening after school, over the bath in the enormous junior dressing room, I stood in queue with others my age. I held a towel and a mug with a soap case in it, wearing only my white petticoat and bloomers like all the rest. The elderly attendant, Vimala *Didi*, suddenly pulled me roughly from out of the queue and turned me all around, noting the black and blue marks all over my body. She asked my classmates and was given a detailed description of what I, the new girl, had encountered in the hands of the teacher who went berserk. She dragged me out abruptly by the hand, out of the bathroom with large tanks of water – leaving everyone to help themselves from them or to go over to the other two attendants. She got me into my frock and marched me to the principal's parlour-office at the far end of the campus, almost dragging me in her anger. There she pulled my dress off assertively and showed the principal the mask of blue-black my body, face and ears were.

"The teacher even hit her on the head. The other girls told me." She hurled at Mother Superior in rage, and then added "What is going on here?"

Then Vimala *didi* dragged me away, still in shock, to the medicine room and left me to the care of the sister-in-charge.

The next day, after classes in standard one, I was again marched to the principal's office. There I saw my mother standing opposite Mother Superior, nodding slowly, while she kept apologising to my mother. The teacher, who had mercilessly beaten me – such that if I were not strong enough, I could have even died of it, was standing with her head bent apologetically. I looked at all of them with no feeling whatsoever, not even the physical pain – it was all a haze of numbness. I'm not sure if I was given analgesics. I looked at my mother hoping that at least now she would take me home.

But all she said, that too without even a look at my state – the blue-black bundle that I was, instead looking at Mother Superior was: "Since you have already taken up the matter, what more can I say?"

I remember looking at her once, shutting myself to her, perhaps forever – as I would never allow myself to open up to her again. I realised my father would never know of this incident and he truly never did lifelong and perhaps the reason I wasn't taken home. I was rather marched back to the games field and left amongst the girls of class two, who rushed to take me back into their fold. The same teacher incidentally minded our games time, never looking me in the eyes ever, over the many years she was there.

I might have locked this episode away in my mind, as I did so many painful memories of my life thereafter and of those who inflicted them. But a year or so back, much to my shock, this teacher sent me a Facebook friendship request. She might have come across my profile on the timeline of several schoolmates. I accepted, after some thought, as she was so inconsequential now, after all, for me to nurse a childhood grudge. What liberated me emotionally from this incident was that the entire day I spent thinking over, forgiving, and then accepting her request.

But all of the memories came rushing back, when at a school get together recently, a dear friend – a doctor based in London, with a daughter of about five now, suddenly blurted: "How could you accept Ms … 's friendship request?"

She then recounted to our close boarders' group who recalled all the details of this event, as vividly as it was the day before and added: "We reported every detail to Vimala *Didi*, and that is why she pulled you out of the bath queue before your turn."

Then again turning to me passionately, the doctor added, "After all this, did you have to accept her friendship request? How could you?"

The rest of the group lectured me over this too as I kept quiet.

That night, a year back now, which we all spent at a seaside resort, since we'd gone on a trip, all the details of this incident came rushing back to me as a slide show. Thinking of my friends' advice, I was glad I had not divulged to them of my other detractors who'd done more harm, and I'd forgiven and allowed them as friends on my Facebook. They would have thought I've actually lost my self-respect and sanity. But it was their love and concern, their passionate anger even now, and the knowledge they had supported me in their little ways back then, that made me now cry over an incident four decades later, having kept it locked coldly for a lifetime.

Over the rest of the days of this trip, I thought about all the trouble I have had a knack of attracting lifelong, without even being a troublemaker in the remotest sense of the word, which could have made me so bitter about life. But God has given me one thing, even if not the good luck he's given many I know, that is a positive and optimistic attitude – to tide over all the hurdles, and toughen me in the process, without turning me negative and nasty. To me, true emotional strength lies not in not being hurt or not being sensitive to low oxygen levels in life. I'm, in all honesty, immensely sensitive to pain, in spite of all my bravado, but I can wear a life-saving mask real fast. Toughness truly lies in the ability to fight being suffocated from pettiness and vindictiveness, emerging positive from the worst experiences.

Just because you're crushed in love you cannot stay lonely forever to protect a breakable heart. If you've lost a professional battle, have been looked over for a promotion and a raise in spite of all your efforts, you cannot stop giving your best, and hide in fear of being defeated again. Strength to me is the ability to win over life's constant endeavour to crush you menacingly, to stay afloat, however strong the tide is, and then fly high with the strong wind of experiences.

"I have come to the frightening conclusion that I am the decisive element. It is my personal approach that creates the climate. It is my daily mood that makes the weather. I possess tremendous power to make life miserable or joyous. I can be a tool of torture or an instrument of inspiration, I can humiliate or humor, hurt or heal. In all situations, it is my response that decides whether a crisis is escalated or de-escalated, and a person is humanized or de-humanized. If we treat people as they are, we make them worse. If we treat people as they ought to be, we help them become what they are capable of becoming."
— **Johann Wolfgang von Goethe.**

Epilogue: Stand Up to Live

"How vain it is to sit down to write when you have not stood up to live." – Henry David Thoreou

I've spent about two decades, as was expected at several work assignments, in motivating and inspiring people to perform with excellence. This was in often being handed charge of the weakest or most troublesome ones – with 'attitude problems' as was commonly termed, in the system. But I've always looked at preparing my wards not just for the job at hand but for a lifetime – by trying my best to instil ethics, values, drive, and ambition in them, to succeed and soar in life. This was by respecting each one, even when the organisation and external training departments would give them to me as a last resort before showing them the door, either due to poor performance in the tests or due to misbehaviour. I was told I was free to ask them to quit right away, if I did not see they had a chance to sustain the long tough haul, especially in the aviation industry. But I never disclosed to these so called 'misfits' why they were sent to my department, rather I treated them at par with my smartest staff, thus making them first believe in themselves, and that they really matter.

These people, in time, grew wings – strengthening which, they learned to fly and moved on to other departments or jobs. How then, having viewed for myself – what trust and belief in a person – thereby in oneself, can do to one's confidence and performance levels, could I not follow this learning for myself when I took up writing seriously for a literary vocation. This was even when no one believed in me, especially close friends and family, who thought I must be really crazy to throw up the financial security of a long corporate career to pursue an obscure one, that my latest whim, however passionate it was, was propelling me into. But I was not deterred. I kept myself motivated and inspired, though it has often been exasperating.

Shuvashree Chowdhury

Now let me share another case of my confidence in the philosophy – of persisting when no one will believe in you. After a year or so of working in an airline, this after a stint with a travel company, I decided to test my intelligence and numerical skills and aptitude, by applying and joining a reputed multinational bank. After six months of working there, though having won the trust and confidence of my boss who not only appreciated, also demonstrated to others, as example, my organisational skills, that he intended to make mandatory, in handling documents – be it cheques, the vault and stuff, also cash, I was bored to death of the job.

This feeling was pronounced since meeting the sales team of the airline I had just left, at a New Year's eve party at a premium club and being teased by the general manager – that I must surely be bored at the bank after the airline stint. He told me how I had left just when there was a great opportunity coming my way, from a new business plan. He knew well of my previous travel company stint from clients and was, thus, aware I would not be kept at the fresher level job I had opted to join to learn from scratch at the airline for long, unless elevated soon. Lured, I decided to return to the airline. Now when I handed in my resignation at the bank, I was summoned to the vice president's cabin, after my immediate boss could not convince me to stay on.

"You see, when you join a new job, your equity falls to zero or so at the start, that is why you tend to want to return to your comfort zone and a growth certainty," said the middle-aged, elegant looking man with curly hair and steel-rimmed glasses.

He was looking into my eyes earnestly, also in seeking my trust in his words, from lifting his head from the notepad on which he was graphically sketching this to explain, convince, and thus retain me at the bank. In response to my silence, he began to draw with firmer strokes on the sheet again and continued to speak.

"If you will only allow some time to cross the most difficult stage of unease and uncertainty at the new job, when people have not yet learned or appreciated your skills – for which you will have to diligently prove your worth over time, you will see that your equity at the new job will double and grow manifold. This is taking into consideration your past experiences, too, that others here at your current level do not have."

In spite of being totally convinced with his words, more so with an elevated sense of esteem and confidence now from his sincerity, I returned to work for the airline. I had already accepted the offer letter and promised to return and join immediately. But I never forgot the valuable lesson that I learned from the bank's VP that would stand me in good stead throughout my career in changing industries several times, but much more when I would give it all up for an untried climb.

When I started to write initially, people would treat me like I was a fresher, as one taking up a new job, this even after two decades of my corporate communications – by way of emails and reports even to top-level executives as a head-hunter being well appreciated. It was like any writer, blogger, journalist (I tend to meet plenty in being married to one), even with a few months or a couple of years of experience, acted like they were so superior – ready to advise and talk with a condescending air. After all, I was the 'wannabe' writer, while they were one. But I swallowed my pride every time from the comments, in all maturity, and stuck my ground quietly, recalling the bank VP's words – that they could not take away all the experiences I bring to my writing, can they? One day, that's going to give me headway over all those people who mocked me, I am confident.

So never allow anyone to steal your esteem and self-confidence, even if you are a late bloomer or entrant to any vocation or creative pursuit … just keep marching steadily. Soon you will leave behind people's taunts, laughter, smirks, even those who then tend to ignore you out of their inherent or growing insecurity. You will walk onto a carpet of acceptance and then cheer. As for the laughing, mocking, bleating brigade, who've obviously never tried anything themselves but the mundane, they will find another scapegoat.

The End